"Did your mo... about traveli..."

"I always prefer to fin... myself." Quinn gave ... a lopsided smile. "To be honest, I don't remember the last time I took my mother's advice about anything. I'm a little stubborn, I guess."

And a whole lot attractive, Rebecca thought. That slanted smile had sent a tingle of awareness right down to her toes. And she still didn't know very much about him. Except that he wanted the old trunk. If he'd set out to captivate her with his roguish smile, she didn't think she could have been more charmed, and she'd responded like an innocent to the charisma of a reckless pirate prince. By the time she'd finished dinner, Rebecca knew her common sense needed a respite.

"You'll excuse me for a moment, won't you?" Rebecca pressed her napkin to her lips, and taking her evening bag, she pushed back her chair.

Quinn rose to assist her. "Of course," he said softly, his mouth forming a smile that was neither suggestive nor innocent, but stunningly attractive all the same. "But don't be long. You won't want to miss dessert."

ABOUT THE AUTHOR

Karen Toller Whittenburg, a native of northeastern Oklahoma, lives in her hometown with her two children. In her leisure time she enjoys reading, playing the piano and needlework, and is involved in her children's school activities.

Karen reports that she has been a reader of romance novels since she was a teenager, and that she is the typical writer who said, "One day I'm going to write one of those." This is Karen's ninth romance, her first for Harlequin. She says that her ideas come mostly "from things I read, or observation of what is happening to my friends, or events in my community."

Summer Charade

Karen Toller Whittenburg

Harlequin Books

TORONTO • NEW YORK • LONDON
AMSTERDAM • PARIS • SYDNEY • HAMBURG
STOCKHOLM • ATHENS • TOKYO • MILAN

For Don,
who helped me believe again.

Published May 1987

First printing March 1987

ISBN 0-373-16197-2

Prologue

"A looker," the old man confirmed with a nod of his balding head. "Classy, too, but she had a nice smile. Good teeth." He rubbed a hand along his scruffy shirt collar and rolled a stubby cigar from one side of his mouth to the other. "You know, a real knockout."

Quinn Kinser smiled, as if he did indeed know. "But you don't remember her name or where she planned to have the trunk delivered?"

Rocking back on his heels, the old man appraised Quinn's neat, dust-free suit with a measured gaze. "I don't pay much attention to names...just faces. She was the only one to bid, and she acted real cool about the whole thing. Not excited like most women at this kind of auction. Afterward, she paid for the trunk and told me she'd have it picked up in a few days." His mouth puckered into a grin, hampered only slightly by the protruding cigar. " 'Please don't let this out of your sight until then,' she asked me, real nice. And it's been right in this office ever since."

Quinn skipped the trivia and considered his options. "Is there any way at all you could help me?" He softened the question with a note of entreaty and wished he had a stogie to offer as bribe. "I'm sure you can understand how important that trunk is to me. It's impossible to put a monetary value on sentiment. It would mean so much to my family if you could just put me in touch with the buyer...."

There was a slight hesitation, and Quinn maintained his smile with effort. Damn! Why had he taken his sweet time about tracking down Molly's trunk? If he'd arrived a couple of days sooner, he'd be the legal owner, not some "knockout" with good teeth.

"Well," the old man drawled, "I don't suppose it could hurt to give you the address." He turned and shuffled to an ancient scarred desk in the middle of the room.

"Address?" Quinn repeated, trying to contain his impatience with the grizzled manager of the mini-storage units. "You mean you know her address?"

"Yeah, it's right here on the copy of the sales receipt, if I can find it." He opened a drawer and began sorting through a stack of papers, finally taking one from the group. "This is it. Rental space number fourteen, large metal and wood trunk, locked." Looking up from the page, the old man grimaced as he worked the cigar back to its starting position. "Funny your aunt rented all that space just for a trunk. Too bad she forgot to pay the rent. Would'a saved you a lot of trouble, if she had."

"Yes, it would have," Quinn agreed, his eyes seeking the other information written on that piece of paper. "But at least you can tell me the name of the person who bought it, and maybe I can get the trunk back... for my family."

A stubby finger pressed the sales slip onto the desk. "Rebecca Whitaker. That's the one. Pretty, with big brown eyes and a dimple. Not the type you'd think would want something as big and ugly as that trunk. My wife tells me you can refinish things like that, though. Maybe that's why she bought it...." He looked down at the papers in his hand with a reminiscing smile, and Quinn couldn't hold his impatience any longer.

"The address, please?" He was jotting it down on his notepad before the old man could change his mind. Rebecca Whitaker, 2642 South Benton, Unit 3-J, Glenacre, Missouri. Thank goodness for small favors, Quinn thought. At least she lived in the area, even if it was across town and a world away from the older, more traditional part of St. Louis where he lived. Glenacre was a growing suburb of St. Louis. An attractive little town of expensive subdivisions and shopping malls. The perfect place of residence for a classy-looking woman who spent her leisure hours attending out-of-the-way auctions. Quinn snapped the lid on his fountain pen. He'd bet the old man was wrong about the dimple.

Not that it mattered. Rebecca Whitaker had—or would soon have—one thing he intended to get. By hook or by crook. Quinn slipped the pen into his shirt pocket and looked up to see the glint of curiosity in the manager's faded blue eyes. He smiled in self-defense. "You've been a great help," he said. "Now I can contact Ms. Whitaker, repay her for the trunk and return it to its place of honor among the family heirlooms." With a glance at the heirloom in question, he had a hard time maintaining a sentimentally affectionate expression.

The trunk was of the 1950s vintage, hardly old enough to qualify as an antique and too awkward and bulky to be of much value in the eighties. In a way it reminded him of Molly Summer with her air of ill-kempt elegance, red hair wisping from beneath a turban hat, fusty fur coat and patent leather pointy-toed shoes. If she'd lied to him about the contents of this ridiculous-looking trunk . . .

"My family and I will never be able to thank you enough for your assistance." Quinn started for the doorway of the cluttered office, eyeing the trunk critically as he passed. How much easier things would be if he could simply steal it.

Of course, that option was out, considering the watchful gaze that hadn't, he was sure, missed even one glance at the object of this discussion. Frustration welled again as it had several times during the hot September afternoon. With a muffled sigh, Quinn reached the door and turned. "When did you say the trunk would be picked up?"

"Didn't say. Maybe Tuesday. Or Wednesday. Depends on what trucking company she plans to use. If she called a moving van, it might be a week or more before they get a full load goin' that direction." The manager chewed on the cigar, his jaw working back and forth. "It don't make much difference to me. I'm here every day. I told her, too. 'I'll make sure that trunk stays put till you make arrangements,' I said." The blue eyes looked suddenly less faded as the old man smiled and patted his rounded belly. "Yep. I'm taking good care of it for her."

Quinn nodded his understanding and stepped outside, forcing another insincere thank-you over his shoulder before closing the door behind him. The sunshine made his eyes ache, and he squinted at the metal building that stretched in ten-foot sections to the end of the property. How had Molly come to choose such an unlikely spot to store her most valued and, as far as he knew, her only possession? If she wanted to hide the thing, why had she rented the storage unit in her own name?

He rubbed at the perspiration forming along his neck. Hell, he didn't even know if Molly Summer was her real name. This could be the biggest wild-goose chase he'd ever been on. But then, wasn't that what he'd come here to find out? She could easily have lied about everything and might, at this very moment, be in the St. Louis airport having a stiff drink and a good laugh at his expense. On the other hand, one part of her story, at least, was true. The trunk was real enough. No denying that. And no denying that it belonged, contents and all, to one Rebecca Whitaker.

Turning, he assessed the possibilities of getting the trunk before it was moved. The place didn't look too well protected, and it wouldn't be inordinately difficult to break into that office. As he stared, the door grated open.

"You still here?" The old man shuffled out into the afternoon, pulling the door to and slipping the padlock into place.

The bolt slid home with an ominous click, and Quinn shook his head in decision. Whatever was inside Molly's trunk might be worth a few sacrifices, but prison wasn't among them. "Just leaving," he said thickly. "Is there any place around here where I can get something to eat?"

"Try the truck stop on the highway. 'Bout ten, fifteen miles from here." A suspicious shadow furrowed the old man's brow all the way up to his balding head. "It's right on your way... you are goin' back to St. Louis tonight, aren't ya?"

It didn't sound like a question, and Quinn was quick to agree. "Yes, I am." Without another word, he walked to his van, unlocked it and got inside. The engine purred to life, and he drove away, feeling the suspicious gaze that followed his license plate.

"You're getting too old for this sort of thing, Kinser," he said aloud as he flipped down the visor and groped for the sunglasses on the seat beside him. "And you're damned lucky he gave you that address. Damned lucky!"

Quinn grimaced as he adjusted the side mirror. Lucky? He must be crazy. He was hot, hungry and had one hell of a headache. He'd driven almost a hundred miles to search for a trunk that could very well be empty or that could contain nothing more than useless sentiment. He'd lied like a tongue-tied trooper and left without getting the trunk and without an alternative.

Lucky? He was out of his mind.

Chapter One

Sugar Plum

                                         Barely Blueberry

                  Lemon Tart

Pepper Mint

                                  Pink Lemonade

                  Vanilla Crème

Rebecca sank back onto her heels and studied the lingerie laid out across her sofa. There was no getting around it, she decided. The entire color collection of Honey Bare teddies was going to have to go in her case, even though it meant leaving something else out.

With a considering frown, she turned her attention to the lace and satin camisole and matching tap pants draped over the chair's arm. As an ensemble in black, white, or beige, the outfit was certain to be a popular item, and since it was new to the line this season, there was no question of leaving it out. The same held true for the Star Shine series of bikini briefs and bras that, in various colors, was carefully arranged on the love seat behind her.

Rebecca ran an assessing glance over the displays and resisted the impulse to use the "eenie, meenie, minie, moe" method of elimination. This sales trip was too important for that. With just one more year of record sales commissions, she would be assured the position of sales rep supervisor with Lady Laura Lingerie. A couple of years in that office, and she could reasonably expect to be offered a vice-presidency. She entertained no doubts that it would happen in the not too far distant future. She'd planned her career, step-by-step, and everything was going like clockwork. She didn't intend for it to change now.

Reaching up, she pulled the ribbon from her hair and combed her fingers through the long auburn waves. It was becoming more of a nuisance every day. Maybe she ought to get it cut in an easy-care and more sophisticated style. Maybe she ought to quit procrastinating and decide what went and what stayed behind on tomorrow's sales trip.

The doorbell chimed a welcome respite, and with one last glance at the samples, Rebecca levered herself to her feet and moved to the door of her apartment. She closed one eye and positioned the other at the peephole, but all she could see was brown-and-red plaid. And a blurry plaid at that. Her hand went to the door handle. She was going to call the building superintendent in the morning and complain about the status of her peephole. It needed to be replaced.

She lifted her right hand to check the security chain as she leaned forward. "Yes?" she asked through the door. "Who is it?"

"Oh, uh..." It was a male voice, muffled, obviously hesitant, and whoever it was, quickly, audibly cleared his throat. "You don't know me, Miss Whitaker, but I—" There was another throat clearing. "It is Miss Whitaker, isn't it? Rebecca Whitaker?"

"Yes, what is it?"

"Could you open the door? I'll only take a few minutes of your time."

Her fingers tightened on the chain. Just what she needed. A salesman of some sort. Who else would be knocking on doors on a Sunday afternoon? He was probably peddling encyclopedias and was, undoubtedly, as green as a baby grasshopper about sales technique. She smiled slightly, thinking of the advice she could give him if she had the time or the inclination. "Sorry, I'm not interested."

"What?" The voice dropped a gruff notch.

She moved her mouth closer to the door. "I'm not interested."

"Interested? In what?"

"In whatever you're selling."

"Selling?" The voice sharpened a disbelieving decibel. "I'm not selling anything. I came here to buy—"

The rest of his words were distorted by the sound of a squeaking door down the hallway. Rebecca frowned. Mrs. Albridge was eavesdropping again. There was nothing to do but open the door and tell the salesman he was wasting his time trying to sell anything in this apartment complex. She opened the door, keeping the chain in place, and looked around the frame. "I'm not selling anything, either," she said with a courteous smile. "And I doubt that you'll do very well in this apartment. Most of the people are..."

He was not a salesman, she realized suddenly. He didn't look like one. Or dress like one. The brown-and-red plaid was a sports shirt, a well-made, well-fitting sports shirt with just the right amount of give across the shoulders and chest. It was tucked neatly into slim-fitting faded blue jeans, cinched at the waist by a worn leather belt. Her gaze dropped to take in the nondescript boondockers on his feet, then quickly lifted to his face.

Definitely not the clean-shaven, eager face of a fledgling salesperson, she thought. The last she'd heard, even attractive, neatly-trimmed beards like his were discouraged in the sales department. He had dark hair, heavy eyebrows, and the most incredibly blue eyes she'd ever encountered. He was frowning slightly and looked a little impatient.

Rebecca allowed a small apology to slant across her lips. "I thought you were an encyclopedia salesman."

He stepped to the side, apparently trying to see more of her. "Why? Were you expecting one?"

"Oh, no. But I'm overly suspicious when my horoscope mentions a tall dark stranger bringing travel and opportunity to my door."

He smiled then. "Well, I don't have any encyclopedias or travel brochures up my sleeve, but opportunity is another matter. May I talk to you for a few minutes?"

"I'll give you one. Talk fast."

He pursed his mouth. "Could I come inside?"

"I don't think so."

"What if I show you my diner's club card?"

"Why? We're not going out to dinner." She was beginning to enjoy this afternoon interruption. Her fingers slid away from the chain. "Your minute is going fast."

The door down the hall squeaked again, and he glanced uncomfortably in that direction. "Look, Miss Whitaker, I can appreciate your concern. It pays to be careful these days, but I really do need to talk to you. My name is Quinn Kinser. I've been gainfully employed for several years, pay income tax with a minimum of complaints, and have a modest retirement plan. I'm six feet and one-half inch tall, weigh one hundred sixty-two pounds—" His hand made a conciliating gesture. "All right, maybe it's closer to one hundred seventy, but I've recently switched to diet soda. I'm thirty-five, divorced, but I like being single. I'm interested in buying the trunk you bought last week at an auction in Jefferson City. And now that your neighbors know more about me than my neighbors, could I come inside and talk to you?"

Rebecca unlatched the door, thoroughly intrigued by the man and his forthright presentation of facts. Or fiction. She didn't know, but she did trust her instincts about people. Mrs. Albridge was probably shaking her head at the impetuosity of today's single women, but Rebecca knew that any man who openly admitted an eight-pound infraction at least deserved a respectful hearing.

"The trunk?" she asked as she opened the door and waited for him to enter her apartment. "Are you interested in antiques?"

Quinn stepped through the doorway, trying not to show his curiosity about the woman in front of him. Rebecca Whitaker, with her russet hair and fair complexion, sparkling brown eyes and—by God, she did have a dimple—was not what he'd expected to find behind this door. She was smaller, younger and didn't look at all like the Yuppie sophisticate he'd imagined. She was dressed casually, but expensively, in black, cuffed shorts and a yellow embroidered knit shirt. The old man had been right. She was a real "looker." And at the moment, she was looking at him with a degree of expectancy.

"Antiques." He repeated the only word that had stuck in his mind and nodded an accompanying agreement. "No, I'm not interested in antiques. Just the trunk." Quinn realized as the words left his mouth that he was forgetting his well-rehearsed lines. "No, actually, I *am* interested in antiques, but *especially* the trunk you bought."

An inquiring frown creased her forehead as she closed the door and took several steps toward the living room before stopping and glancing over her shoulder at him. "How did you know about that? And how did you locate me?"

He strove for a casual expression. "The man at the mini-storage place remembered you. He gave me your name and address."

"Oh, really?" Rebecca half mumbled the sarcasm as she moved into the room. "How silly of me to believe a business transaction would be treated with confidentiality."

Quinn was ill at ease. He hadn't had much experience at fabricating a story from whole cloth, and he didn't want to jump feetfirst into a lie before he even got a chance to sit down. "It was the circumstances," he said, hoping she would be reassured. "Very special circumstances."

She was intrigued. He could tell by the curious sparkle in her eyes and the way she stood—with one fist at her slender waist, bare feet spaced slightly apart, lips pursed—as if she were debating with herself. Quinn shifted under her direct gaze, but kept smiling.

"There isn't any—uh—problem, is there?" she asked. "I mean, there isn't a body in the trunk or—?"

He laughed. He couldn't help it. "No, of course not. I don't know what's inside the trunk, but I'm confident that it isn't a body."

"Well, that's a relief." She turned toward the sofa. "I thought for a minute you might be FBI or CIA or something official like that."

"Not me. I avoid acronyms whenever possible."

Her lips curved in amused acknowledgment as she picked up some clothing from the sofa and made a place to sit. "If you don't know what's inside the trunk, why do you want it?"

She was holding women's undergarments, he realized. And what's more, there were dainty bits of lacy apparel all over the room. He glanced at the love seat where he supposed she intended for him to sit. More lingerie. Bras and panties, if one wanted to stretch the term to include these tiny scraps of sheer fabric. He ran his tongue along suddenly dry lips and hoped to God he didn't look concerned as he cleared a space and sat down.

As he placed one of the bras on the chair arm, he forced a nonchalant tilt into the corners of his mouth. "Couldn't decide what to wear?"

She pressed a finger against her lips, but not before Quinn saw the amusement tugging at her mouth. "Something like that," she answered. "I've been trying to reach a decision for the past hour. And at the moment, I'm open to any and all suggestions. Do you have any?"

A leading question, if he'd ever heard one. He glanced at the bikini briefs beside him, thinking that he definitely was out of touch with today's woman. He hadn't done a lot of dating in the three years since his divorce, and apparently he had a lot of catching up to do.

"Can I have a private showing?" There, he thought, that wasn't such a bad comeback, considering he was out of practice.

"Be my guest." Rebecca made a sweeping gesture with her hand. "But this is as private as it gets. And I won't make any promises that we're alone, either. Mrs. Albridge might very well be listening at the keyhole. I've always suspected she has her eye on my lingerie samples."

His eyes met her laughing ones. "I didn't see your neighbor, but I can't believe she'd look half as good in—" he resisted the impulse to hold up one of the garments "—these things as you do."

"Oh, I don't know. A frilly pink curler cap might be an interesting accessory, don't you think?"

He didn't know what to think but he had an idea she was pulling his leg, and he also had an idea that she could be caught in the game. "Shall I see if I can borrow one for you?"

"I'd much rather have you borrow a suitcase for me. My sales case is already packed, and I'm down to the final decision on what goes and what stays. Now do you have any suggestions?"

"How about a trunk? You have one, don't you?"

"Yes, but I'm afraid it's going to be a little bulky for air travel. And since it won't be delivered until next week sometime, I can't use it this trip."

"You're going away?"

"A business trip to the West Coast."

"You're a traveling saleslady," he said, with a wry glance at the piece of lingerie in her hands. "I've always wanted to meet one."

"Why?"

There was a haughty note in her voice, and Quinn was quick to smile away any offense. "My mother warned me about traveling salesladies, and I've been hoping to meet one ever since."

She didn't say anything, just regarded him thoughtfully, and he decided to change the subject. Fast. "Did you call a trucking company about picking up the trunk?"

Her brows edged together. "A mover. A slower, but less expensive alternative than hiring a truck. Did you want to apply for the job of truck mover?"

"Oh, I have a much better offer for you."

"And that is—"

Quinn wished she wouldn't come quite so much to the point with her questions. "Money. I want to buy that trunk."

"Why?"

"Sentimental reasons." He clasped his hands and leaned forward, trying for a sincere expression. "You see, that trunk belongs to my aunt, Aunt Molly, and it's very important that I get it back. For her, I mean. You understand, I'm sure."

Rebecca leaned against the cushions and watched him with renewed interest. "Well, to be honest, if it's so important to her, I don't understand how she could let it be sold at a public auction."

"It is difficult, isn't it?" Quinn nodded solemnly. "She's in poor health, though, and can't be held responsible for forgetting about the trunk. She has trouble remembering things, especially with all the trips she's made in and out of the hospital in the past year. It's sad, but Aunt Molly is really showing her age."

"It's sad that your family...or you...didn't take charge of her business affairs for her, while she was in and out of the hospital."

Was there a note of doubt in her voice? Or was he imagining it? "Oh, we did, of course. But Aunt Molly's an independent little lady—and well, she just didn't tell us everything."

"So how did you know about the trunk?"

"Oh, it's been in the family for years. So we all *knew* about it, of course, but no one knew exactly *where* she'd put it."

Rebecca shifted on the sofa, tucking one tanned, slender leg beneath her. The curve of her hip drew his eyes, and his thoughts took a new and potentially dangerous turn. She was very attractive, and he wondered if there was any possibility of getting to know her better on a more personal level. His gaze wandered along her arm to her shoulder and to an odd little throbbing at the base of her neck. Interesting, he thought. And there was just a hint of challenge in the set of her chin. Getting to know Rebecca Whitaker on a personal level was certainly an idea with possibilities, an idea worth pursuing. His eyes met the cool expression in hers, and he added a judicious amendment...an idea worth pursuing *carefully*.

"My aunt is quite eccentric," he said, as if his mind had never strayed from poor Aunt Molly. "It doesn't surprise me that she rented a mini-storage unit for that trunk."

Rebecca frowned consideringly. "I'm surprised that you were able to track it down. It must have taken a lot of detective work on your part."

"Oh, I never would have found it if Molly—*Aunt* Molly—hadn't told me where to look. One day at the airpo—at the *hospital* she mentioned the trunk and how much she wished she could have it with her. So I questioned her, and after several false starts, here I am, hoping you'll agree to sell the trunk back to me." Quinn stroked his thumb across his moustache and along the line of his dark beard. He hoped she was buying this story, because he didn't think he could repeat this performance if his life depended on it. "You'll make an old lady very happy."

Which was about the hokeyest line she'd ever heard, but Rebecca was just too curious about this man to protest. He was either less intelligent than he looked, or he was lying through his most attractive beard. And either way, she wasn't about to let him get his hands on that trunk, at least not until she'd investigated the contents for herself. But she saw no reason to let him know that now. "There really isn't much I can do until the trunk arrives," she said. "If you'd like for me to phone you when it does, I'd be happy to talk with you then."

"Maybe we could discuss it over dinner?"

She smiled, thinking that for a man who was interested in an old trunk he was displaying a definite interest in her. He probably *had* heard something about traveling salesladies, and in that case, it would be her pleasure to enlighten him. "That would be nice."

"Good." He sounded somewhat surprised, and she hid her smile as he clasped his hands, then unclasped them, then settled back against the love seat. "When will you be back from your sales trip?" he asked.

"Later in the week. But I don't have an evening free until next Tuesday."

"The trunk should be here by then." He seemed to relax, as if he believed everything was settled.

Rebecca felt a pang of conscience, but it quickly passed. "Yes," she agreed. "I certainly hope so."

"Tuesday, then. We can finalize the details over dinner." His hand moved to rest on the cushion—and a bit of lingerie—beside him. His fingers flexed idly against the satiny material, then as if he realized what he was doing, he quickly moved his hand to rest on his knee. "In the meantime, I'll tell my Aunt Molly not to worry, that her precious trunk will soon be in my possession." He looked smug and self-satisfied for a fleeting moment before a frown wiped off the expression. "Of course, I'll give it to her immediately. Then it will be in her possession."

"Providing that she remembers to pay the storage fee this time." Rebecca smiled in an attempt to keep the conversation light. She was uneasy about "finalizing details" when she had no idea what those details might involve. Something about Quinn Kinser—other than his contradictory body language and afterthought reassurances—unsettled her. Made her a little nervous, a little excited. Possibilities, she thought. Or sheer undiluted sex appeal.

"Oh, we'll make sure of that this time."

Rebecca ran her finger along the lacy strap of the Vanilla Crème teddie. "Funny that you don't know what's in the trunk. I would have thought she'd tell you of at least one or two things."

"She couldn't. Her mind is going, and details escape her." Quinn felt a surge of confidence. Rebecca believed him. The trunk—and the journal that Molly had said was hidden in it—would soon be his to explore. "Aunt Molly drifts in and out of reality. I was even reluctant to look for the trunk. I thought she'd imagined the whole thing or that perhaps, in a lucid moment, she'd invented the story just to entertain herself. Older people do act oddly at times you know."

"Oh, I don't think age has a monopoly on that. I know a few people in the mid-twenties age bracket who have very odd behavior."

Quinn catalogued that information with the other impressions he'd gathered about her. She, he guessed, was in her late twenties, only a year or perhaps a few months removed from the age group she'd mentioned. "Well, I don't want to give you the wrong impression. My aunt has lived a colorful life, and she's a delightful person."

"In her lucid moments." A thread of laughter ran through Rebecca's comment, and Quinn searched her expression for amusement, but met only her sincere smile.

"Molly is delightful all the time, even when I'm absolutely sure she's lying. I wish you could meet her to see for yourself."

"I'd like that. Which hospital is she in?"

Now why had he opened himself up to that? "Perhaps we could visit her next Tuesday," he lied. "After dinner."

"I'll look forward to it," she said in a pleased tone that still held a note of laughter. "She sounds like quite a character."

Quinn offered only an enigmatic smile and resolved to test his charm on Ms. Whitaker's composure. "You know, Rebecca, I'm very glad that she forgot to pay the rent. Otherwise, I might never have met you."

Her fingers stilled on the narrow lingerie strap. She knew a setup when she heard one, and she was a bit disappointed to hear such an unoriginal line from him. Surely after the story he'd just told, he could do better. "It was probably our destiny, Quinn," she said, with tongue firmly in cheek.

He grimaced. "I asked for that, didn't I? Sorry. It must be all these . . . undergarments lying around. Makes it hard to think clearly."

Laughter rippled past her lips. "I hope the buyers on the West Coast feel the same way."

"With you presenting a case full of these?" He waved his hand to encompass the lingerie samples. "How could there be any doubt?"

"Easily. You see, you're assuming that all the buyers are male and susceptible to a pretty face. Lady Laura Lingerie is an equal-opportunity company. We sell to women *and* men who are not only *not* susceptible, but who are downright hard-sells."

He drew his fingers across his bearded chin as his mouth framed a wry admission. "What can I say? I did tell you I'd never met a traveling saleslady before. I hope you won't hold it against me."

"On one condition." Rebecca arched her brows in a subtle challenge. "You will resist the urge to tell me any jokes that concern traveling..."

"Salesladies." He said the word with her and laughed. A husky, rich-sounding laugh that pleased her. All the way to her toes. "You have my word, Rebecca, that such a breech of humorous etiquette will not interfere with our Tuesday night dinner. But in return, I would like your word that you won't do something feminist and insist on paying half the check. I'm a little old-fashioned about that kind of thing."

She was a strong supporter of the feminist movement, and she had, on several occasions, insisted on picking up the entire tab for a dinner date. But she found something charming in the way Quinn had stated his position. Outdated, perhaps, but completely charming. "I will be pleased to be your guest," she said easily. "And I suppose you're going to insist on picking me up here?"

A slow smile parted his lips, revealing strong white teeth between the thick, dark moustache above and the carefully tended, equally dark beard below. Rebecca wondered why she'd ever thought she preferred clean-shaven men. Quinn

Kinser was a nice-looking man, even if he was somewhat of a traditional male. "All right," she said with a contrived sigh. "What time shall I be ready?"

"Seven-thirty?" He stood, ready to take his leave, and of all things, Rebecca recognized a twinge of regret.

"Fine." She stood, too, but made no move toward the door. "I'll look forward to it." She was repeating herself—something she rarely did—but at the moment, she didn't know what to say. "And I hope your aunt's condition improves."

"Oh, I don't have a doubt of it." He thought of Molly's quaint little smile and the prim frailty of her appearance, which was every bit as misleading as the lies he'd spun in order to get his hands on that trunk. Improve? If Molly could have heard him this afternoon, she'd be laughing the most enthusiastically healthy laugh the world had ever heard. "Good luck on your trip."

He took a step toward the door. So did she. "Thank you. I'm glad you weren't selling encyclopedias."

"I'm glad you were so understanding about the trunk. It will make all the difference in the world for my aunt." He was beginning to sound like the dutiful nephew he'd pretended to be. Time to cut the small talk and escape before he said something really dumb. "I can't wait to tell her."

He walked purposefully to the door, and Rebecca followed, trying to imagine what she was going to find inside that trunk. It had to be something valuable for Quinn to go to so much trouble. He really was a terrible liar, although she couldn't quite put her finger on the reason she was so sure he'd been lying. Past experience with slick sales personnel, she supposed, had given her a better education than she'd realized. She opened the door and then couldn't resist offering him a handshake. "It's been an...interesting...afternoon," she said evenly.

"My pleasure, Rebecca." A seductive sincerity warmed his eyes to a gentle blue as he took her hand, engulfing her fingers with his palm. His lips curved just slightly, and a slow awareness swirled across her senses. She watched with quiet surprise as he raised her hand and pressed a kiss against her skin. It was an old-fashioned gesture, lost in the new wave of women's rights and men's resulting uncertainties. If anyone had told her she could be captivated by such a gesture, she'd have laughed in their face. But at the moment, she was charmed. There was no other word to describe the warm way she felt.

"Goodbye, Quinn." It was all she could think to say, and she was amazed that it sounded so rational.

"Until Tuesday." He stepped into the hallway of the apartment building with a confident smile, and she closed the door, perhaps a bit quicker than was necessary.

With a disbelieving sigh, Rebecca pressed her back against the door and wondered what had possessed her. She was a woman of the eighties, a career-minded woman who was going places. Oh, she liked men. Freethinking men, who weren't threatened by her independence and who didn't interfere in her well-ordered life. She didn't know how freethinking Quinn Kinser might be or how much of an interference he might create, but she knew for certain that she didn't pose any threat to his self-confidence. He was a con man and not a very good one, at that. And still she'd not only *let* him kiss her hand, but she'd been silly enough to *like* it.

Pushing herself upright, Rebecca walked into the front room, determined to resurrect her own freethinking independence. She had his number now, and to her way of thinking, Quinn Kinser owed her a dinner. Despite the fact that she had no intentions of allowing him within ten feet of her trunk and its mysterious contents.

IN THE HALLWAY, Quinn pushed the elevator button, then turned abruptly and walked to the stairwell. In the background, he heard the click of a closing door and smiled to himself. Mrs. Albridge, he thought, Rebecca's eavesdropping neighbor and owner of the pink frilly curler cap. For a moment, Quinn considered going back and asking the nosy neighbor if she'd keep an eye on Rebecca's apartment for him. He could say he was with the FBI or CIA or some other impressive group. Then he'd know the moment the trunk arrived.

As he started down the stairs, he called a halt to the ridiculous musings of his imagination. One success did not make him a candidate for *Truth or Consequences*, although he felt a measure of misguided pride over the way he'd presented his case to Rebecca. He felt a little guilty, too.

It was against his nature to deceive anyone, even though he couldn't see the harm in this particular deception. Molly's journal couldn't be of much value to anyone, with the possible exception of another ambitious journalist, and he refused to feel any remorse about getting his hands on it any way he could. After all, he intended to pay Rebecca for the trunk and the shipping charges. And he was taking her out for dinner, too. Not an entirely altruistic gesture, he admitted, but it ought to count for something.

Quinn reached the lobby and strode purposefully toward the door. The amazing thing, he thought, was that she'd believed him at all.

Anyone so gullible deserved a good dinner.

Chapter Two

"I'm glad you're back, Rebecca. This apartment building is very boring without you." Wally Sherrow stretched out on the bed and put her hands behind her head. "Our apartments may have identical color schemes, but your bed is ten times better than mine." She closed her eyes and released a mighty yawn. "I don't know why I ever thought I wanted a water bed."

Rebecca didn't glance up from her desk. She wanted to total the sales figures one more time before she put the West Coast trip out of her mind and tackled the unpacking. "You wanted a water bed," she told Wally absently, "because you said that every successful psychologist should have one."

"You must be mistaken, dear. I wouldn't have said anything that neurotic."

"Hmmm." Rebecca pushed the Total key and watched with satisfaction as the numbers printed out onto the paper. With distinct pleasure she tore the strip from the calculator and clipped the paper to her sales folder. A good trip, she congratulated herself. A very good trip. "You'll be happy to know, Wally, that I made more sales on this five-day trip than I made in the entire month of August. And August was a darn good month." She moved away from the desk, still keyed up from the hectic pace of the past few days, but just a little bit tired...in a pleasant, satisfied way.

Wally opened her eyes but didn't move any other muscle. "Congratulations. Does this mean you get the key to the executive washroom?"

"The only key I want is the one that opens the executive suite."

"Good for you! You and I think alike, Rebecca. If the truth were known, we were probably born twins but were separated at birth by a cruel twist of fate."

"Twins?" Rebecca couldn't resist a dubious laugh, considering that she and Wally wouldn't pass for distant cousins. A natural platinum blonde, Wally was several inches taller, possessed an enviable shape and had a droll, occasionally off-the-wall sense of humor that went well with her unusual name. Rebecca lifted the suitcase onto the bed and unlocked it. "Now, *that* sounds neurotic. Have you been getting enough sleep lately?"

"There is no such thing as enough sleep."

"Maybe you need to take extra vitamin C."

"Oh, sure. You're beginning to sound like the women in my Tuesday night therapy group. Vitamins, exercise and men. The panacea of the eighties."

"Oh, really?" Rebecca hung a couple of dresses on the closet door and made a mental note to drop them off at the dry cleaners. "Is there a choice, or do we have to accept the combination?"

"There is a wide range of opinions regarding the first two, but the consensus of the group is that men are the essential ingredient to happiness."

"And healthy sleep patterns."

Wally groaned and rolled onto her side. "You know, lately I've been thinking that I should have chosen a career in business, like you did. Travel, insurance benefits, no office overhead, a regular paycheck, and a key to the washroom. Rebecca, you have it made. Let's trade jobs."

"No, thanks. You'd set my career back a couple of years, and I'd tell your Tuesday night group the awful truth about vitamins, exercise and men."

"What a great idea. Why don't you come with me Tuesday night, and together we'll exorcise the ancient fable that a woman without a man is like a night without stars."

"Sorry, can't make it. I have a date." Rebecca walked into the adjoining bath, turned on the faucet and filled the sink with warm, soapy water. She walked back to the bedroom and found Wally sitting cross-legged on the bed. "I have to wash my hose," she explained as she gathered the nylons and started again for the bathroom.

"Which just proves my theory."

"Which theory is that?" Rebecca called, up to her elbows in suds. "The one about dirty laundry? Or the one about psychosomatic allergies in males?"

"Very funny. Especially coming from a woman who would rather go out with a man than spend the evening with a group of woman who are learning about independence and self-sufficiency."

"Next to you, I'm the most independent, self-sufficient woman I know. But what can I say? I'm a pushover for a dinner invitation."

Wally's sigh was audible from the other room. "I suppose he's paying the check, too."

Rebecca smiled at herself in the mirror and wondered what Quinn Kinser would think of Wally's ultrafeminist views. "Will it make you feel better if I tell you we have some business to discuss?"

"So he's a prospective account? Why didn't you say that in the first place?"

"*Actually*, he has business to discuss with me. I'm only going along for the food." And a bit of fun, she told her reflection.

"In other words, you're allowing him to buy your attention."

"He thinks he's going to buy the trunk I got at that auction in Jefferson City."

"Oh, God! You've met a man who has the same affliction for useless junk—excuse me, priceless antiques—as you do. You'd better be careful, Rebecca, or you'll be riding off into the sunset on a bicycle built for two."

Rebecca laughed as she dried her hands and moved to stand in the doorway. "Relax, Dr. Sherrow. I'm not a candidate for your Tuesday evening sessions just yet. To be honest, I don't think Quinn Kinser has any interest in antiques at all. There's something in the trunk that he wants, but so far I haven't been able to figure out what it could be."

"Where is the trunk?" Wally took an enameled comb from her hair and pulled it through the pale strands before tucking it into place again. "Let's open it and find out what he's after."

"The trunk is on a moving van somewhere in this state. I phoned the moving company before I left on Monday morning and told them not to deliver it until I contacted them next week."

"Why the delay?"

Rebecca tapped her fingers against the doorframe. "I don't really know, except that I haven't met a man so attractive or so entertaining in years."

"And?"

"He has extraordinary blue eyes."

Wally put a hand to her forehead. "Come on, Rebecca. You're not impressed by good looks and a smooth line. What did he do to charm you out of your normal good sense?"

The back of her hand tingled with the memory of his kiss, and Rebeca stuck it into the pocket of her robe. Wally would never buy that excuse. "He told me the most amazing story about his aunt, who is the original owner of the trunk and who forgot to pay the storage fees and who—in a moment of unclouded thought in a haze of ill health—asked him to rescue her property.''

"An amazing story," Wally agreed in a tone of heavy patience. "Which you obviously didn't believe."

"No." Rebecca tried to prevent a hint of a smile from settling on her lips, but couldn't. "I didn't believe a word of it. Then or now. You'd have been proud of me, Wally. I read his body language like a pro. And he was so eager to have me believe him. It was funny actually."

"So why are you going out to dinner with him? Just call the movers, get the trunk and find out what's inside. Simple."

It should have been. Rebecca knew that. But she didn't want it to be simple. She'd thought about Quinn a lot since Sunday. She'd wondered and imagined and even entertained a moment of fantasy about him. Once she opened the trunk, all of the possibilities would vanish into the truth, and she'd know why he'd lied. "I'm not ready to do that yet," she told Wally, before turning back to the stockings in the sink. "I want to find out what he has to say Tuesday night."

Wally came to the doorway. "One of these days, Rebecca, that streak of romanticism in you is going to get you in big trouble. You'd be better off coming to my therapy session."

"Why?" She began wringing water from the stockings and hanging them across the shower rod. "I'm in no danger from Quinn Kinser."

"Which brings us right back to my theory. Any woman, including you, given a certain set of circumstances, will fall victim to the Barbie-Ken Syndrome."

Rebecca laughed. She couldn't help it. "Oh, Wally. How did the women's movement ever get off the ground before you came along?'' She shook her head as she hung up the last pair of hose and released the drain stopper. "I thought the Barbie doll had matured and become a career woman."

Wally ignored the laughter and the skepticism. "But what does she wear to the office? A tweed suit that transforms into a wedding gown in the blink of an eye. I'm telling you, Rebecca, we're not out of the dark ages yet. Inside every woman, there is a frantic little voice yelling 'I'm not successful unless I have a man of my own.' "

"Don't tell me you hear it, too?" Rebecca whispered in mock horror.

"The frantic little voice *I* hear belongs to my mother, who is terrified I'll die unloved and unsung." Wally walked back to the bed and sank onto the edge. "Which translates into, 'without giving her grandchildren.' "

"Give her a Barbie doll and tell her your theory." Rebecca opened her cosmetic case and began putting away the contents. "I'm sure she'd be glad to punch holes in it for you."

"You laugh, but if you'd counseled as many women as I have, you'd see the same pattern I see. They start out with a declaration of independence and career goals, and end up forgetting it all when they see that 'you-need-me' look in a man's extraordinary blue eyes."

"I'm sure the same could be said for men."

"Men don't have to choose. They've always had it all. Career, independence, and a woman to take care of life's little details." Pulling her feet up onto the bed, Wally put her arms around her knees and watched Rebecca in the dressing-table mirror. "Men are easy. Any woman can get any man she wants if she follows a few simple steps."

"You should write those down in a book, Wally, and give them to the women in your Tuesday night group. I know it's against your principles, but in the long run, you'll make more people happy and healthy. Not to mention the added benefits to your checkbook if the book is a big hit. It might help your sleep patterns, too."

Wally pursed her lips and rocked gently backward, then forward again. "I could do it, you know."

"I was only kidding." Rebecca turned to share a good laugh at the absurdity of the idea, but Wally wasn't laughing.

"In fact, the more I think about it . . ."

"Oh, Wally. You don't want to—"

"No, I think I do." Her voice picked up interest and energy. "A book for today's woman: *How to Get the Man You Didn't Think You Wanted* or *Barbie plus Ken: the Ultimate Fantasy*."

"How about *Love Is a Scientific Impossibility*?"

Wally arched her dark blond brows. "Now I like that, Rebecca. You're getting into the spirit of this. Do you want to be the co-author?"

"Count me out, thanks." With a sigh, Rebecca closed the cosmetic drawer and sat in a wicker chair, watching in disbelief as the ridiculous idea took root. Wally was usually sensible to the point of fanaticism. She seldom gave in to impulse and never took any of the men she dated seriously. So Rebecca couldn't imagine what was going through her head now . . . unless it was a whirlwind of brain activity brought on by lack of sleep. "You're not really serious, are you?"

"Don't you think I can do it?"

"Oh, I have no doubt you could do it. I just can't believe you want to write a book about how to catch a man."

Wally wrinkled her nose. "I'll approach it from the scientific angle. As if I were conducting an experiment on how certain situations create the illusion of an emotional involvement, and how a woman can manufacture the 'right' conditions."

"And just who will be the subjects for your experiment?" Rebecca still had hopes of laughing at the whole idea. "You can't ask any of your patients."

"Of course not. I'd never do something so unprofessional. I'll be the principle subject and then—" she paused slyly "—there are always friends' experiences to draw from."

"You can leave me out of this," Rebecca said firmly. "I'm not interested."

Wally only smiled as she stood and did a couple of side stretches. "Right. You take vitamins and exercise, Rebecca. You can be my control group."

"And what lucky man gets to help you with your research? I can't think of anyone you've dated who could hold your interest for that long a time."

"Oh, it won't take long. A month, maybe. Six weeks if I keep up with my regular caseload. And the man will have to be a stranger. More of a challenge that way." She walked to the bedroom doorway. "What about your Tuesday night date? No, forget it, that would be an unnecessary disadvantage since he's already got his eye on you."

"My trunk," Rebecca corrected. "He has his eye on my trunk. And I'm not going to assist you with this experiment in any way. I'm sorry I mentioned the idea."

"Don't be. I haven't felt this enthusiastic in a long time. Just think, I'm going to write a book, proving scientifically that love is no more than a set of circumstances."

She was going to prove that she could be as crazy as some of the other tenants in this building, Rebecca thought, but there didn't seem to be any point in saying so. "For my part, I hope you fall madly, hopelessly in love with the first encyclopedia salesman you meet."

Wally laughed. "Not a chance. But if I were you, Rebecca, I'd take heed of my warning. That romantic streak is going to get you in trouble."

Rebecca laughed, too. But not for the same reasons. She wasn't the one who was about to get in trouble. No Complications had been her motto for a long time. And she wasn't about to mess it up by conducting experiments, scientific or otherwise. "Right now, I'm taking my romantic streak to bed."

"Well, I'm going across the hall to my apartment, and then I'm going to make some notes. Check with you later." With a wave of her hand, Wally left.

Rebecca heard the front door click shut and went to set the security chain. She was suddenly tired. Wally took a lot of energy, and though Rebecca enjoyed her friend's company, there were times when she felt drained by it. As she slipped into bed, she wondered for the second time just what Quinn would think of Wally. There was no question that Wally would find Quinn attractive but too traditional for her taste.

For that matter, Rebecca thought, he wasn't really her type, either. So why was she looking forward with inexplicable eagerness to seeing him again? And why didn't she simply have the trunk delivered before Tuesday night and end this guessing game she was playing in her mind?

She turned onto her side, knowing the answer but hating to admit Wally was right. In her heart of hearts, Rebecca did hear a little voice. It wasn't frantic and it wasn't yelling, but she sometimes heard the whisper and wondered if she was putting too much of herself into her career. Was there more to living, perhaps, than living alone could offer?

A year ago, maybe even a few months before, she'd have stamped out that whisper with logic and the full weight of her carefully planned goals. But tonight, in the soft, warm darkness of her bedroom, she listened and wondered and finally restlessly told herself to stop being an idiot and get some sleep.

ON MONDAY MORNING Rebecca was still thinking about Wally's experiment, which had blossomed over the weekend into a major undertaking. Wally had decided she would "catch" a man, just to prove that it could be done in a systematic and scientific manner. If everything went according to plan, she would organize her experience into a cause-and-effect, how-to manual for the husband-hunting career woman. Rebecca had tried to discourage the idea, but Wally was too immersed in theorems and hypotheses to listen.

Woe to the man who knocked at Wally's door, Rebecca thought as she left her apartment building for work. And with the thought, her lips curved in soft memory of Quinn and his appearance at her door. She wondered if he worked in St. Louis, and if he was on his way to work, too. He'd said he was gainfully employed, but that was as much as she knew about him. Except for his height, weight, age and marital status.

Divorced. The word played through her mind, evoking questions about the man and his life before he'd arrived on her doorstep. Rebecca found it odd that she had agreed without hesitation to see him again when she knew so little about him. She was very choosy about the men she dated, and in general, avoided going out with divorced men. They usually came with extra complications...emotional scars or financial deficits or an aversion to any kind of commitment.

Quinn Kinser hadn't struck her as the typical divorced man, though. He had seemed comfortable with himself and with her, despite the awkward circumstances surrounding their meeting.

As she drove onto the company parking lot, Rebecca smiled at her own imaginings. Who did she think she was kidding? Quinn wanted something from her...an ugly, old trunk...and she was ninety percent sure that he had lied in order to have a chance at getting it. She gave her common sense a good shake, locked her car and put Quinn Kinser firmly in the back of her mind. He stayed there, for the most part, until later in the day when she received a long-distance phone call.

"Is this Rebecca Whitaker?" asked a gravelly voice that sounded far-off and indistinct. When she affirmed her identity, the voiced pressed for more. "The Rebecca Whitaker who came to an auction in Jeff City and bought a trunk?"

She frowned but admitted a tentative yes.

"Well, Ms. Whitaker, I'm the one that sold it to ya. Sam Ellis, that's me. You might not remember, but I run the storage units, and you told me to keep an eye on that trunk till you had someone pick it up. I did, too. Right up to the last minute . . ."

"Mr. Ellis," Rebecca said, her frown clearing. "Of course, I remember you." He'd been the only man at the sparsely-attended auction. In fact, she remembered, sparse was a flattering estimate of the number of people who had come to the storage units that day. To the best of her memory, there had been a handful of women . . . herself, Wally, a couple of collectors who left before the bidding began, and an elderly lady, who had looked out of place. Perhaps out-of-date would have been a better description, Rebecca thought. "What can I do for you? There wasn't any problem with the movers I hired to pick up the trunk, was there?"

A gruff chuckle answered her. "Nope. No problem. They picked it up some days ago. Say, haven't you got that thing, yet?"

"Oh, it's all taken care of, Mr. Ellis. Thank you."

"Well, that's good to know."

There was a minute of silence, and Rebecca tapped a pen on the report in front of her, leaving an ink dot on the paper while she waited for him to continue.

"You, uh, wouldn't by any chance want to sell that trunk, would ya?" he asked finally, clearing his throat and mumbling around the cigar she imagined he had stuck at the corner of his mouth. "Ya see, I got to thinkin' that my wife'd like to have something like that for her keepsakes. You know, all that stuff women collect for no reason? Well, anyway, I thought about it too late. After you were gone. But then I thought maybe you'd be willin' to sell. I could pay you for your trouble." The pause was slight before he added, "My wife'd really like to have that trunk."

Rebecca wanted to laugh. Same story, different verse. "I'm sorry, Mr. Ellis, but the trunk isn't for sale. I have a few 'keepsakes' I intend to put in it." She added another ink dot to the report. "I appreciate your offer, though. If I ever do decide to part with it, I'll certainly give you a call."

"Okay." He didn't sound pleased. In fact, if it hadn't been for the mumbled tones, she'd have sworn he sounded angry. "Well, goodbye, then." And with that, the conversation ended.

Rebecca sat for several minutes, pondering the call and wishing she had the trunk at that very minute. What fool notion had possessed her to delay its arrival in the first place? Without hesitation, she looked up the moving company's number, dialed, and asked that the delivery be made the next day. A second later, she changed the day to Wednesday, confirmed the arrangements and hung up the phone.

"Now why would Mr. Ellis want the trunk?" she mused aloud. "And why now?" The possibilities were myriad, she supposed, all depending on what she would find when she unlocked the trunk. Wednesday seemed suddenly too long to wait, but she didn't want the trunk and Quinn Kinser in her apartment at the same time.

She stared at the report, thinking that if she'd known an out-of-the-way auction would thrust her into such an intriguing situation then she'd have been searching the newspapers for them years ago. What luck that she'd chanced onto that particular one on that particular day. It had netted her an as yet unknown treasure, a prospective dinner date, and at least a hundred questions she couldn't begin to answer.

But Quinn Kinser was going to answer a few tomorrow night, one way or another. Two could play charades, and she was ready for the game to begin.

Chapter Three

When Rebecca opened the apartment door just before seven o'clock on Tuesday evening, Quinn caught his breath. She looked...sensational, and for the life of him he couldn't figure out why he was surprised. He certainly hadn't found her unattractive on Sunday afternoon. But now, with her casual cotton attire replaced by evening linen and silk, with her willful tangles brushed into tantalizing obedience, she looked...well, sensational. And he must look as speechless as only a journalist at a loss for words could look.

"Rebecca," he finally managed to say. "Hello. How are you?"

"Fine, thank you. How are you?"

She tried to hide the amusement that tugged at the corners of her mouth, but he saw it and shifted uncomfortably from one foot to the other. "Unoriginal, but give me a few minutes to get over it, and we'll begin this conversation again."

Her lips completed the smile as she held open the door for him to enter. "Don't worry about it. There's nothing wrong with 'hello, how are you?' It's pretty standard fare on occasions like this."

"I wanted to be different."

"Really? Why?" Her slender brows lifted, forming a tiny crease across her forehead.

Quinn stepped into the entryway just as he heard a door squeak down the hall. "You're the first traveling saleslady I've met." He shrugged casually. "I wanted to make an impression."

"Oh, you have. You're the first bearded man who has ever darkened my doorstep."

"Sounds ominous, not exactly the impression I wanted you to have of me."

"Does that mean you're going to shave off the beard?"

She was teasing, he realized. Stringing him along like a tuneless violin. Why hadn't he noticed the laughter in her eyes? They, at least, looked just as intriguingly familiar as he remembered. "No. The beard stays because I like it, but I have every confidence that you will come to like it, too."

"I might, at that." She already did, although she thought it might be just a momentary lapse in her usual preference for clean-shaven men. She certainly didn't want to start changing long-established tastes on such brief acquaintance. But Quinn Kinser was a very attractive man, and Rebecca had to admit that his appearance alone made a strong argument for beards in general and his in particular. "Would you like to have something to drink before we go to dinner?"

He glanced toward the living room. "I'd love to, but I'm afraid there won't be time. I've made reservations for seven forty-five, and the restaurant is on the other side of town." He grimaced wryly. "I don't know your side of St. Louis as well as I know mine."

She laughed and reached for her evening bag. "I think that's a problem easily overcome, as long as we don't discuss which side of town is best."

He stepped ahead of her into the hallway and waited as she followed and closed the door behind them. "Agreed. Let's discuss how you came to live on the wrong—whoops! I mean *this* side of the tracks."

With a chastening frown, she pushed the elevator button. "I moved here four years ago when I began working for Lady Laura Lingerie. It isn't as close to my office as I'd like, but it's certainly closer than I was before."

"And where was that?"

"Columbia." She smiled at his concurring nod. "Where did you live before?"

"I've lived in the same house for more years than I care to count." The doors opened, and he followed her into the elevator. "But I like it. The house is in one of the older neighborhoods, and what it lacks in modern architecture, it more than makes up in roominess and comfort. They don't build houses like that anymore."

Rebecca let her lips curve in complacent agreement before she pressed them together and decided the only way to find out what she wanted to know was to start asking questions. "Do you live close to your work, Quinn?"

"I work at home."

"Oh. And what kind of work do you do?"

"I write."

Nice, short answer, she thought. No embellishment, and maybe just a little evasive. "Fiction or nonfiction? For fun or profit?"

His release of breath might have been a resigned sigh, but she couldn't be sure. "Nonfiction, basically, and I manage to have some fun with it, although I always strive to make a profit."

"I'll bet it's hard to work at home, isn't it? It must take a lot of self-discipline."

"I try not to think of it like that, but I do keep strict office hours and generally keep outside distractions to a minimum."

"Do you write books or what?"

"'Or what' about covers it," he said. The elevator doors opened onto the lobby of the apartment building, and

Quinn tried not to look relieved. He didn't like talking about his work. Built-in caution, he supposed, from early training in the investigative field. Not that he had anything to hide, but something about Rebecca's persistence made him uncomfortable.

He wondered if he could claim the Fifth Amendment and then decided that was silly. She was curious about him. That's all. And her curiosity was certainly understandable. He hoped that when Emily was grown she would be as inquisitive in the same situation. Keep that in mind, he told himself as he pushed open the glass doors for Rebecca. Once outside, he took her elbow and guided her toward his parked van. "Actually, I write anything I think will sell," he said. "Magazine articles. Newspaper articles. Special assignments. Any kind of free-lance work."

"Which magazines?"

He named several, and before she could ask, he named a couple of newspapers, too, then added a note of humor to his voice. "Recently, I've been thinking about doing a story on traveling salesladies, but I don't know. It's going to be hell doing the research."

She wrinkled her nose in response to his teasing. "You're right, Quinn, and you don't even know the half of it." He unlocked the door of a blue and beige van and opened it for her. "Believe me," she continued as she stepped up into the van, "whatever your mother told you about traveling saleswomen, she could only have touched on the high points."

"I always prefer to find things out for myself." He closed the door and walked around to the driver's side. Once inside, and with the seat belt fastened, he gave Rebecca a lopsided smile. "To be honest, I don't remember the last time I took my mother's advice about anything. I'm a little stubborn, I guess."

And a whole lot attractive, Rebecca thought. That slanted smile had sent a tingle of awareness right down to her toes.

And she still didn't know very much about him. Except that he wanted the old trunk. Yet he hadn't asked about its delivery. She glanced at him but decided to pursue more general topics of conversation for now. She would work her way up to the subject of Aunt Molly and the value of the trunk. After all, she thought, the evening was just beginning. There was plenty of time.

But time got away from her over the course of dinner, and Rebecca didn't know how it had happened. On the drive to the restaurant, she'd managed to gather some background information: his place of birth, his family, and his educational history. But Quinn had eluded any real in-depth discoveries and had kept turning the same questions back to her, asking about *her* family, *her* education, *her* interests. And she'd talked, answering in far more detail than she'd ever intended.

If he'd set out to captivate her with his roguish smile, she didn't think she could have been more charmed, and she'd responded like an innocent to the reckless charisma of a pirate prince. By the time she'd finished eating, Rebecca knew her common sense needed a moment's respite.

"You'll excuse me for a moment, won't you?" Rebecca pressed her napkin to her lips and, taking up her evening bag, pushed back her chair.

Quinn rose to assist her. "Of course," he said softly, his mouth forming a smile that was neither suggestive nor innocent, but stunningly attractive all the same. "But don't be long. You won't want to miss dessert."

Rebecca swallowed and told her suddenly weak legs to move. This dinner had been unlike any dinner she'd ever had. She barely knew what she'd eaten. She was sure the taste had been wonderful—the restaurant was one of St. Louis's finest—but her attention had not been on food. Quinn Kinser was a charming and worthy opponent. Although the trunk had not as yet been mentioned, she had asked a lot of questions about his work, which surprisingly, he'd answered with witty sincerity. And despite her better judgment, she believed him. It was definitely time to powder her nose and adjust her perspective.

"I'll be right back." Her chin up, head back, shoulders straight, she walked away from the table, determined that after a few minutes of reflection in the ladies' room, she'd be back to normal and in control of the fluttery awareness inside her, which at the moment seemed to have the upper hand.

Quinn watched her go and sank, with a slow sigh, back onto his chair. *You, my boy,* he told himself, *are in deep trouble. She's quite a lady...someone you could really like, someone with depth and the ability to laugh.* She was beautiful, too. He couldn't help but observe the confident way she moved through the crowded restaurant and the interested gazes that followed her. Rebecca Whitaker was a definite bonus in what, so far, had been an empty quest. Like finding fourteen-carat gold inside a box of Cracker Jacks.

But she was on to him. He sensed it in the cautious way she'd watched him all evening and in the careful phrasing of her questions. *What kind of work do you do, Quinn?* she'd asked almost before the elevator doors had closed behind them. On the drive across town, it had been questions about his family and schooling. And as soon as they were seated in the restaurant, she'd begun a series of *Where did you work before?* and *What made you decide to...?*

He'd been honest with her, as there was nothing in his background worth hiding, and he'd managed to turn the tables a couple of times and discover more about her. But no matter what interesting direction the conversation took, she eventually returned to the subtle inquisition. She was working her way up to Aunt Molly and the trunk. He could feel it coming.

Yes, something had given him away. He thought back over his Aunt Molly story and couldn't pinpoint anything he'd said that first Sunday afternoon. In fact, he still believed he'd done a masterful job, considering it was his first attempt at blatant storytelling. Maybe, though, he should just have been truthful.

Quinn frowned and reached for his water glass. If he'd told her the real story, she sure as hell wouldn't have believed him. If someone had told *him* that a little old lady, who, for all practical purposes, lived at the airport, had a buried treasure hidden in an old trunk—

Quinn drained the glass and set it on the table with an unnecessary thump. No one in their right mind would believe the stories Molly Summer had told him. Not without the proof that she *said* was inside the trunk. He hadn't believed her at first, either, but the more he'd talked with her, the more intriguing details she'd added, and the less sure he'd become that she was just a fanciful old woman.

The first time he'd seen her, she'd been sitting at a corner table in the airport coffee shop, dining—there was no other word for it—on prepackaged crackers and coffee. Or hot water. He hadn't been close enough to see more than the steam escaping the top of the paper cup. She had smiled at him, and he had smiled back before looking quickly away, feeling embarrassed at having been caught watching her. He'd assumed she'd just arrived in the city and was waiting for someone to come for her. Since he'd been on his way to Washington, D.C., to a conference with a well-known political journalist for whom he'd done some investigative work, Quinn had soon forgotten the encounter.

But on his return a few days later, he saw her again. This time she was sitting in the arrival-departure waiting area. She was wearing the same clothes she'd worn before: same fur coat, same purple dress, and the same matching turban hat secured with a gaudy brooch. Wispy strands of bright red hair escaped the turban, little strands of defiant youth against an aging complexion. And on her hands she wore fine, white gloves.

She was a sight, an oddity in a place where the unusual wasn't uncommon. As he left the terminal, Quinn concluded she was now on her way out of town, although it bothered him that she apparently had no one to see her off. The feeling didn't linger, though, and he again forgot about her.

A week later he was back at the airport with his daughter, Emily. Putting an eight-year-old on a plane for the required two-week visit with her mother in a town five hundred miles away was an unsettling task at best. This year Emily had made it worse by being so grown-up about the whole thing. Usually he'd accompany her on the flight, but she'd insisted that his presence was not necessary. So he handed her over to a smiling flight attendant and walked back to the waiting area with a lump the size of Dallas in his throat.

And there was Molly. Same clothes. Same smile. Same inquisitive expression. There was a shopping bag at her feet, an old-fashioned clasp purse in her lap, and the white gloves on her hands. His concern for Emily, and the peculiar aloneness that was always with him when she wasn't, channeled itself into a curious concern for this frail-looking stranger. "Hello," he said as he cautiously approached her. "Are you seeing someone off, too?"

Alert, green eyes smiled up at him. "Oh, no. I'm just enjoying the day. But I can see that you're not. That was your daughter, wasn't it? She looks like you."

Quinn had expected a less observant answer and a less friendly, vibrant voice. He didn't know quite how to respond. "Yes, people often comment on our resemblance."

The old woman nodded, and one gloved hand patted the black purse. "Where is she going?"

"Minneapolis."

"That's a nice place. She'll like it."

"You've been there?"

The green eyes danced with an amusement Quinn could see but couldn't understand. "Young man, I've been everywhere."

It was the perfect thing to say to an investigative journalist who, at that moment, was lonely and in need of a distraction. Within a very few minutes, Quinn was seated beside her, and the next thing he knew, he'd forgotten about her eccentric mode of dress and was thoroughly enchanted with her. Molly Summer was quite a character. And the stories she had to tell . . .

From that initial meeting, their acquaintance had stretched into a curious friendship. He began making trips to the airport just to see if she'd be there. She usually was, in one area or another. She told him she liked the hustle and bustle, the conversations, the hellos and goodbyes that took place there. Whenever he offered to take her home, though, she refused, and he eventually formed the idea that she had no home to go to. He often bought her dinner in the airport restaurant, but she told him she had plenty of money and didn't want for anything.

He didn't believe her, but he was convinced that any attempt on his part to help her find housing or financial assistance would result in her disappearance. Just as he'd reached the point of deciding he had to do something, she told him about the journal.

"I once knew a man named Quinten," she announced one afternoon in the coffee shop. "Of course, no one dared to call him Quinn. He was Quinten. Thomas Quinten Williams, the third."

Quinn choked on his soda. "You knew Governor Williams?"

"I knew him when he sold fish in an open market on the outskirts of town." Molly wrinkled her nose and chuckled softly to herself. "He was as smelly then as he was in politics. I never liked him much. And I certainly never voted for him."

Thomas Q. Williams, the third, had been party to one of the biggest political scandals in Missouri history, and Quinn was immediately interested in what Molly knew about it. After a couple of pointed questions, he realized she knew quite a lot, not only about the late governor, but about several other prominent state politicians as well. She evaded his attempts to find out just how she knew, but she said enough to convince him that she had once been on the inside of a very elite circle.

On later reflection, Quinn decided she could be reciting bits and pieces of information she'd read in newspapers or heard in general conversations years before. Her mind was agile and quick, despite her years, but he had to consider the possibility that her memory had woven the facts she knew into a part of her own past. And so, when she'd told him she'd kept a journal, he'd been dubious, and even more so when she coyly refused to tell him exactly where it was.

But then, two days later, as if she'd made a major decision, she'd told him the journal was in the trunk and that the trunk was in Jefferson City. He'd listened with a skeptical ear and humored her by saying he'd get right over there and check on it.

He'd delayed acting on the information, though, and now look where he was...in a very expensive restaurant, waiting for a very beautiful, very intelligent woman, and facing a dilemma of his own making. If he admitted his deception, he risked losing the trunk and any chance of getting better acquainted with Rebecca. If he didn't admit the deception, he risked the same consequences. And Molly, who could have saved him all this trouble, had vanished.

"Did I keep you waiting too long?" Rebecca startled him, and he almost knocked over his chair in getting to his feet.

"No, no." He managed a smile of greeting as she seated herself at the table. She was, if possible, lovelier than he remembered, and she'd only been gone a few minutes. "It only seemed like a lifetime."

"You could have ordered dessert without me." Rebecca ignored his flattery and wished it were as easy to discount the chemistry of attraction. Quinn Kinser was having an inexplicable effect on her normally steady equilibrium. Actually, she thought, it wasn't so inexplicable. And that was the problem. "I really don't care for any," she said and was glad he couldn't know she wasn't only referring to dessert.

"Are you ready to go?" he asked politely, and then, at her agreement, he asked the waiter for the check.

While he took care of that, Rebecca glanced at her watch and then brought her inquisitive gaze to his neat, wiry-looking beard and the intriguing tilt of his mouth. She didn't know which fascinated her more, the beard or the mouth, and she wondered what it would be like to touch. Soft, she guessed, and sensual. Maybe before the evening was over she would know.... No! What was she thinking? Much more of this, and she would be a candidate for Wally's therapy group.

When he pulled back her chair, she stood and walked ahead of him through the restaurant to the entrance and then stepped outside. Turning toward where they'd left his car, she set an easy pace and made a general comment on the coolness of the evening. He replied in kind, and it wasn't until they were driving away that she remembered her doubts. "Does your Aunt Molly know we're coming to visit her?"

She knew by his quick frown that he'd forgotten the proposed visit, and it reinforced her budding suspicion that there was no Aunt Molly. Disappointment followed the reinforcement, but she doggedly pursued her advantage. "Is she doing better now?"

Quinn hesitated, knowing he was at a crossroads. "To be honest," he began, then paused. "Well, I don't really know how she's doing. I haven't seen her for several days."

"Is she still in the hospital?"

"I don't know where she is."

Rebecca shifted uncomfortably in the seat. Why didn't he just admit he'd lied in the first place? Was there something illegal about his reasons for wanting the trunk? She recognized an unsettling reluctance to believe Quinn could do anything outside the law, which just showed she was as susceptible to outward appearances as the next person. What would Wally make of that? she wondered and at the same time determined not to let Wally know.

The ride to her apartment was quiet. The building was quiet, too. Rebecca felt distinctly at odds with herself. She wanted to pretend this was an ordinary first date, although it was the most out of the ordinary evening she'd experienced in a long time. And she wanted to stop pretending that she had no idea what Quinn was really after. In the hallway outside her apartment, she turned, deciding to end the conflict one way or the other.

"Quinn, I—"

"Rebecca, there's something—" He'd begun at the same moment, and they both stopped, looked at each other and laughed awkwardly. "You first," he said.

"I—I just wanted to thank you for dinner. It was very nice."

His hand enclosed hers, and a warm shiver ran through her body. "It was my pleasure. When can I see you again?"

Tomorrow. She bit her tongue to keep from saying the word. Perspective. She had to keep her perspective. "Oh, I'm very busy this week."

"Are you going out of town?"

"No." Her breath hung precariously in her throat. He was so close, and his voice was so soft, so sensuously near. "No, I'll be home."

"Then I will see you." It was a promise, and she met his eyes, feeling more unsteady than she'd ever felt before.

"Maybe." She managed only a whisper as his mouth made the slow descent to her lips.

"Not maybe." His breath warmed her, his arms pulled her against him, and she stopped listening to the cautious voice of reason in her head. His beard brushed at her chin, a softly persuasive prelude to the equally soft pressure of his kiss. He tasted her with just enough restraint, just enough eagerness, to send a pulsing wonder through her. Her reservations melted away, and she lifted her hands to his shoulders and eased them around his neck.

She'd been kissed before. Many times. She'd responded before, too. But not like this. Not with the same swirling awareness, the sense of discovery that she now experienced. Her lips parted beneath his, and his tongue stroked the sensitive inner curves of her mouth. She returned his tentative exploration and would have set her hands to discovering the tactile pleasures of his chest, but she heard a familiar squeak from down the hall. Mrs. Albridge.

Rebecca and Quinn pulled guiltily apart and exchanged a regretful look. For her part, Rebecca knew she ought to be grateful for the interruption. Quinn Kinser was still an unknown quantity, and she was being foolish to pretend otherwise. She didn't know how he felt, but she knew it was time to say good-night.

Quinn felt both frustrated and annoyed. Normally he never let a good-night kiss get out of control, and normally he didn't need an eavesdropping neighbor to end a potentially hazardous situation. He should have realized the danger. And he should have finished what he'd started to say and admitted the truth about Molly and the trunk. If she believed him now, it would be more than he had a right to expect. "Rebecca, I want to tell you—"

She put a finger to her lips and shook her head secretively. "Not out here. Let me open the door and—" She turned, inserted the key and stared in stunned surprise as the door swung open without assistance. A quick prescience preceded her glance into the apartment, and a tight knot of alarm formed in her stomach as she realized that the lock had been broken.

Chapter Four

Quinn sensed the change in tension almost immediately. It was more than the look of consternation on Rebecca's face. It was the quick, sure recognition that something was not as it should be. He moved forward, taking the key from her and passing an assessing eye over the damaged lock. Her hand fell limply to her side, but he noticed that only with a vague awareness.

"I locked the door," she said, her voice fraying slightly on the words.

He nodded. "Stay here."

Her fingers closed on his coat sleeve in protest. "You shouldn't go inside."

"I shouldn't?" Quinn purposely lightened his tone. "How else am I going to impress you on such short acquaintance? This could be a once in a lifetime opportunity." He didn't allow time for any further protest but stepped inside the apartment, hoping his survival skills were in peak operating condition. He had no sense of danger, only a heightened alertness, an uneasy caution, as he moved toward the living area and the soft glow of a table lamp.

With a flick of the switch, he increased the light in the room and relaxed a little at the reassuringly normal appearance of the room. There was no lingerie decorating the furniture, and he smiled to himself at the memory of his first introduction to Rebecca's apartment. He cast a probing gaze into every shadow, every crack and cranny in the room and saw nothing that looked out of place. Of course, he wasn't that familiar with Rebecca's life-style, but it seemed apparent that nothing had been disturbed. Not in this room, anyway, he thought.

From there he backtracked through the hallway into the kitchen, only to find the same lack of disturbance. The counter was cluttered by a single coffee cup. Nothing more. Quinn turned and made his way through the living room to the bedroom beyond.

This room, he immediately decided, was definitely Rebecca's favorite. It wasn't cluttered, but there was a comfortable disarray, a certain studied disorder, as if she spent more time here than in any other room of the apartment. Her desk was small and obviously well used. A large case sat on the floor beside it. Her sample case, he assumed, and passed a curious gaze past it to the rest of the room. Soft colors, blue and a dusty pink, wove across the papered wall and were picked up in the adjoining bath. The bedspread and curtains blended the same combination of colors and were reflected back by the oval mirror above the dresser.

Quinn had to remind himself that he was looking for signs of a theft, or at the very least, a random search. He was not standing in Rebecca's bedroom to discover her taste in decorating. It didn't matter if he liked what he discovered. He was there in the role of protector, and he would do well to remember it. He moved matter-of-factly toward the desk top and a closer examination of its apparent neatness.

Outside in the hallway, Rebecca stood uncertainly, her mind seething with questions. This couldn't be happening. She clearly remembered locking the door. And besides, why would anyone want to break into her apartment? There was nothing worth stealing. Except, maybe, the stereo equipment, although that would be very awkward to move. The television set was an older model with a small screen, but her thirty-five-millimeter camera was sitting in plain view on the bookcase. And there was a pair of diamond studs in the top drawer of the dresser. Her mind clicked off several items of possible theft value, and with each one the hollow feeling in her stomach filled with a righteous anger.

With a falsely confident set of her shoulders, she made up her mind that she wasn't going to stand around while some burglar stole her prized possessions. This was a matter for the police. Even as she took a purposeful step forward, she realized that her thoughts were not entirely logical. Still, reassuring illumination was now pouring from the front room into the hallway, and when she pushed the door inward, she could see there was a light in the kitchen, as well. She paused, listening for sounds of conflict or disturbance. The only thing she heard was Quinn's movements, which were quiet but not stealthy. Releasing her breath in a slow sigh, Rebecca entered the living area and picked up the telephone.

In the bedroom, Quinn tensed as he heard noise beyond the doorway and then relaxed as he recognized Rebecca's voice. With one last glance around the room—a room that, despite his practical reminders of his role in this adventure, still pleased him with its soft blend of color—he turned in the direction of the sound.

She was replacing the receiver as he entered, and he took a second to admire the pert tilt of her nose and the glint of copper in her hair. Rebecca was a very beautiful lady, he thought, not for the first time that evening. He'd gotten off to a bad start by lying to her, and he wasn't sure that simply setting the record straight would make amends. But being man of the hour during this would-be break-in just might put him over the hurdle. He quietly cleared his throat. "All clear."

She jumped in startled surprise, and her palm flattened at the base of her neck. "Oh! You scared me."

He smiled. "I didn't mean to."

"I guess I'm a little jumpy."

"Perfectly understandable, under the circumstances."

Her glance darted past his shoulder to the bedroom behind him. "I called the police."

"What did you tell them?"

Her eyes met his, and one slender brow arched questioningly. "That I'd been burglarized." There was an expectant pause, but he let it pass without comment. "Well," she continued, "I have been, haven't I?"

"That's hard to say. The lock, certainly, has been broken, but other than that, I can't see any sign of disturbance. Of course, you'll need to look around. It could have been Tidy Tim, the famous burglar who cleans house during every robbery."

She lowered her raised eyebrow with a frown. "I don't see anything funny in this situation."

That was more than apparent, Quinn thought and wished he hadn't released his tension with attempted humor. The man of the hour was slipping by the minute. "You're right. I'm sorry. It was just a nervous reaction. My detective skills aren't exactly honed to a fine level of confidence."

Rebecca pursed her lips in a considering line before letting a tiny smile relax the corners of her mouth. "Thank you for looking around. I do appreciate it, even though we probably should have called the police immediately."

"Probably so," Quinn said, although he reserved the right to doubt that the police were going to be of much assistance. He had investigated enough break-ins during his early days as a reporter to know that this one was hardly worthy of the description. "Why don't you check for missing items before the officers arrive?"

She agreed with a quick nod and then glanced around as if she didn't know where to begin. "Do you think anything was stolen?"

Realizing she needed reassurance and direction, Quinn moved closer to her. "There's only one way to find out."

Again she nodded, but made no move from the middle of the room. He caught the subtle scent of her perfume and forced himself not to lean closer. Instead he took her hand. "Now, what in this room is out of place?"

She turned in a slow, careful circle, looking, narrowing her gaze several different times. Finally, she looked at him again and shook her head. "Everything looks the same."

"What about the stuff on the bookshelves?"

Again she turned, visually checking the two floor-to-ceiling shelves. "My camera is there. And my grandfather's pocket watch is still in its case. The books look okay, too." She paused to frown. "I don't suppose anyone would want the books. They wouldn't have much value in a black market."

Quinn suppressed a smile. "You're probably right. But whoever broke into the apartment might look through them for cash. I've heard that some people keep their savings hidden in a collection of books."

"I keep money in my purse or in the bank. There isn't any cash in the sugar bowl, either."

"Somehow, that doesn't surprise me. You seem like a very practical young woman." Quinn rubbed his beard and guided Rebecca toward the kitchen. "But just to be on the safe side, let's check."

The inspection of the kitchen took very little time, considering that it was readily apparent that the pans, plates, and other cooking paraphernalia were all in place. Looking through the bedroom, from desk drawers to dresser drawers, took much longer, and Quinn could tell that the search bothered Rebecca more than she wanted him to know.

When she finally closed the closet doors with a heavy sigh, shaking her head to indicate that she could find nothing missing, he wanted badly to be able to offer some comfort. He just wasn't sure it was the right moment, and while he silently debated the question, there was a knock on the front door.

The police officer was a brash young man, fresh from the academy and determined to go strictly by the book. He wasted no time in removing his hat and any doubt that he was in charge from here on in. Quinn wasn't impressed, but he obligingly stepped back, giving moral support to Rebecca as Officer Cook ran through a list of questions with the efficiency and feeling of a professional interrogator. "Name?" he asked brusquely, his pencil poised.

"Rebecca Whitaker."

"Spell it, please."

"R-e-b-e-c-c-a W-h-i-t-a-k-e-r."

"Address?"

"2642 South Benton, Unit 3-J. Glenacre, Missouri." Rebecca paused for a moment, then, with the merest whisper of humor in her voice, she proceeded to spell out the words. "That's G-l-e-n-a-c—"

The police officer looked up with a patient smile. "Yes, I know. Thank you. Now could you tell me the last time the apartment was secured?"

"Secured?" Rebecca shifted position on the sofa, betraying her uneasiness to Quinn and giving Officer Cook another chance to be condescending.

"When is the last time you locked the door upon leaving the apartment?"

"Tonight." Rebecca glanced at Quinn, as if confirming the fact. "Around seven o'clock."

"And at what time did you return?"

"Just a little while ago... a few minutes before I called you."

The policeman nodded, looked at his watch and wrote something on his tablet. "Is that when you discovered the broken lock?"

"Yes."

He tapped the pencil, with the eraser end down, against the paper. "Would you show me the apartment, please?"

Quinn wanted to show him the door—the full force of it against his backside—but resisted the urge. It was hard to sit still while the policeman walked through the rooms, following Rebecca and making squiggly notes, asking questions about her neighbors and whether or not she'd received any suspicious calls or visitors lately. Quinn was relieved that she didn't mention him in either category.

When the tour was finished, and Officer Cook stood once more in the center of the living room, Quinn watched the closing flip of the notepad and the grim expression on Rebecca's face.

"If you think of anything else, Miss Whitaker," Cook said smoothly, "give me a call. Other than that, there isn't much the police department can do. I suggest you call the janitor and get a new lock put on. Until then you should find somewhere else to stay." He looked purposefully at Quinn. "Ordinarily a burglar won't return, but I don't encourage people to take any chances. These days, it pays to be careful, if you know what I mean."

Quinn knew, and he could have cheerfully throttled the policeman for needlessly frightening Rebecca further. "Thank you for your assistance," he said. "We certainly will be careful." Within the space of a minute and a half, Quinn had walked the officer to the door, sped him on his way and closed the door carefully behind him. The door, however, wouldn't stay closed. It soundlessly opened a vulnerable inch. As he turned, he saw the quickly masked concern that creased Rebecca's forehead.

"Friendly guy, wasn't he?"

Her nervous question found an answering chord in a forgotten corner of his emotions. He wanted to gather her into his arms, tell her she would be safe with him, comfort her, protect her. If he'd known her longer... What the hell? he thought, he'd already made the mistake of lying to her. Why balk at moving too fast? She needed to be held, whether she realized it or not.

"Oh, he was a great guy," Quinn said as he moved forward and placed his hands on her shoulders. "A real credit to the force." He drew her toward him, feeling her resistance, sensing her wish not to resist. Ignoring the mixed signals she was giving him, Quinn gathered her close in his embrace and hoped she would accept his comfort for the simple human gesture that it was. She couldn't seem to relax, though, and Quinn loosened his hold, allowing her to move away if she chose. When she didn't make any attempt to leave his arms, he smiled softly and pressed a fleeting kiss into the warm summery scent of her auburn hair.

After a moment in which she still stood somewhat stiffly in his arms, he loosened the embrace a little more and attempted to put her at ease once again. "I'm surprised, Rebecca, that you didn't tell Officer Cook about your 'suspicious' neighbor down the hall... the one who is after your lingerie samples."

Rebecca looked up, fully into his face, and her lips curved ever so little. "Mrs. Albridge? Now why didn't I think of that?" As she straightened away from his attempt at comfort, Rebecca's expression became purposeful and considering, her uncertainty momentarily displaced. "Let's ask her."

"Ask her what?" Quinn was confused. "You don't really think that woman in the pink curler cap had anything to do with this?"

Rebecca smiled as much for herself as for him. "No, of course not. I've never seen her outside her apartment, but nothing and no one gets past her. She must have seen whoever broke my lock. At the very least, she can probably give us a detailed description.''

With an agreeable, if somewhat skeptical nod, Quinn followed Rebecca out into the hallway, although his arms felt cheated and empty. Rebecca was obviously a determined woman when it came to getting answers. He liked that, and he wondered what it would be like to be the focus of so much determined energy. Good, he thought. It would probably feel very good.

Mrs. Albridge opened her door almost before the knock had a chance to resound in the narrow hallway. She kept a hand braced on the knob, Quinn noticed, as if she expected trouble and wanted to be ready to secure the door if necessary. He hid his amusement at the sight of the neat cap of gray curls wisping around her head. She might have been sixty or sixty-five. It was hard to tell.

''Hello, Mrs. Albridge,'' Rebecca said with as much friendliness as she could muster at the moment. ''I wonder if we could talk to you?''

''We? Who's we?'' The voice wasn't overly friendly; the small dark eyes were openly suspicious.

Rebecca had a curious impulse to laugh. ''My...friend and me. You see, while we were out tonight, someone broke the lock on my apartment door, and I wondered if you...?''

''As a matter of fact...'' Her suspicion vanished with interest, and Mrs. Albridge opened the door another, less hesitant, inch. ''There was a man here earlier. I saw him myself. He was tall and very dark...could have been from one of those sheikh nations.''

''*Sheikh nations?*'' Quinn whispered, and Rebecca shushed him with a wave of her hand behind her back.

''He looked Arabic?'' Rebecca encouraged her neighbor to say more. ''Was there anything else you remember about him? Was he near my door?''

"Yes." Mrs. Albridge nodded with enthusiasm. "He and Dr. Sherrow stood right outside your door and talked for a long time before they left."

"Did they leave together?"

"Yes, they did."

It probably meant nothing. The man could have been one of Wally's patients or a fellow psychologist. There was always someone coming or going at Wally's apartment. "You didn't notice anything—" Rebecca paused "—unusual?"

Mrs. Albridge wrinkled her forehead in thought. "Well, I did think it was odd for Dr. Sherrow to leave the building with a strange man."

"Was he strange?" Quinn asked. "Or just strange-looking?"

Rebecca frowned at him, but Quinn didn't seem concerned, and Mrs. Albridge missed the humor, anyway. "He was strange-looking," the older lady said, giving the question a legitimacy it didn't deserve. "Not at all Dr. Sherrow's type. Too dark."

"Oh, I see." Quinn stepped confidingly closer. "And from your observations, what is Miss Whitaker's type?"

Rebecca interfered before her neighbor could answer that, too. "Thank you, Mrs. Albridge. I'll talk to Dr. Sherrow myself." She started to turn, then paused. "You didn't see anyone else in the hallway this evening?"

Mrs. Albridge patted a curl at her temple. "Just you and this gentleman here."

With a quick grin, Quinn caught Rebecca's eye. "Well, I certainly hope you don't think *I'm* strange-looking, Mrs. Albridge."

"No." The door started to close on the words. "Just strange."

Rebecca laughed, letting the tension of the past hour slip away for a moment. "You asked for that."

Quinn leaned against the wall, watching her, enjoying the sound of her laughter, admiring the composure she exhibited in this unsettling and frightening situation. Now that he knew nothing had been damaged, other than the door and perhaps Rebecca's sense of security, he wanted to concentrate on getting to know more about her. But before he could even formulate the thought, she was turning away, moving down the hallway toward her apartment.

Rebecca kept her gaze from straying to the door and the pry marks visible on the wood beside the knob. She didn't want to see the evidence of intrusion into her life, but she couldn't suppress the shudder that rippled across her shoulders as she walked past the entrance to her apartment on her way to Wally's front door. She knocked and then glanced at Quinn, who was still down the hall, still standing with his back to the wall, his arms crossed at his chest.

A nice chest, she thought. Broad and muscled and strong. She had almost, *almost*, laid her head against his chest and sought comfort in his arms. If he hadn't mentioned Mrs. Albridge, Rebecca was sure she would have done just that. There was something about Quinn that made her feel safe, made her feel as if she could depend upon him. It was ridiculous, really. She hardly knew him, and it wasn't as if she went around *looking* for someone to depend upon. But here he was, just when she needed him most, and she was grateful to whatever fate had brought him into her life. He winked at her, his mouth forming a bearded smile that was half cheeky, half charming. Rebecca's lips curved in answer as she raised her hand to knock again.

"I don't believe anyone is at home." Quinn straightened and approached her as she stood in front of Wally's door. "Is this Dr. Sherrow's apartment?"

"Yes. I can't imagine why she doesn't answer. Wally is usually home by this time on Tuesday nights."

"It's only a little after ten o'clock."

Rebecca lowered her hand to her side. "It seems later."

"Because of all the excitement, I imagine." Quinn nodded toward Apartment 3-K. "Can you spend the night with your friend?"

"Oh, sure." Rebecca heard the breathiness in her voice and felt a beginning tremor of panic, but she hoped that Quinn wouldn't notice her nervousness. "Wally won't mind. But I don't have a key. I'll just wait until she comes. Then I'll ask." The words tumbled out, too fast, too thick. "She'll be home soon, I'm sure. She's usually home by now."

Quinn pursed his lips and frowned thoughtfully. "You're not worried about . . . anything, are you?" He shook his head. "That was dumb. Of course, you're worried. You have every right to be. Is there someone else we could call to come over? A family member, maybe?"

"No. I'm fine." She managed a quietly unconvincing smile. "Wally should be here any time now." Her hesitation filled the space of a heartbeat. "Would you, uh, mind staying with me until she comes home?"

"Of course. I'll be glad to." He would not, Quinn decided, look at his watch. The actual time didn't matter, anyway. It was the thought of Emily that tugged at him, reminded him of other responsibilities. Even though he knew his daughter was—or should be—sound asleep, Quinn felt an inner pressure to go home, to be in the house should she awake and call to him. Colleen, the live-in housekeeper, was there, of course, but it wasn't the same. Emily depended upon him to protect her, and asleep or awake, she took his presence for granted and basked in the security it offered. He took that innocent trust seriously, although the appeal in Rebecca's eyes made him wish he wasn't quite so sensitive. He wished it even more when he noticed the tight lines of tension around her mouth and heard the bravado in her voice.

"I shouldn't ask you to stay," she said with a regretful tone. "That wasn't very thoughtful. I'm sure you have other commitments, and I'm sorry I..." She stopped and gave him a smile. "I can wait for Wally by myself. There really isn't any need for you to—"

"I'm not in a tremendous hurry, Rebecca. We can go back into your apartment and wait." He let his lips part in a reassuring grin. "When your friend returns, I'll return to Emily, and everyone will be happy."

Rebecca didn't feel happy at all. "Emily?" she questioned. "Who is Emily?"

"My eight-year-old daughter."

"You have a daughter?" She tried to hide her surprise and knew she didn't succeed. Quinn had a daughter. An eight-year-old daughter. Rebecca hadn't considered that possibility. She realized suddenly that for all the questions she'd asked him during the evening she'd neglected to find out about his past relationships. "You told me you were divorced, didn't you? How long has it been?"

"More than three years now. It seems longer."

"You have only one child?"

"Yes. I wanted another, but—" He ended the sentence with a shrug. "Don't you think we ought to go inside?"

"Oh, of course." Rebecca took a step toward her open apartment door and stopped. Quinn watched the series of expressions that floated across her face, and he interpreted her hesitation as a severe case of overwrought nerves.

With a lift of her chin, Rebecca moved forward and pushed open the door. It swung back silently, and she stood looking at the pry marks on the door panel. "You don't have to wait, Quinn. I'll be fine. Really." She touched the doorknob, twisted it once, then let her hand drop. Taking a deep breath, she groped for firmer control over the helpless feeling inside her. After all, nothing had been taken, noth-

ing disturbed except the lock, and she could prop something against the door to keep it closed.

But as she looked inside the apartment, she had the sense
of an unwelcome presence. Someone, some stranger had
invaded her home. It didn't matter that nothing had been
stolen. It only mattered that her privacy had been violated.
"Why my apartment?" she asked aloud. "What could
possibly prompt anyone into breaking in?"

"Burglaries are random crimes, Rebecca. There isn't
often a solid reason to steal from one person as opposed to
another. It just happens. Luckily, whoever tried your place
left before any damage was done."

"You're right." She turned, with an attempted smile
tucked at the corners of her mouth. "I won't worry about
it. With Officer Cook on the job, I should feel perfectly
safe, shouldn't I?"

The humor fell flat, and she wished she had another opportunity to seek the protection of Quinn's embrace. But she
wouldn't, of course, because that would be too revealing of
her state of mind. "Thanks, again, Quinn, for a lovely evening. I enjoyed the dinner very much. And I am sorry for all
the trouble here."

"Don't apologize. It has been a long time since I've had
a date end with such excitement." It had been a long time
since he'd felt this seesaw of emotion simply because of a
woman, and he wasn't quite sure how to handle it. The moment didn't seem right to take her into his arms, and yet he
felt that she needed more than just his presence. He certainly couldn't say good-night and walk away, leaving her to
face the night alone. "Would you like me to help you secure the door?" he asked, saying the first thing that came
to mind and realizing immediately it was the wrong thing.
"While we wait for your friend," he amended.

Rebecca took a step inside her apartment, but allowed him no room to follow. "No. I can manage. You've done more than enough already. Thanks, though, for offering."

Quinn looked at his watch. It was getting late, and he wanted to be home. He wanted to stay with Rebecca, as well. Why did she have to be brave? She reminded him of Emily when she tried to act so damned independent. Emily had traveled alone on the airplane because she was "growing up." Rebecca would stay alone, waiting for a friend who might not be home for hours, because she was "grown-up." So why did he feel guilty? With a sigh, he quit trying to understand the female mind. "Why don't you come home with me, Rebecca? I have locks on every door in the house and an extra bedroom. I have a live-in housekeeper, if you're worried about propriety, and an eight-year-old who keeps my conscience on its toes. You can rest securely, and I'll bring you back here in the morning."

"That would be too much trouble for you." Rebecca had intended to refuse outright and was surprised at the wavering tone of her voice. Did she want him to persuade her? "I'll be fine here."

"No, you'll be frightened or at the very least, too tense to sleep. Even if you stay across the hall, you'll spend the night listening for the burglar to return. Now don't argue. Just get your toothbrush and come with me."

Rebecca opened her mouth to protest but closed it soundlessly. He was absolutely right. She wanted to get as far away from this place as she could. "Are you sure it will be all right?"

For a moment his eyes centered on her lips, then lifted slowly to meet her questioning gaze. "It will be fine, Rebecca."

She believed him. She didn't know why, but she did. Tomorrow, undoubtedly, she was going to wonder what had possessed her to abandon her independence. But for tonight, she didn't care. Quinn had offered her a secure haven, and she was going to accept it. "It will only take a minute to get my things," she said.

Chapter Five

The Trunk.

Rebecca didn't know why it hadn't occurred to her earlier, but almost two hours after discovering the broken lock, when she was safely and comfortably ensconced in a leather recliner in the den of Quinn Kinser's home, she remembered. "Do you think someone wanted the trunk?" she asked him.

"The trunk?" Quinn had hoped she wouldn't bring that up. He had thought of the possibility and discarded it. There couldn't be anything worth stealing in that old trunk. Molly would have told him. Wouldn't she? The awful possibility that the trunk had been taken from Rebecca's apartment, and that she had forgotten it had been there in the first place, flashed through his head. "I didn't see it anywhere in your apartment."

"It hasn't been delivered yet." She lifted the coffee mug to her lips and inhaled the sweetly rich smell of chocolate. "Still too hot."

Quinn glanced sharply at her, and Rebecca smiled as she set the mug back on the end table. "The cocoa," she explained. "It needs to cool a little more."

"You don't have to drink it if you don't want to." He started to reach down and slip off his shoes, but he stopped. Much as he would have liked to relax and stretch out on the

sofa, he thought the situation warranted a degree of deco-
rum. Rebecca looked far too comfortably feminine sitting
there in his favorite chair. He shifted his position and com-
promised by resting his feet, shoes and all, on the coffee table. "When Emily is upset about something, I make cocoa
for her. I guess that's what I was thinking of when I made it
for you. I should have asked you if you wanted any first."

"Oh, no. I love it, thank you. No one has made cocoa for
me since…" She paused, remembering, thinking it had been
a very long time since anyone had treated her with such
tender thoughtfulness. "Well, I probably wasn't much older
than your daughter. She's a lucky little girl to have you."

His eyes, his expression, even the strong, stubborn angle
of his bearded jaw went soft with affection. "I'm the lucky
one. Emily is—" He broke off with a rueful grimace. "You
probably ought to change the subject, Rebecca, before I pull
out her baby pictures."

She laughed, and Quinn thought how good it sounded.
This room hadn't heard a woman's laughter in years. Diane, his ex-wife and Emily's mother, looked at life, and
everything else, as a serious matter. He only hoped that his
daughter would grow up to laugh as easily, and as naturally
as Rebecca did.

"I would love to see Emily's baby pictures." Rebecca let
her glance drift to the walls of the den where photographs
of a dark-haired, blue-eyed child at various ages and in a
myriad of poses smiled back at her from several different
angles. "Assuming, of course, that there are others."

His chuckle was soft as his gaze followed hers. "Thousands more, but I won't do that to you tonight."

"Has she always looked so much like you?"

"For the first six months of her life, she looked very much
like a little monkey. No one, except her mother, was rude
enough to point out any resemblance between us then." He
paused to review the wall of photos. "I can't bring myself

to take down some of the earlier photographs in order to put up current ones, so this portfolio of parental pride keeps expanding. The wall is getting a bit cluttered, isn't it?''

It was, but somehow it looked right. The rest of the house—at least the part Rebecca had glimpsed briefly on her arrival—was lovely. Old, traditional, and welcoming. But it was this room that was most like Quinn. Comfortably cluttered with a melange of varied interests, the room whispered secrets about him. And she liked what she heard. "It's a charming room, Quinn. I wouldn't change a single picture frame."

He settled easily against the sofa cushion, relaxing with her despite his self-imposed restrictions, wondering why he wasn't in the least bit sleepy. "So," he said, cautiously reintroducing a touchy subject, "the trunk hasn't been delivered yet. What's taking so long?"

"I haven't been home." Rebecca picked up the mug and sipped the pleasant-tasting cocoa. "I couldn't have it delivered to an empty apartment."

"You could have had it delivered to me and saved us the trouble of moving it a second time."

"But you have to move it to your Aunt Molly's, anyway." She watched his reaction closely and wasn't surprised to see him frown.

"Aunt Molly," he muttered. "Right. But you see, Rebecca, I—"

"There isn't an 'Aunt Molly,' is there, Quinn?" She had known it intuitively, but she wanted his confirmation.

His eyes met hers, held, and then he looked away. "Oh, yes, there is a Molly. She's every bit as real as you or me, and the trunk does belong to her."

No, Rebecca thought. *It belongs to me. Fair and square.* Still her conscience vacillated between right and wrong, keeping the trunk or giving it back, and she finally told herself firmly that she had every right to at least see what was inside it before making that decision. "Well, if it's her trunk, then there can't be anything more than sentimental things inside. So I guess that rules out the possibility that whoever broke into my apartment was looking for the trunk."

"I think you're right. Whoever broke the lock probably was looking for money or jewelry and was frightened away before having a chance to steal anything. The burglar could have heard Mrs. Albridge open her door. Or maybe it was your friend and her sheikh."

Rebecca smiled above the rim of the cup before taking another drink. "Mrs. Albridge has a lively imagination. Wally will have a fit when I tell her about that. She has a rather eccentric view of men, especially those from countries where women are second-class citizens."

"A feminist."

"Absolutely. And you can spell it in capital letters, too. I adore Wally, but she is definitely an extremist."

"So you don't share her views?"

"I didn't say that." Rebecca placed the half-empty cocoa mug on the table. "I'm as involved in my career as she is in hers. It's just that I'm more mellow about traditions."

"Your career is very important to you?"

"Very." She said it simply, wanting there to be no misunderstanding from the beginning. Although she wasn't sure if this was actually a beginning or not. She nodded toward the wall. "I don't have any photographs on my walls. Only awards for sales achievements."

And there, in a nutshell, Quinn thought, was the problem. He'd lived with a "career woman," thank you. He'd sometimes thought it would have been easier if Diane had left him for another man, rather than for her work. At least, Rebecca was upfront about it. Better to know now than later when the comfortable feeling she evoked in him had progressed to a dangerous level. "You have no ambition to get married, have children?'' he asked, mostly from a desire to have the question settled firmly in his mind.

"Not at the moment." She pushed the lever and eased the recliner to an upright position. "I can't say I don't think about it, but for now..."

"You're satisfied." His voice was threaded with a regret she couldn't interpret.

"Satisfied? I don't know about that." Lately she had been feeling distinctly dissatisfied. "For now, I'm just avoiding complications." Which, she realized, was a ludicrous thing to say, considering that Quinn represented a whole passel of complications to her plans, and yet she was sitting quite contentedly in his house long past midnight.

"Well, if we don't get to bed, you're going to be too sleepy to deal with all of tomorrow's complications." He stood, wishing he'd done something besides bring her home with him. What was Emily going to think in the morning? What was *he* going to think while he lay in his own bed knowing that Rebecca was only a couple of doors away?

She stood, too, stretching her arms just a little. A stirring attraction rippled through him, and he quickly moved toward the doorway. "I'll show you your—the guest room." He made the amendment and consequently gave the words far too much emphasis.

Rebecca noticed and wondered at his sudden restless movements. Had she said something? Was it her commitment to her career that bothered him? Maybe he was looking for a wife, someone to share his life and his daughter. The idea wasn't entirely unappealing, and she hesitated to let it stay in her mind, but it seemed in no hurry to leave.

As she followed him, she decided perhaps she was simply tired and not thinking clearly. Sleep seemed suddenly very necessary. But when she walked past him as he stood in the doorway, Rebecca caught a lingering scent of the cocoa he'd made for her, and she wanted to rest her head on his shoulder. Just for a minute.

Her eyes met his, transferring the thought to him as surely as if she'd spoken it aloud. There wasn't room for indecision, and her lips parted with a ready invitation. Quinn had done something for her this evening that she wasn't about to underestimate. He had been understanding, thoughtful and considerate, tenderly so, and she was grateful. The kiss she offered was a simple thank-you, wasn't it?

This was the last thing he needed at the moment, Quinn thought. It was late. She was seductively disheveled and more vulnerable than she knew. His hands closed over hers tightly, hoping to squeeze some sense into her, get her to withdraw the kiss she offered so freely. But she only moved closer, tilting her face up to his, waiting in that quietly exciting way a woman has when she knows she won't be rejected. He ought to press a fleeting and friendly kiss at one corner of her mouth and be done with it. Hell, all things considered, he was in a much more vulnerable position than she was. If Emily woke up and wandered downstairs...

His gaze fell to the tempting slope of Rebecca's lips, and it became harder to remember his paternal responsibilities. Emily wasn't going to awaken. And it was, after all, nothing more than a good-night kiss. Rebecca swayed toward him, and his arms, with hardly any urging, slipped around her waist. When her palms came to rest against his chest, a warm, familiar feeling moved inside him, and Quinn knew he'd never really had any other option.

As his lips came to hers, Rebecca released her breath in a soft quiescent sigh. She wanted his kiss, needed the reassurance of his arms around her. The reason had as much to do with the events of the evening as with her sincere longing to be close to him. With the sensuous brush of his beard against her face, Rebecca lost the ability to weigh her reactions. She merely relaxed and enjoyed the delicious sensations pouring through her.

Quinn tasted minty and sweet, with the faintest scent of chocolate still clinging in the thickness of his moustache. Rebecca wanted to smile, but his lips were requesting a response that took all her concentration. How had she managed, in the space of a fairly short evening, to experience such a range of emotions? From curiosity to alarm, from apprehension to cozy relaxation, and from simple awareness to a complicated attraction. But in his arms, it didn't matter very much. Only the pressure of his lips on hers, only the strength she found in his embrace mattered.

When he loosened his hold on her, Rebecca was reluctant to let the moment end. Which was silly, she told herself. Hadn't she already received more support from him than she had any right to ask of an old friend, much less a new one? It was time she stopped being a weak sister and took charge of her emotions. With a determined smile, she stepped outside the circle of his arms. "Quinn, I want to thank you one more time for being so—"

He interrupted her with a shake of his head. "I didn't do anything that any other red-blooded American male wouldn't have done under the circumstances. We're all heroes at heart, you know, just waiting for the call of a damsel in distress. I should be thanking you."

She laughed. For no good reason at all. She hadn't been a damsel in distress since the fourth grade when the class bully had thrown her favorite doll into the prickly hedge. She'd waited hours for a rescuer and finally had braved the thorns herself. After that experience, she had wasted no more time looking for white knights. But now, looking into Quinn's extraordinary blue eyes, her lips still tingling from his touch, she wondered if perhaps she'd missed out on a pleasant bit of fantasy.

"Good night, Quinn."

His finger brushed her cheek, hesitated at the corner of her mouth and then, as if he thought better of the idea, he dropped his hand to his side. "It's morning, actually, but there are still a few good sleeping hours yet. Come on, I'll show you the guest room."

Switching off the downstairs light, he guided Rebecca to the stairs by the dim glow of the moon spilling through an overhead skylight. The house was midnight-quiet, and their footsteps created a soft squeak as they climbed the stairs. At the top landing, Quinn moved ahead of her and opened a door. Within seconds, he had turned on a bedside lamp and bathed the room in muted shadows.

"There's a bath across the hallway," Quinn said. "And breakfast is anytime you're ready for it in the morning." He backed toward the door. "I'll see you then."

She nodded, and Quinn left the room, carefully closing the door behind him. Rebecca ran a hand over the chenille spread and released a long-held sigh. She didn't usually sleep well away from her own bed, but she suspected tonight would be different. As everything seemed to be different when Quinn was nearby. Without a second thought, she pulled back the covers and prepared to test the theory.

Down the hall, in his own room, Quinn looked balefully at his bed. He didn't think he had much chance of catching any of those good sleeping hours still left before daybreak. Knowing that Rebecca was in his house made him restless. He kept wondering how Emily would react to sharing breakfast with a stranger. Not just a stranger, a woman. But it was too late to worry about that now. He could hardly ask Rebecca to stay in her room until Emily left for school, could he?

Without bothering to take off his clothes, Quinn lay on the bed and stared at the ceiling. All in all, he decided, it had been one hell of a first date. The only problem he could see was what did he do as an encore?

REBECCA AWAKENED, feeling refreshed and rested. She took in the contours of the bedroom from the cushioned luxury of the bed. Accustomed as she was to waking in strange hotel rooms, Rebecca felt no sense of being out of place, and she was in no hurry to leave the comfortable bedroom. She stretched lazily and squinted at the window, trying to judge the time by the amount of morning sun trickling through the gauzy curtains. With the light, the night shadows had disappeared, and the room was now an easygoing beige color with occasional splashes of buttercup yellow to add contrast. By the lack of personal touches, Rebecca knew it was a guest room, but still she felt very much at home.

There was a tranquillity in Quinn's home, a sense of happy times and family bonds, that Rebecca recognized without being able to analyze. Maybe that was why she'd slept so soundly. Or maybe it had been the cocoa. Or the security that Quinn provided simply by his nearness.

With a yawn, Rebecca decided she was feeling far too relaxed in this house. It was time to get out of bed and bring last night's unsettling events into focus. She was glad, very glad, that she didn't have to go into the office. She didn't think she would have been able to keep her mind on sales figures and projected sales trips. Not today. The first thing she needed to do, she supposed, was to find the apartment building's elusive superintendent and arrange to get the lock fixed.

Sitting up, Rebecca fought another yawn and finally gave in. No, she thought, the first thing she needed to do was to dress and follow the mysterious scent that was at that very moment tickling her nose. She hoped it was a cup of coffee calling her name, and she hoped Quinn would be there to share it with her.

When she found the kitchen a short time later, Quinn was nowhere to be seen, but the aroma of coffee was definitely real. Rebecca sniffed appreciatively as she paused in the doorway to observe the sole occupant of the kitchen. Perched on a stool beside the breakfast bar, the child was studying the back of a cereal box. With one foot tucked beneath her and one foot swinging free, her expression one of total concentration, she could have been posing for an ad promoting a vitamin-enriched cereal, "part of a well balanced breakfast." Rebecca smiled, thinking that Quinn's daughter was just as pretty as her pictures. She was dressed all in blue with only a flashy neon-pink belt and matching hair ribbon for contrast. Emily was, Rebecca decided, a very stylish eight-year-old.

"Hello," she said. "You must be Emily."

Wide blue eyes, much like Quinn's, glanced at Rebecca in surprise. "Hello."

So far so good, Rebecca thought as she stepped forward. "I'm Rebecca Whitaker... a, uh, friend of your father's."

There was an infinitesimal hesitation before the foot that had stopped swinging started again. "It's nice to meet you," Emily said in well-trained, polite tones. "Would you like some breakfast?"

The thought of presweetened cereal made her stomach churn, but Rebecca knew better than to say so. "Hmm. Maybe after I've had a cup of coffee."

"I'll get it for you." Emily slid from the stool and walked around the bar. She jumped up, balanced herself on her knees on the countertop and opened a cabinet door. With a mug in her hand, she repeated the action in reverse, and within a minute she'd set the coffee on the kitchen table. "There," Emily said with obvious satisfaction.

"Why, thank you, Emily." Rebecca pulled out one of the wicker-type chairs and seated herself at the table. Lifting the cup, she braced herself to sip the steaming hot coffee, realizing that Emily expected immediate approval. It was hot. It also had the consistency of weak tea. "Mmm." Rebecca pressed her stinging lips together. "Did you make the coffee this morning, Emily?"

The pert elfin mouth parted in a gap-toothed smile that could only belong to an eight-year-old. "Yes, I did. For my daddy."

Rebecca nodded. "I'm sure he'll appreciate it. Do you make coffee for him very often?"

"No. But I watch him do it every day." With a toss of her dark ponytail, Emily placed her hands over the back of a chair. "It isn't hard, you know."

"I've heard that." For good measure, Rebecca judiciously took another sip. "What school do you attend, Emily?"

The child named a local elementary school, and Rebecca nodded as if she knew exactly where it was. "And I'll bet you're in the—" Rebecca tilted her head to one side, as if debating the question "—eighth grade. Right?"

Emily's chuckle was spontaneous and skeptical. "Second," she corrected with childish patience. "I'm in the second grade."

"Emily Kinser, did you turn on that television?" A tall, slender, and stern-looking woman appeared in the doorway, with her arms wrapped around a stack of towels. "You know better than—"

Emily looked over her shoulder. "Colleen, this is Daddy's friend, Rebecca." She rolled the syllables, lending them an air of importance. "And I made coffee for her."

"Good morning." The housekeeper acknowledged the introduction, even as her gaze whipped across the counter. "I hope you didn't make a mess, Emily." Colleen seemed more concerned with locating scattered coffee grounds than with finding a stranger in the kitchen.

"I didn't." Emily's chin sank onto her hands, and Rebecca felt a tug of sympathy.

"Well, you better go brush your teeth." Colleen walked past the kitchen table on her way to the opposite doorway. "It will be time to leave for school in a few minutes. I'll be back in a minute to fix you some breakfast," she said to Rebecca.

"That's okay," Rebecca began, "I don't—"

"She can't hear you." Emily regarded Rebecca pensively. "Colleen doesn't hear anything she doesn't want to."

Rebecca turned her gaze to Emily and the matter-of-fact statement. She didn't know too many children of this age, but Quinn's daughter seemed very mature. Was that what divorce did for children? Rebecca wondered. Give them insight beyond their years and of dubious value? "Does she take care of you?" Rebecca asked.

"When Daddy isn't here. And she fixes my hair in the mornings. Daddy can't do that very good."

Rebecca smiled and sipped the coffee. Oddly enough she was beginning to enjoy the taste. "Hmm. I had the idea there wasn't anything your daddy couldn't do."

Emily wrinkled her nose. "Unless he just doesn't want to. Do you like him?"

"Yes."

"A lot?"

Rebecca thought seriously about lying but decided against it. "A lot."

"Are you going to live with us?"

Whoa! She hadn't expected that. "No, Emily. I stayed here last night because..." Pausing to choose the right words, Rebecca wondered where Quinn was at the moment. "Well, you see, someone broke the lock on my apartment, and I..." she began.

"Really? Who?" Emily's expression of disdain conflicted with the energy and eagerness of her questions. "Did the police come? I'll bet you were really scared."

Rebecca began clicking off the answers on her fingers. "Yes, someone really broke the lock. I don't know who it was. A policeman came and asked a hundred questions. And yes, I was a little bit scared; wouldn't you be?"

Emily pursed her lips in exaggerated thought. "No."

"Do I smell coffee?" Quinn stood in the doorway. He wore a slightly wrinkled knit pullover shirt and a pair of faded jeans. He looked as though he'd rolled out of bed, pulled on the first clothes he saw and hurried downstairs.

"Good morning, Daddy." Emily's face had brightened with the sound of his voice, and now she ran to him and hugged him.

"Hi, sunshine," he said, giving her ponytail a tug. Above her head, his eyes met Rebecca's, and he smiled slowly.

As a sensation that was far too pleasant for so early in the morning rippled down her back, Rebecca curled her fingers around the mug and raised it in greeting. "Emily made coffee for you."

"Great." His hand squeezed his daughter's tiny shoulder, but he continued to smile at Rebecca. "I need a cup to wake me up this morning."

"Didn't your alarm go off, Daddy? I had to eat cereal for breakfast."

"*Had* to?" Quinn shook his head as he moved toward the kitchen cupboard. "That's a crock, Emmy, and you and I both know it. Colleen would have fixed you anything you wanted to eat. All you had to do was ask."

Rebecca watched as Emily considered that with a pout. "Colleen combed my hair, and it hurt. She meant to, Daddy. I know she did."

"My, your morning has gotten off to a bad start, hasn't it?" Quinn glanced at his daughter, then at Rebecca before he turned his attention to pouring coffee into a cup. "What about you, Rebecca? Did you have to eat cereal for breakfast, too?"

"Emily offered, but I'm not a big fan of eating anything this early." She smiled at Emily. "Maybe later."

Quinn pulled out a chair and sat opposite to Rebecca. Emily was on his lap before he had time to get settled. "Did you sleep all right?"

A sudden and inexplicable shyness rippled through Rebecca, and she lifted her mug then set it down again. "I didn't have any trouble at all, which is surprising, considering..."

"She has an apartment," Emily said, leaning her head against Quinn's chest. "Someone broke it."

"Yes, I know." Quinn met Rebecca's eyes and thought how very pretty she looked. He wondered if morning always agreed with her and wished he'd taken the time to find some other clothes. "I'm glad you felt safe here."

Rebecca's lips curved. *Safe.* What a warm feeling the word gave. What a quiet, welcome glow it added to the morning. "I think I can handle whatever the day brings."

"I never doubted it." Across the table, their eyes held, and a sweet, uncertain tension spiraled through the air.

"Do you like the coffee, Daddy?" Emily grabbed Quinn's hand and pressed it between her smaller ones. "I'll make it for you every day from now on."

"That'll be great, sunshine." Quinn took a drink and wrinkled his nose over Emily's head. "Are you all ready for school? Have you brushed your teeth?"

Emily narrowed her gaze at Rebecca. "Yes. I'm ready to go."

Rebecca arched her brows not wanting to point out that Emily hadn't brushed. Emily might be only eight, Rebecca thought, but she was obviously feeling somewhat threatened, and either consciously or not, she was staking first claim on Quinn's attentions.

"Smile when you say that, partner," Quinn captured Emily's chin and turned her face toward him. "Let's see those teeth—all five of them."

"Daddy...." Emily posted a plaintive protest. "I have more than five teeth."

"So you do. And they're all in need of brushing." He scooted her off his lap. "Take care of it. Quick."

It was apparent that Emily didn't want to leave the room, but Rebecca decided from Quinn's easy, authoritative manner that this was a common morning ritual. "She doesn't like to leave you," Rebecca commented when Emily had departed from the kitchen.

"She just doesn't like to go to school." He smiled wryly. "Actually, she *does* like school. She just doesn't want me to *think* she does. She's at that age." He swallowed a mouthful of tepid coffee. "Thanks for not mentioning the—uh, special flavor of your morning beverage."

Rebecca laughed. "It kind of grows on you, though, doesn't it?"

"Emily has the same effect. She isn't at her most charming today but, if you're not careful, she'll have your heartstrings wrapped around her finger."

Would she? Rebecca wondered. Children had never held the number one place on her list of priorities, but after spending only a few hours in this home, with this family of two, she felt the stirring of an unfamiliar yearning. And Emily, young as she was, had recognized a threat, however minor. Was it possible, Rebecca thought, that a child could sense emotions between adults that perhaps the adults weren't even fully aware of as yet? Had the indisputable attraction she felt for Quinn communicated itself to his daughter and aroused a possessive jealousy? It was definitely something Rebecca intended to think about . . . later, when she was alone.

"I suppose I should see about getting the lock fixed first thing this morning," she said, choosing a diversion for her thoughts. "Surely it won't take the building superintendent long to do it."

"I'll change the lock for you. That way, you won't have to worry about any delays. We can pick up a new lock on the way to your apartment." A passing frown creased his forehead. "Or do you want me to take you to work?"

"No, I'm taking the day off." Rebecca ran a palm over her linen slacks, which were a little worse for the wear. "I'd have to change clothes, anyway, but I'd already arranged to—" she paused, not sure why she balked at mentioning the delivery of the trunk, but certain that she didn't want him at her apartment when it arrived. "I'd arranged to be away from the office today. And really, there's no need for you to bother with the lock. That's the superintendent's job. He may as well earn his keep just like the rest of us."

Emily bounced back into the room, distracting Quinn from any argument he might have offered. "Bye, Daddy. Colleen's taking me to school." She kissed him on the cheek, then rolled her lips apart for his inspection. "I brushed my teeth and—" She straightened her shoulders. "I made my bed."

"Wow," Quinn said as he hugged her again. "You must be trying to impress Rebecca. Is that it?"

Emily's blue eyes turned shyly toward Rebecca. "I always make my own bed."

"A good habit," Rebecca said with a friendly smile. "I'm glad I got to meet you, Emily. Maybe we'll get to have breakfast together again someday soon."

Emily said nothing, just pressed another kiss against her daddy's beard. "Bye, Daddy. See you this afternoon." She skipped out the door, and in a couple of minutes Rebecca heard the slam of a car door and the sound of the engine as it moved out of earshot.

Silence, steady and soft, filtered through the room. There was only the two of them. Quinn and her. She ought to go home. She wanted to stay. A lazy grin cut through the thickness of his beard, and for no reason at all, Rebecca found herself laughing. As if she belonged in this kitchen, as if she had any number of good reasons for being there. With him.

"How do you feel about three-egg omelets?" Quinn asked. "And you can be honest. If you prefer Emily's cereal...?"

"No. Eggs will be fine." What was she saying? She rarely ate breakfast. "As long as you're the one who's cooking them."

His grin deepened and eased into a self-assured and reassuring smile. "What can I say? When a women's rights advocate is staring me in the face, believe me, I cook." He stood and reached for her cup. "Would you like more coffee? *Real* coffee?"

"Yes. If you don't mind."

"My pleasure. Just sit back and let me take care of you for a little while."

Take care of her? She hadn't needed anyone to do that in years. How odd even the words sounded. And yet, how comfortable she felt. "All right, Quinn," she said with a rueful tilt of her lips. "Show me your stuff, but be careful. I've never met an omelet I liked this early in the morning before."

"Then you, darlin', are in for a treat."

Chapter Six

There was a first time for everything, Rebecca thought later that morning as Quinn drove her home. If anyone had told her yesterday that she could not only face, but also consume the major portion of a three-egg, double-cheese omelet with onions and tomatoes, she'd have sent them directly—do not pass Go—to Dr. Sherrow for therapy. Of course if Quinn continued to have that overzealous effect on her appetite, *she* would be a candidate for counseling herself.

"Are you sure you don't want me to take care of—"

"I'm sure," Rebecca interrupted him decisively. She needed a degree of perspective before she allowed him to "take care of" anything else in her life. And the narrow confines of his van was not the place to get it. "You can just drop me off in front of the apartment complex, and I'll be able to handle things from there."

"Okay, fine." His tone was short, clipped, and wounded.

"Quinn," she began, unsure how to communicate her doubts or even if she should. "You've been wonderful, and I can never thank you enough, but I can't impose any more. Really, I—"

"It wouldn't be an imposition." He glanced sideways at her and wondered why he was so reluctant to let her get on with her life. He had done more than etiquette demanded for a dinner date. So why did he feel rejected because she didn't want to spend the next twenty-four hours in his company? What was it about Rebecca Whitaker that made him want to take on the role of superhero? *Crazy.* "I'm kind of at loose ends today, anyway." What was he saying? He had a million things to do. "And it wouldn't take long to put a new lock on that door."

Rebecca resolutely kept her smile to a discreet level. In recent memory, she couldn't think of anyone, other than her mother, who had expressed such concern for her well-being. It was a good feeling, but she recognized that her pleasure in it was a bit exaggerated. "I'll call you at home as soon as I talk to the superintendent about the door. If he can't get to it immediately, maybe I'll take you up on your offer. Agreed?"

What could he say? "Agreed." As he pulled the van to the curb in front of her building, he took hold of his good judgment and determined he would say nothing more than a casual goodbye. But he couldn't help it. "You'll be all right?"

"Yes." She opened the car door, then leaned toward him and kissed him on the lips . . . a swift, gentle and tantalizing kiss that made him want to offer her more than his skill as a locksmith. "I'll call you." She stepped out of the car, and because he was left with no other option, Quinn drove away.

Rebecca stood for a minute on the sidewalk, enjoying the fresh smell of morning and the soft touch of breeze and the lingering memories of being with Quinn last night and this morning. She didn't know why a man with such obviously traditional ideas about protecting women had this very *untraditional* effect on her, but she recognized her vulnerability. She had never enjoyed a morning more, or perhaps it was simply that she had never enjoyed anyone's company more than she did Quinn's.

But close on the heels of that possibility came a cautioning thought, and she reminded herself again of a major complication that came hand in hand with Quinn Kinser—his daughter. Would Emily present an insurmountable obstacle? Rebecca wondered and then scoffed at the idea with a shake of her head. An insurmountable obstacle to *what*? She hardly knew Quinn, even if she had spent the night in his home.

As she turned toward the apartment building, she experienced the odd but definite sensation of being watched. A glance around revealed no evidence. The sidewalk in front of the building was clear, as it often was in the middle of a weekday morning. She looked across the street, but there was only a small amount of traffic, and on the opposite sidewalk, an elderly lady stood at the crosswalk. Rebecca wondered if the woman needed assistance in crossing the street, but there was an air of independence in her posture, and Rebecca decided the lady was just waiting on the Walk light.

Inside the building, Rebecca forgot about everything else and concentrated on locating the janitor. She informed him of the broken lock and of the temporary measures Quinn had taken the night before to secure the apartment until the door could be fixed. The building super was a rotund man with a fat leather tool belt draped below his overgrown belly, and at least four or five weighted key rings jangling at his hip.

"I'll get to it sometime today," the janitor told her after accompanying her upstairs and checking the damage. "Nothing to worry about, Miss Whitaker. It'll be right as rain before bedtime this evenin'."

"I certainly hope it will be," she countered, letting him know she would not be silent if the problem wasn't corrected. "In fact, I would be very grateful if you could fix it within the hour."

"Nope. Can't do that," he explained, rocking back on his heels. "I got a backed-up toilet in number 7B and an electrical problem in unit 4's air conditioning." His grin widened, and the keys at his waist jingled noisily as he shifted his weight. "You know how people get when the plumbing doesn't work or when they get too hot."

"I'm sure it's difficult, Mr. Shumacker, to keep all the tenants happy, but I know I can depend on you to change the lock very soon." Rebecca watched him from her doorway as he shuffled down the hall, muttering under his breath about the day's hectic schedule. She smiled to herself. The smile faded somewhat as her glance fell again on the doorframe and the pry marks on the wood. Determinedly she looked away, glancing across the hall to Wally's door. Maybe Wally could shed some light on last night's events, Rebecca thought as she walked over and tapped lightly on the door.

"No luck," Rebecca said aloud a silent minute later, although there was no one else in the hallway. "Where are you, Wally? At the office? Did you even come home last night? It's a cinch you're not home now, isn't it?"

Down the hall, Mrs. Albridge's door squeaked as it was being closed, and Rebecca felt suddenly a little shy and embarrassed at getting caught talking to herself. Maybe she could question Mrs. Albridge again. Ask her if she'd remembered any other details about the night before, or if she'd seen anyone else . . .

"You, Rebecca Whitaker," she said to herself, her voice softer this time, more like a whisper, "are afraid to go inside your own apartment. Why else would you be standing out here in the hall carrying on this one-sided conversation?"

It was true, and although she hated to admit it, the realization did seem to help direct her thoughts and action toward her own apartment. An uneasy feeling accompanied her past the doorway and into the living area, and try as she might, Rebecca couldn't shake it. Someone had invaded her privacy, and even though nothing had been stolen or bothered, that invasion had altered her security in her own independence. She wasn't sure she would ever recapture it. At least, not in this particular apartment.

Drawing a deep, determined breath, Rebecca began a visual, thorough inspection of the rooms, touching objects as she went, trying to adjust her sense of alienation to a comfortable familiarity. When she had checked everything she could think of, she sank onto the edge of her bed and surveyed the room around her. Why did she feel as if she'd missed something? A clue, maybe, or a reason for...

Why did her mind persist in rejecting Quinn's explanation of a random burglary? Why did she continue to seek a motive? *"Has anything unusual happened to you in the past few weeks?"* the police officer had asked her. She'd said no, but now she wondered. Within a week after she'd attended an out of town auction and purchased that trunk, Quinn had appeared at her door with an offer to buy it. A little more than a week later, she'd received the call from Mr. Ellis, who worked at the mini-storage. And now, two days later, she had to wonder if there could be a connection.

The possibility formed a lump in her throat. Quinn couldn't be involved with the burglary. After all, he'd been with her.... What did that prove? her pragmatic conscience argued. He could be working with Mr. Ellis or someone else to get the trunk. He could have gotten her out of the apartment so his accomplice could break in and—

The telephone rang, and she started in surprise, realizing how far imagination had carried her in a matter of seconds. She was jumping to all sorts of hasty conclusions. In the first place, she was a better than average judge of character, and she would testify under oath that Quinn had nothing to do with the broken lock. Why would he try to *steal* the trunk when he could acquire it through diplomacy . . . a much less risky approach?

The phone rang again, and Rebecca absently reached for it. "Hello?"

"I'd like to know what you're doing home on a perfectly good working day," Wally said. "I called your office first, but that receptionist is as stingy with information as my mother. You're not sick, are you?"

"No. I'd planned to take the day off, anyway."

"Anyway, what?" The sound of shuffled papers came through the phone wires.

"Well, it's the middle of the week, I'm caught up with my sales calls, and I wanted to be here when the mover arrived."

"Movers? Oh, you're expecting your antique trunk to be delivered, aren't you? I'd almost forgotten about that. Well, tell me the truth now—don't you wish you'd gone with me last night? Your date couldn't possibly have been as entertaining as the discussion that took place in my therapy group."

Rebecca lay back on the bed, cradling the phone against her ear. "Let's not take any bets on that, Wally. I had quite an evening myself. In fact, I was just getting ready to call you and tell you—"

"You've met the man of your dreams," Wally stated flatly. "Give me a break, Rebecca. That's not entertainment."

Rebecca tried not to let her friend's dry humor bother her. "Someone pried open the lock on my door last night. Is that entertaining enough?"

"What? You're kidding!"

"Believe me, it isn't something I would joke about. Someone broke into my apartment."

"When?"

"While I was at dinner."

"That's odd."

"Odd isn't the word I use to describe it."

"No, I meant it's odd that someone should try to break into your apartment while you were out on a date."

Rebecca closed her eyes, preparing an answer in case Wally somehow managed to rationalize that the break-in wouldn't have occurred if only Rebecca had gone to the therapy session instead of having a date. "Well, it would have been more odd if they'd tried to break in while I was at home."

"You're missing the point, Rebecca. You are often away from your apartment for days at a time when you take sales trips. If someone was watching your apartment—and don't ask me why they would, but for the sake of argument let's say a burglar was keeping an eye on your comings and goings—it makes sense to attempt a break-in while you're out of town, not just out for an evening."

"But when I'm not in town, the building security guard knows and keeps watch on my apartment."

"Pardon my skepticism, but if you're counting on him to protect your interests, you're more gullible than I think you are." Wally cleared her throat, ready to press her point. "Besides, that isn't what I'm getting at. Why *your* apartment? And why last night? I just think the whole thing is very odd."

"I can't argue with you there."

"Hmm." There was a pause over the phone lines while Wally was thinking and Rebecca pursed her lips, waiting. "You don't suppose this man you've met...the one with the wonderful blue eyes, the one who wants to buy that old trunk, the one who took you out to dinner *last night* could have—"

"No," Rebecca interrupted. "I don't suppose that at all."

There was a momentary offended pause. "Well, I was only suggesting that it's possible your date was in on it. He could have arranged the whole thing. After all, you did tell me that you were sure he'd lied to you about the trunk, and there's always a chance..."

Trust Wally to go straight for the off-the-wall possibility. Rebecca sighed. "I already considered that, but Quinn was as surprised to find the lock broken as I was...maybe more."

"He didn't act suspicious at all?"

"He acted like a perfect gentleman." Rebecca made a genuine effort to be patient, but she didn't like discussing Quinn this way. She couldn't explain it, but she knew she didn't like Wally's line of thinking. "He even insisted that I spend the night at his house, since the lock couldn't be fixed until today."

The ensuing silence was worse than Wally's pointed comments. "How long have you known this man?"

"Long enough." Rebecca's voice brooked no further argument, and she hoped Wally would honor that. "He lives in a charming home in the older part of town. He has a full-time housekeeper and an eight-year-old daughter."

"A daughter." Wally rolled the word on her tongue with some prejudice. "I take it she's full-time, too."

Rebecca paused to give her patience time to catch up. "I didn't ask about custody arrangements, but then it really isn't any of my business."

"Ah, now *that's* the Rebecca I know and admire." Wally laughed...alone. "Let's get back to the attempted break-in," she said in a more serious tone. "Did you call the police?"

"Yes, but the officer wasn't much help. He just looked around, made a lot of notes and advised me to spend the night with a friend."

"Lucky there was one available. I'm sorry I wasn't home, but you're probably not. After all, I don't have extraordinary blue eyes."

"Or a beard. Or any number of other—"

"I get the idea," Wally said. "Let's not get personal."

Oddly enough, Rebecca felt herself begin to relax and enjoy the light conversation. Maybe Wally was as good a psychologist as she claimed she was. "Nothing was taken or disturbed," Rebecca said, returning to the subject at hand. "So the popular theory is that whoever broke the lock was frightened away before he could enter the apartment."

"Or she. It could have been a woman, you know."

Rebecca closed her eyes at the triviality. "Yes, I suppose so. But Mrs. Albridge said she saw you with a man and thought that you might—"

"I can imagine what she said. But I don't remember seeing anyone...oh, wait. The pizza man." Wally's voice grew distant, then strengthened with the memory. "As I came out of my apartment last night, there was a man walking down the hall, and he asked me what time it was. I remember now. He had on a white uniform with a red logo of some sort above the pocket. Petey's Pizza, I think. Hell, I'm not sure. I didn't pay close attention, although I thought he was the best-looking deliveryman I'd ever seen. And he was wearing an expensive watch. Now why would he ask me the time if he had a watch on his wrist? And come to think about it, it didn't look like the type of jewelry a pizza deliveryman would wear, either."

"Are you sure?"

"Well, no. I can't say that I know much about the tastes of pizzeria employees. Who knows? Maybe he gets a commission, or his wife bought him the watch as a birthday present."

"Are you sure about the *uniform*?" Rebecca allowed a hint of exasperation into her voice. "Would you recognize him if you saw him again?"

"Oh, sure. He's in every pizzeria in the country." Wally's tone dripped with skeptical patience. "I can't remember a single distinguishing feature of how he looked, but I'd know that fragrance anywhere. He smelled more like pepperoni than pepperoni.'' There was an audible sniff, and despite everything, Rebecca smiled. ''No,'' Wally continued. ''I wish I could help you, but I'm not even sure I recall the color of his hair.''

''It was dark. Like a sheikh's.''

''What? Why would you think that?'' There was a brief pause and then a rueful sigh. ''Mrs. Albridge. I do wish I could get that woman into therapy. What a subject...a woman who lives her life through a crack in the door, a peeping Thomasina, complete with paranoid tendencies.''

''And a pink curler cap,'' Rebecca added, remembering what Quinn had said and smiling.

''Yes, well, that's what makes my work interesting. That's why I'm going to write the book that will free women forever from—'' A buzz interrupted, and Wally broke the sentence in two. ''I've got another call, Rebecca. I'll have to fill you in on my research plans the next time we're together. And if I remember anything else about the pizza man, I'll call you immediately. In the meantime, don't give the time of day to anyone who smells like pepperoni.''

''Thanks, Wally, I appreciate...'' Looking at the receiver in her hand, Rebecca shrugged at the abrupt end to the conversation. She wondered if she should phone Quinn and let him know about Wally's encounter with the delivery man. It really wasn't much information, she reasoned, but he might think it had more significance than she could find.

With a frown, Rebecca replaced the telephone receiver in its cradle. She was making something out of nothing and using it as an excuse to call him, which was not like her. She tried never to make excuses for her actions. So why didn't she simply pick up the phone and let him know— What? That she missed him? It hadn't been an hour since she'd seen him. Perspective, she reminded herself. She needed time to gain perspective. And she needed time to investigate the contents of her much-talked-about and very mysterious trunk.

As if her decision had signaled the all clear, the telephone rang again. When she answered, a representative of the moving company informed her that the trunk was on its way and would be delivered within the hour.

Perfect, Rebecca thought as she hung up the phone for the second time. She couldn't have scheduled it better. Quinn was safely out of the picture for the moment, and she decided he probably ought to stay that way until after she'd checked the trunk. But as she walked from the bedroom into the living room and then to the kitchen, there was a knock at the door, and her first thought was of Quinn. An uneasy excitement gripped her. It was too soon to be the movers, but surely Quinn wouldn't have come back . . . would he?

He not only would, she discovered when she opened the door, but he had. "Immediately isn't soon enough," he said with a slow, unassuming smile. "I'm going to fix this lock right now."

The tensions of the past hour ebbed as she stood facing him, sensing his eagerness to be with her and feeling her own breathless response. How did he do that? she wondered. How did he make her forget her resolution of not five minutes before and be glad, to the exclusion of good common sense, that he was here?

"The building superintendent will take care of it," she said, knowing it didn't sound much like the protest she'd intended.

"Now he won't have to." Quinn stepped into the entry and knelt in front of the door. Setting a small toolbox down beside him, he narrowed his attention on the lock. "Piece of cake," he said, his smile slanting upward at her. "You'll be locked in before you know it. Are you enjoying your day off?''

"So far." Rebecca leaned her shoulder against the wall and watched the play of muscles across his back and in his upper arms. Attractive, she thought. Definitely attractive with a sensual, appealing strength. Not handsome, exactly, but more intriguing than any other man she'd ever met. Maybe it was the steadiness, the security she saw in him that captivated her... the idea that he was confident of who he was and his place in the scheme of life. Real confidence, she decided, was a rare commodity in men these days. It was usually a cover-up for insecurities, but somehow, she didn't think that was true of Quinn. He was what he was, and she liked that.

He dropped the screwdriver he'd been using and picked up another. "Did you ever find your friend? The doctor. I've forgotten her name."

"Sherrow. Wally Sherrow. I talked to her on the phone just a few minutes ago."

Quinn glanced up. "Did she see our strange-looking suspect?"

"The only person she saw was a man delivering pizza. She doesn't remember much about him except that he smelled like pepperoni and was wearing an expensive watch."

"Would she recognize him if she saw him again?"

"She says no, only the smell, but I imagine if she saw him under similar circumstances in the same clothing, she probably would. And knowing Wally, she could recognize that watch anywhere."

"What kind of clothing?"

"A uniform. White, I think Wally said, with a red logo."

A frown crinkled his brow, and Quinn sat back on his heels. "I'm trying to recall which pizza franchise uses that kind of uniform. It can't be that hard to find out."

"Wally mentioned Petey's Pizza, but I'm not familiar with—"

"Yes, there is one called Pete's." Quinn frowned harder. "At least, I think that's right. I'll have to ask Emily. She's a regular consumer."

"And you're not?"

He grinned a little sheepishly. "On occasion, but I'm not selective, you see. I just like pizza. I take it you're not a fan?"

"I don't know, really. Pizza isn't something I eat that often. On the road I usually have meals with clients, and when I'm home, I cook."

Quinn shook his head in admiration. "A traveling sales-lady *and* a cook. A rare combination. No wonder pizza de-liverymen are trying to break down your door."

Her lips curved slightly, but it was still hard to find hu-mor in the broken lock. "Do you think the man Wally saw could have been...?"

"Your guess is as good as mine." The old lock came free of the doorframe and fell into Quinn's hand. "I think it's worth investigating, though. Surely those places keep rec-ords of orders and deliveries. The trouble will be in locat-ing the right pizza parlor."

"I'll get the phone book and look up—" Her voice broke and she straightened away from the wall. *The trunk,* she re-membered suddenly. *The movers are on their way.* The last time she'd looked up anything in the phone book had been to arrange transport for her auction purchase. And now that it was finally going to be delivered, Quinn was here.

Rebecca caught the question in his expression, but she turned as if she were simply preoccupied with getting the information. What should she do? she wondered. Ask Quinn to leave? Or would it be all right if he stayed? No. She still had a lot of unanswered questions regarding the con-tents of that trunk. If he were with her when it was opened ... well, she might never discover what, if anything, was so important. Besides that, she reasoned, the trunk was hers, and she had every right to evaluate its contents. With Quinn present, she knew she wouldn't be able to do that. So she had to get him out of the apartment.

Easier decided than done, she thought some fifteen minutes later as she suggested for the third time that he should talk to the manager of Pete's Pizzeria.

"I'll do that." He gave a last approving twist to the new doorknob and lock assembly, tested it to make sure all the parts fit and then opened the door again. "After I'm finished here."

"Aren't you finished now?"

He cut her a sharp glance. "Not quite. Are you in a hurry?"

Rebecca walked to the doorway of the living room, then walked back. "They might not keep records for more than twenty-four hours. Maybe not that long. I think you ought to check it out now."

"It's only a matter of making a few phone calls." He raised a puzzled gaze, but she didn't want to meet his eyes. "I don't see any need to rush."

"Easy for you to say. It wasn't your apartment that was broken into."

He frowned, then slowly stood. "All right. Where's the phone book? I'll call right—"

"No," she interrupted, a trifle desperately. "I think ... I mean, don't you think it would be better to talk to Pete, or whoever the person in charge is, in person? Face-to-face is better if you suspect that there's something criminal going on."

"Face-to-face? Listen, Rebecca, if there really is something criminal going on, I'd a lot rather be talking long-distance."

That made sense to her, but she wanted to argue. Anything to get him out of her apartment. "What could happen in a public restaurant?"

"Right." Quinn shook his head and touched the doorknob again. "What am I worried about? If Pete tries to mess with me, I'll put a pizza pie in his face." His lips quirked in a wry smile. "You know me. Always the hero."

Rebecca was suddenly ashamed of herself. "Maybe it isn't such a good idea. Forget I said anything. It's just that I'm..."

"Concerned, I know. And it's perfectly understandable. At least the lock is fixed. You won't have to be concerned about that anymore."

"It looks nice," she said. "Thanks for fixing it."

"You're welcome." With a considering frown, he bent to pick up the toolbox and set it out of the way. "Would you like to have lunch? Maybe together we could beard the pizza man in his—?"

"No!" Rebecca realized the word was too harsh and tried to soften its impact with a smile. "I—uh, have some things I need to do and..." Her voice trailed off, and she wondered why she didn't simply say that she wanted him to leave, at least for a little while. "I do appreciate your help, but..."

He nodded, a wry grin cutting between his beard and moustache. "Sometimes a little help goes a long way. Sorry, I know you have your own life, and I don't want to intrude." The grin tucked down into a rueful, heart-tugging half smile. "Except that I do want to. I guess it's just been a long time since I felt needed."

It was a sincere expression of his feelings, and Rebecca was caught unprepared. Although her heart melted at his willingness to be vulnerable, her mind spun with a new line of possibilities. Last night she had definitely needed *some-one*. Would anyone else have been as understanding, as comforting? Maybe. Maybe not. Did she need Quinn? Not yet, she decided. Could she begin to need him? Very probably she could. Which was a scary thought, but not too scary.

"I didn't realize I was making my insecurities so obvious," she said, because vagueness seemed a legitimate compromise.

"And I didn't mean to make you uncomfortable. Forget what I said. It was probably only wishful thinking."

As he turned, preparing to leave, Rebecca suddenly wanted to begin the moment again. Maybe she had been hasty and overly defensive. Wasn't it possible that Quinn had seen past her independence to a tiny corner of her heart that wasn't entirely satisfied? "Quinn, I..."

"No, listen." He lifted a hand to silence any explanation she might feel she had to offer. "I'll leave, go to the pizza place and talk to the manager, maybe have some lunch, and call you later. That way you can continue with the plans you made, and I can—" The smile reappeared with all the eager charm of an early spring. "I can make plans to be with you this evening. Or tomorrow. Or maybe both."

Rebecca laughed, forgetting everything for the moment except her delight in him. But just as his laughter joined hers, there was a noise in the hallway outside, followed by a knock at the partially open door and a deep, burly voice announcing "Modern Moving Company. Where do you want this trunk?"

Chapter Seven

It was one of Rebecca's most embarrassing moments, and she stood, facing Quinn's slowly comprehending expression for what seemed like years. She knew that *he* knew why she had been anxious for him to leave, but she couldn't seem to break the strained silence. The two men outside her apartment, however, had no compunction about pushing open the door and interrupting. "Are you Ms. Whitaker?" one of the movers asked in a voice that far outweighed the slender proportions of his body. "Have we got the right apartment?"

For a split second she thought about denying it. "Yes. Yes, that's my trunk." Putting her hand on the door and avoiding Quinn's eyes, she indicated that the trunk should be brought inside. "You can take it through there." She indicated the living area. "To the bedroom."

The trunk was bulky, and the moment was awkward, but Rebecca followed the movers into the bedroom to show them where to set it down. Quinn didn't make any attempt to follow, and as she wrote out the check to the moving company, she wondered if he had left. She felt bad about the situation, but after all, he had no right to expect her to tell him everything.

In the entryway, Quinn leaned his shoulder against the wall, just as Rebecca had done earlier. She hadn't wanted him to know the trunk was being delivered. That, he told himself, was obvious. The reason, however, was more obscure. He'd thought they were getting along famously: he already felt as if he'd known her for years rather than a few days. But this episode made him rethink his approach. What he'd suspected before, he now knew for certain. She didn't trust him, at least not when it came to the trunk and his story of Aunt Molly's sentimental attachment to it. He should have gone with his gut instinct in the beginning and simply told the truth.

So? He'd just tell her. His shoulder twinged a protest at the pressure he was putting upon it, and he shifted to turn his back to the wall. *And why would she believe you now?* his practical nature inquired. *It takes more than good intentions to establish trust in a relationship.*

He knew that, of course, but since his divorce—no, even before that—he'd considered that trust was a given, something built into the fabric of friendship. He had an established circle of friends and family; all the women he'd dated since the divorce were in some way related to someone he knew and who knew him. What he kept forgetting, though, was that Rebecca had no prior knowledge of him, no basis for trusting him, except what he told her and what she could observe. He *had* lied to her—however innocently—and obviously she realized it.

"Yes, ma'am, thank you." The movers stalked past him like hunters making their way through a jungle. One of the men, who would have nothing to fear from an eight-hundred-pound gorilla, paused to eye Quinn with suspicion. "If you have anything else you want moved, Ms. Whitaker, just let us know, and we'll see it moves."

"That's a comfort," Rebecca said as she held the door for the men to exit. Her glance strayed to Quinn.

Damned if she wasn't smiling, he thought, straightening his shoulders in self-defense.

"I'll keep that in mind," Rebecca said as she closed the door and fiddled with the lock.

Was she nervous? The possibility made him feel a little better. "So..." He kept his voice steady, pretending he had little, if any, real interest in the delivery of Molly's trunk. "The trunk is here."

"Yes."

She met his eyes squarely, and he knew this was going to be tricky. But maybe honesty—to a point—was the best option. "If you didn't want me to be here when it arrived, you should have told me to leave. I would have gone peacefully."

"I didn't know that."

"Well, now you do."

"Yes." She didn't look away. Neither did he. There was an argument hovering... He could feel it, but he wasn't sure he wanted to pursue it. Where was his confidence when he needed it most? Nowhere to be found in the tide of ambivalent emotions swirling inside him. He wanted Molly's trunk, or more precisely, the journal that was supposed to be in it. He also, much to his own consternation, wanted Rebecca to trust him. The two shouldn't have been mutually exclusive, but at this exact moment, he felt fairly certain they were. So he simply had to choose which he wanted more.

"I just want to ask one—"

"Don't, Quinn. I'm not going to let you have the trunk...not yet, anyway. It isn't fair for you to ask."

"You don't even know what I—"

"Oh, yes, I do. I knew you were lying the first time we met. You sat there on the sofa, moving around so restlessly that body language alone gave you away. And every time you mentioned Aunt Molly, you stumbled over the words."

He felt he should make a stab at defending his integrity. "Sitting on a sofa that's been decorated in ladies' lingerie tends to make me restless. Comes with the territory, so to speak." He thought there was a perceptible shortening of her frown, but he couldn't be sure. "And as to Molly..."

Rebecca stopped him cold with some body language of her own, and with her chin set at such an angle, he was hesitant to proceed, so he waited for her to cue him. "Come on, Quinn. Why don't you admit there isn't an Aunt Molly? You made her up just so you'd have an excuse to get the trunk."

Her tone dared him to contradict her, and he felt an answering annoyance rise to the occasion. "Well, if you believe *that*, you certainly won't believe the real story."

"Try me."

"Oh, no. If you think I'm going to set myself up for another inquisition like this, you're wrong. There *is* a Molly. And that *is* her trunk."

"You made her up. Just tell me what you want out of the trunk, and I'll—"

"I want you to believe me, damn it!"

"But you just now *told* me that you lied."

"I did? No, that's not the point. Molly is a very real person."

"It *is* the point, and if she's so real, I want to meet her."

Quinn realized he was fast losing ground. "You can't...at least, not now."

Her eyebrows lifted in a disbelieving arch. "Whatever you say."

Damn, but she could be as aggravating as Emily when she got an idea in her head. "I'd be happy—ecstatic, in fact— for you to meet Molly, but..." His words trailed away in frustration, and Rebecca took up the slack.

"But what?"

"I don't know where she is."

Rebecca rolled her eyes and turned away.

"No, wait, Rebecca. I'll take you to Molly as soon as I locate her. You see, I went to the airport day before yesterday, and she—"

"Spare me the explanation. When you find her, bring her here, and then—*maybe*—I'll be ready to listen. In the meantime, I do have things to do and…" For the life of her, Rebecca couldn't finish the sentence and simply sent Quinn out the door and away from her. Why couldn't he just trust her enough to tell her what was inside that trunk before she found out for herself?

She walked into the living room, and Quinn wasn't slow to follow. He didn't say anything for a few minutes, and she pretended not to notice as she busied her hands with straightening magazines on the coffee table. If he recognized the significance of her closed bedroom door, he gave no sign. He cleared his throat, and despite her frustration, her lips curved ever so little. She turned her back so he couldn't see.

"Rebecca, I'd like to explain about the trunk." He jammed his hands into his pockets, then quickly pulled them free again, as if he was afraid his body language would contradict his words. "It's not really all that important to me. I mean, it's not as if there's anything of real value involved…at least, it wouldn't be of value to anyone else. At any rate, I can't believe—"

The phone rang shrilly, and Rebecca sighed her impatience. Just when he'd started to talk. Just when she felt the tenuous threads of trust were forming between them. She considered letting it ring, but Quinn paused expectantly, and so she walked to the telephone and lifted the receiver. "Hello?"

"May I speak with Rebecca Whitaker, please?" The male voice was a crisp tenor with the clipped tones of a northern accent.

"This is she."

"Good. I'm so glad to find you home. My name is Scott Forsythe, and I hope I'm not phoning at an inconvenient time."

He was, but her curiosity led her to deny it. "No."

"This may sound like an unusual request, Ms. Whitaker, but I would like to meet with you to discuss a family heirloom, an old trunk to be exact, that I understand you have in your possession."

Rebecca swallowed hard, not knowing whether to laugh or cry. *What was going on?* "Oh?" she said, as if she didn't have a clue as to what he was going to say next.

"You see, it belongs to my Aunt Molly, who had it in storage, and I only recently discovered that she hadn't paid rent on the storage unit. By the time I—"

He continued with his story, but Rebecca stopped listening with any degree of concentration. After all, she had heard it all before. Her gaze went to Quinn. He was trying hard to appear as if he had no interest in eavesdropping. She was trying hard to appear as if it didn't matter whether he heard the telephone conversation or not. Nonchalance would have come easier, she knew, if she hadn't been considering a more pertinent question—whether to hit him with the receiver in her hand or whether to throw the entire telephone.

Quinn had stood right there not five seconds earlier and told her that the trunk wouldn't be of value to anyone other than himself. Either he didn't know the value of whatever was inside, or he didn't want her to know. She didn't like this, she thought, pursing her lips to contemplate the sudden shift in the situation.

As far as she could see, she held all the aces but one. Quinn had momentary possession of the ace of hearts—*her* heart—and all evidence aside, she wanted to confide Scott Forsythe's story, in all its similar detail, to Quinn. For all the good that would do. He would probably concoct some ridiculous story to explain *that*. She supposed she had little choice but to keep her own counsel.

"So I'm sure you understand my desire to restore the trunk to Aunt Molly as soon as possible," Scott concluded his presentation, and Rebecca turned her back to Quinn.

"I'm not sure I can help you," she said.

"You do have the trunk, don't you?" His hard tone sharpened.

Without hesitation, she added a caution to her voice. "Well, I can't put my hands on it at the moment."

"Oh, you mean it hasn't been delivered from the auction yet. The old man at the storage units told me you'd had some trouble with the moving service. He was kind enough to give me your name and telephone number, though."

Mr. Sam Ellis had a lot to answer for, Rebecca thought. "I see," she said.

"Could I take you to dinner tomorrow?" He sounded polite but not overly enthusiastic. "We could discuss it then."

"I'm afraid I'm busy. What about the afternoon? Say four-thirty?" She gave directions to a popular café not far from her office building. "Second booth from the window. I'll look for you there."

"Good. Thank you, Ms. Whitaker. I look forward to meeting you in person."

She wasn't so sure she reciprocated the feeling, but she ended the conversation with a similar platitude. As she replaced the receiver, Quinn cleared his throat behind her. She turned, unsure of what her reaction to him should be at this moment. When he smiled with just that hint of shyness, she knew she was treading a narrow line.

"Business?" he asked, as if he were expressing only a polite interest.

"Something like that."

He nodded, lifted his hand to his beard and stroked it thoughtfully for a moment. "I've been thinking, Rebecca, and I have a proposition for you." He grimaced at his choice of word. "No, not a *proposition*. More like a proposal . . . well, not a *real* proposal." His rueful expression tugged at the corners of her reluctant mouth. "I have an idea."

"An idea?" She didn't want to smile, and she didn't want to respond to the soft persuasion in his voice, but she couldn't seem to help herself. "All right. I'll bite. What is it?"

"Come with me. Now. Forget the trunk. Forget that I ever mentioned it to you. We'll locate Pete's Pizzeria and talk to someone about the mysterious deliveryman. After that, I'll buy you lunch—anything but pizza—and if we still like each other, we'll go to a ball game."

A ball game? Surely he was kidding. "I'm not much of a sports enthusiast," she said, skirting the edge of an outright refusal.

"Aw, come on, Rebecca. Give it a try. I guarantee you'll be on your feet, yelling and cheering with the rest of the crowd before the first point is scored."

She doubted it, but he seemed so eager, so hopeful that she found it hard to say no. And, oddly enough, she recognized a little swirl of excitement in her stomach. Because of an invitation to a ball game? No, she knew better than to try to fool herself. She did want to investigate the man Wally had seen in the hallway, and she was getting a bit hungry. But beyond those practical reasons, she was pleased because Quinn had invited her, period.

Even recognizing her pleasure was ridiculous in itself, she thought. Except for the hours she'd spent asleep, she'd been with him almost constantly since seven o'clock the evening before. But the attraction was still working, growing stronger in fact, and she didn't want it to end.

But a ball game? she asked herself. Just when she should be most interested in the trunk and its mysterious secrets? Just when she should be least inclined to believe anything he told her? A ball game?

Well, why not? She wanted to believe him, she wanted to spend time with him, and, surprisingly enough, she really didn't care about the stupid trunk in her bedroom. At least, not when he stood there, smiling, daring her heart to be reckless, just this once. To hell with the trunk, she thought. It would be there when she came back.

But would it? Did she dare leave it? There was always a possibility that whoever had tried to break in once would do so again, and there was also the possibility that the trunk had been the objective of the aborted theft. Would it be safe?

Quinn seemed to read her thoughts. "We'll ask Mrs. Albridge to keep her eyes on your door and call the police the moment she sees a sheikh disguised as a pizza deliveryman."

Rebecca laughed with a mixture of relief and pleasure. "All right, Mr. Kinser, you're on. Just promise me one thing."

His lips curved between the dark moustache and full beard. "Let me guess. The trunk is, from now on, and until further notice, none of my concern."

A little harsher than she would have said it, Rebecca thought, but close enough. "Bingo."

He sighed. "Couldn't I just take one look—" Her chin lifted a firm inch, and he nodded agreement. "You have my word, providing you humor me about the ball game."

"Anything you say. Just let me slip into something more..." His eyes sparkled with hopeful amusement, and she tried to frown at him. "Sporty," she finished with a grand exit to the bedroom.

It didn't take long to change into a pair of cotton slacks, bright print blouse and tennis-type shoes. Turning in front of the mirror, she wondered if her clothing was casual enough for a sporting event. She couldn't believe she'd actually agreed to go. Especially when the trunk was within reach, filled with treasure or, at the very least, an answer to some of her questions about Quinn. But it didn't seem so important. She had no reason to trust him, yet she did. Wally would be horrified at her behavior, Rebecca knew. But she didn't care about that, either. Some corner of her heart told her Quinn was special and that she wouldn't be sorry for taking a few hours out of this one day to be with him.

But as she went to join him in the living room, another corner of her heart—the practical corner—cautioned her to close the bedroom door behind her. Quinn must have noticed, but he only said "Ready?" The look in his extraordinary blue eyes went a long way toward reassuring her.

"Ready," she answered.

IT TOOK ALMOST TWO HOURS to find "Pete" of Pete's Pizzerias, Incorporated, who, as it turned out, was actually not "Pete" at all. Nathaniel Duncan was a fast-moving, fast-talking entrepreneur who had little time for inquiries regarding delivery schedules and even less time to make conversation with Quinn. Rebecca he acknowledged with a courteous nod before discounting her presence and turning his attention entirely to her companion.

"You understand my position, I'm sure, Mr. Kinser." Nathaniel Duncan leaned forward across his desk top, hands clasped in a gesture of sincerity. "We simply cannot help you unless you can be more specific."

Not for the first time since she and Quinn had been ushered into this office, Rebecca straightened her shoulders. "Mr. Duncan," she said in a tone that made it clear she was tired of being ignored, "We have been specific. We have told you the apartment building where the delivery was supposedly made. We have told you the approximate time of the delivery. And we have given you a general description of the person making that delivery. Now, in turn, we would like for you to examine your records—surely you do keep records?—and tell us if the man purporting to be your employee was legitimate."

Impatience shadowed Duncan's thin features but was quickly camouflaged with a conciliating smile. "Now, now. There's no reason for you to worry your pretty little head about this, Miss Whitaker. If you'll just let me discuss this with your friend here, I think we can come to an understanding."

Rebecca thought they could probably come to an understanding more quickly than Nathaniel Duncan could say "insufferable bigot," which in her humble opinion was the nicest label she could give him. "Mr. Duncan," she said in a calm voice that belied the anger in it. "There is every reason for me to worry about this matter. *Someone* broke into my apartment. I have two witnesses who can identify that person as one of your employees. Now, what do you intend to do about it?"

Duncan's face flushed an angry red as he met Rebecca's determined gaze. He looked at Quinn, who shrugged. "I think you, uh, ought to come to an understanding with her," Quinn told Nathaniel, and Rebecca loved him for being supportive.

She pressed her advantage. "All I want to know is whether or not your records show a pizza order from my apartment complex at or sometime after seven-thirty last night. Is that specific enough?"

For a long minute, Rebecca didn't know if Nathaniel Duncan would cooperate or not. His mouth was pursed in such a tight wad that she didn't think any information could get past it. Finally, though, he unclasped his hands and reached for the telephone, never taking his eyes from Rebecca. A couple of clipped commands later, he replaced the receiver. "You can talk to Harry in the personnel department. My secretary will show you the way. Other than that, I can't help you . . . *Miss Whitaker.*"

Rebecca fought a smile at his concession. "Thank you, Mr. Duncan. I appreciate your willingness to cooperate." She stood, and both men followed suit, although she could tell that Nathaniel Duncan did so with the utmost reluctance.

"Well, you certainly gave him what for," Quinn said a few minutes later as they followed the secretary down the hall. "I can't say he didn't deserve it."

Rebecca rolled her eyes. "He deserved a lot more than he got. I only wish Wally had been here. She'd have had his back to the wall in five seconds flat."

"Oh, I think you did a fine job, considering that 'you didn't have to worry your pretty little head' about it."

"Oooh. That made me mad. Mr. Nathaniel 'Pete' Duncan has a bad attitude. I will never eat in one of his restaurants as long as I live."

"And I promise never to phone in a delivery order from Pete's Pizzeria." Quinn held up his right hand in a solemn vow, and Rebecca pushed it back to his side with a wry smile.

"I hope it isn't Emily's favorite franchise, or you could have a hard time keeping that promise."

"You're right, but this is a matter of principle. I want that kind of chauvinistic attitude to make Emily mad, too."

"Maybe she won't ever run into a man like Duncan." Rebecca slowed her steps as the secretary stopped before another office door and motioned for them to go on inside.

Harry, the employee from personnel, was far more likable than his boss, and within a very few minutes Rebecca had explained the situation and what she hoped to discover.

"Nothing to it," Harry said, turning to his computer keyboard. "We keep records of orders all across the city. With this computer system, I can call up any of our several restaurants and tell you exactly how many pizzas were ordered, what time they were ordered, and what time they were delivered."

"But we need to know where the order came from," Quinn pointed out. "A specific apartment complex."

Harry frowned. "I only have records of telephone numbers, not addresses."

"But the deliveries," Rebecca asked. "Don't you have some way of knowing if the pizza gets to the right address?"

Absently scratching his ear, Harry punched another code into the computer. "Let's try..." In a minute he shook his head and pressed another key. The computer whirred, made a ticking noise and Harry smiled. "Sorry," he said. "I don't show any activity in your area." The smile faded. "That isn't good. Glenacre is usually one of our high order areas." He punched another key, but Quinn stood and, with a touch of his hand at her elbow, suggested that Rebecca stand, too.

"Thank you, Harry. You've been a great deal of help." Quinn started for the door, but Harry didn't acknowledge either the thank-you or their departure. Outside in the hallway, Quinn sighed his relief. "It's only my opinion, but offhand, I'd say Pete's Pizzerias, Incorporated, is just this side of losing its edge on the competition. With Duncan at the stern, and Harry, here, paddling for shore, I certainly wouldn't buy stock in the company."

"That just shows your good judgment." Rebecca frowned thoughtfully, then proceeded toward the elevator and exit. "And I guess we now know that whoever it was that Wally spoke to outside my apartment last night, he wasn't delivering pizza.''

"Wally is sure about the uniform?" Quinn asked. "Maybe we have the wrong franchise."

"How many white-and-red uniformed, pepperoni-scented deliverymen could there be? It has to be this particular franchise, and the burglar had to have borrowed or stolen the uniform."

"So, do you want to go back and ask Mr. Duncan if he can give us a uniform count?"

Rebecca laughed. "We ought to, just for the aggravation, but I think he'd probably have us escorted speedily from his office."

"I think you're right. Besides, I have a much better idea."

"Lunch."

"How did you know?"

"Just a hunch, based on the number of times pizza has been mentioned in the past twenty minutes. It was almost enough to spoil a healthy appetite."

Quinn put his arm around her shoulders in a friendly hug as they reached the main lobby of the office building. "Almost," he agreed, "but not quite. Besides, you need to eat. Build up your strength for the ball game."

"How much strength can it take to watch a ball game?"

He grinned. "Just wait. You'll see."

IN THE THIRD QUARTER of the soccer game, Emily almost scored. The goalie was too quick, though, and the play continued, zero to zero. Rebecca had to learn the rules as the game progressed, but she had rarely enjoyed an afternoon more. Was it Quinn's patient explanations and attention or was it Emily's childish pleasure at having Rebecca watch her play?

Probably a mixture of both, Rebecca thought. A sprinkle of Quinn's charm mixed with a dash of Emily's smile resulted in feelings of warmth and contentment. It was, Rebecca had discovered, a potent and pleasant combination.

"Having fun?" Quinn asked, his eyes on the soccer field, his hand holding hers. "Not getting hoarse from yelling, are you?"

"Isn't that the objective?"

"Having fun or getting hoarse?"

She laughed because the sun was shining, the air smelled wonderfully fresh and because he had such incredibly blue eyes. "Oh, I think it could be—" The referee blew his whistle and signaled a penalty against Emily's team. "What does he think he's doing?" Rebecca grumbled. "I didn't see anything wrong."

"It was a hand-ball, I think." Quinn watched the exchange between referee and players, then nodded. "Yes, that's what happened. Only the goalie is allowed to touch the ball with her hands, and anytime another player does it, even if it's accidental, there's a penalty."

"But she didn't mean to touch it. The ball hit her on the wrist." Rebecca turned her frown to the referee. "That isn't fair."

"But it is the rule."

"Well, I don't have to like it."

Quinn smiled broadly. "Trust me, you'll think it's an excellent rule when the ref calls a penalty on the other team."

She was willing to concede a degree of prejudice. "Maybe I will. It just seems like such a lot of rules for these girls to remember. They're only eight years old."

This time, the laughter was his. "Spoken like a true mother."

The words echoed softly in her head and left a lingering wistfulness in her heart. "No, I just haven't forgotten what it was like to be that age."

He turned his head to look at her, captured her gaze with his and held it until she grew uncomfortable and looked away. "You really like kids, don't you?" There was the sound of discovery in his voice, and Rebecca wondered if he was always so easy to please.

"Of course. Doesn't everyone?"

"No." He said it flatly and, she sensed, with experience. "Everyone doesn't."

"Well, there's no accounting for taste."

He was silent for a moment. "You like children, yet you don't want any of your own?"

She wrinkled her forehead in a frown. What did he really want to know? "I don't want any *on* my own, if that makes it any clearer. I am fortunate enough to have two parents who genuinely love each other and who have worked very hard to keep that relationship alive. I won't offer my child less."

"What about your career?"

Rebecca ran a hand beneath the weight of her auburn hair, lifting it so the cooling air could reach her neck. "Tough question. One I'm not sure I can answer. A child would certainly change things." She tensed, ready to cheer the goal that at the last minute missed its mark. With a rueful tilt of her brows, she relaxed. "I've always gone for the challenge, though. I'd like to think I could manage to have both."

She could have sworn he sighed, as if he'd been holding his breath waiting for her answer. Were her views on family life important to him? "Don't you feel the same way? After all, you're juggling more than one role at the moment: you have a career and you have Emily."

"I do, don't I?" He grinned easily, as if the thought were new and unexpectedly pleasant. On the field, the soccer ball bounced once, met a flying foot and sailed into the goal. The cheering section, including Quinn and Rebecca, rose in unison, excitedly yelling for the first score of the game. When they seated themselves again, Quinn caught Emily's eye out on the playing field and gave her the thumbs-up sign. She grinned, looking more like her daddy than she did in any one of her pictures.

"You can't get this feeling from any career," he said to Rebecca.

It was not an arguable point, even if she'd been inclined to disagree. She suspected he was absolutely right, and though she hated to acknowledge it, she felt a degree of envy for Quinn and the other parents sitting around her. At the same time, she felt a stirring curiosity about Emily's mother and about Quinn's relationship with her. Rebecca recognized the potential danger of such thoughts and feelings. She had taken psychology; she lived across the hall from Wally. Two good reasons to proceed with caution. Getting emotionally involved with Quinn—and his daughter—was not in her plans.

Quinn clapped and yelled as Emily booted the soccer ball halfway down the field. Without a second's hesitation, Rebecca enthusiastically joined his cheering section.

Chapter Eight

True to his word, Quinn left her at her apartment door later that night without mentioning the trunk. On the way home, he talked about Emily's soccer team, and he talked about his college days and the spring his fraternity won the volleyball championship. He asked about her education, her family, and why she chose to sell lingerie.

She told him.

Probably, she thought later as she fastened the security chain, she had told him more than he'd ever wanted to know about Lady Laura Lingerie and her own plans for climbing the corporate ladder. There was a certain tension present whenever her career was mentioned. He tried to disguise it, but she felt it as if it were a tangible form of caution. She didn't know why it bothered him and could only assume that his beliefs about women were even more traditional than she'd suspected.

Yet when she thought back over the afternoon, Rebecca couldn't recall a single moment when she'd felt uncomfortable or out of place: the leisurely lunch at an out-of-the-way restaurant where they had lingered with a glass of wine and a nonthreatening discussion of favorite books, music and movies; the drive to school to pick up Emily and the subsequent and impromptu tour of her classroom; the soccer game and the after-game pizza party, which was *not* held at

Pete's Pizzeria. Even Emily had seemed genuinely glad to see her and had left no doubt of her enthusiasm at having someone other than "just Dad" watch her play.

All in all, Rebecca wondered if perhaps she had been a little too comfortable with Quinn and his daughter. She had enjoyed herself, to be sure, but there was definite, dangerous attraction in the idea of a single man raising his child alone. But she, Rebecca reminded herself, was too practical to be swayed by such a predictably feminine response.

Predictably—p-r-e-d-i-c-t-a-b-l-y. She could hear Emily's voice in her head, repeating the word and its spelling as she had repeated other words all evening. *"I'm entered in the spelling bee this year,"* she'd told Rebecca in confidential tones as if it were a secret known only by the two of them. *"My teacher says I should practice."*

Rebecca smiled with the memory of Emily's serious blue eyes and the patient way Quinn had corrected the few words she'd misspelled. Emily. Quinn. A family of two. Where did nontraditional, career-minded Rebecca Whitaker fit in? With a sigh, she resolved to put the two Kinsers out of her thoughts. It wasn't as if she didn't have plenty of other things to occupy her mind.

Putting her purse on the sofa, she walked into the kitchen, poured herself a glass of orange juice and took it with her to the bedroom. The trunk was waiting, just as she'd left it, and a slow building anticipation rippled down her back. At last, she was alone with the infamous long-lost trunk of Aunt Molly—whoever "Aunt Molly" might be.

Rebecca set the juice glass on the bedside table, and pursing her lips, she moved to the dresser and retrieved a small shiny key. One of the movers had handed it to her just as they'd prepared to leave after the delivery. "This must have fallen out of the lock while we were taking the trunk out of the back of the van," he'd explained. "Some lady saw it fall on the sidewalk and told me not to lose it."

Rebecca hadn't thought to question him further, but now she wished she had. There hadn't been a key for the trunk. At least, she was pretty sure there hadn't been when she'd bought it. She must have made a mistake, though, because there was definitely a key now. It could have been taped to the bottom of the trunk, she supposed. Out of sight. Still, it was odd. But then so far everything about the trunk was a little odd. Her fingers closed over the key, and she narrowed her gaze on the object of so much speculation. "One phone call," she said aloud. "Then it's just you and me, *Aunt Molly*."

Wally answered on the second ring with a crisp, no-nonsense, professional "Yes? This is Dr. Sherrow."

"Whatever happened to a simple hello? You're not at the office now, you know." Rebecca sat on the edge of the bed and kicked off her shoes. "You must be working too hard."

"Always. It's my nature."

"Your *compulsive* nature."

"There's nothing wrong with me that having a man of my own wouldn't cure."

Rebecca laughed. "Oh, no. Don't tell me that Wally Sherrow, the last stalwart of independent womanhood, has fallen prey to her own scientific theory? What a blow to the feminist movement."

"Rest easy. I've been working on my book about what women think they have to have to be happy, and when the phone rang just now, I was in the process of listing some of the nonsense I hear at the office. Don't worry about me, Rebecca. I will never succumb to the idea that a man is necessary for the sustentation of life as I know it."

"Regardless of what your mother says."

"She's from the old school and can't be held accountable. Just be glad *you* don't have to listen to her lectures."

"Believe me, I appreciate the fact that you never gave your mother my phone number," Rebecca said wryly.

"How is the book coming along? Has your hypothesis run head-on into any opposition yet?"

"My scientific theory is soundly documented and ready for testing in the outside world. I am ready to prove that opportunity plus situation equals emotion, or in laymen's terms, love is a mathematical equation. All I need to do is match Barbie with Ken."

"What? No volunteers?"

Wally yawned audibly over the phone lines. "It wouldn't work if some man just volunteered. This experiment is going to require careful handling."

An understatement from every angle, Rebecca thought. "I'm sure you'll manage," she said. "You always seem to land on your feet."

"It's my compulsive life-style. You should try it, Rebecca."

"Yes, well, we all have our problems, you know."

"How well I know." Wally paused, which was an effective little trick Rebecca had learned to watch out for. "And how is your problem working out? Are his eyes still incredibly blue? Or has reality grayed the edges?"

Rebecca hesitated for only a second. "As blue as the Hope Diamond."

"I still have room for one more in the Tuesday evening therapy group."

A slow smile curved across Rebecca's mouth. "Thanks, I'll keep that in mind. Listen, I called to ask a favor. Are you booked solid tomorrow afternoon?"

"I don't think so, but I'll have to check the appointment book. Why?"

"It's a long story, which I don't want to go into now, but I'm supposed to meet someone, a man named Scott Forsythe, at Bridgette's Café tomorrow at four-thirty." Rebecca paused to consider the phrasing of her request. "I'd like to have your company and the benefit of an objective opinion.''

"And since I'm the most objective, opinionated person you know..."

"Exactly," Rebecca agreed with a chuckle. "I'll fill you in on the details later, but I need your expert powers of observation tomorrow. If you can just be there, watch, and tell me later if you think he was telling the truth, it will help tremendously. You see, he called me because he wants to buy the trunk, and I—"

"Hell's bells, Rebecca! That trunk is turning into a real treasure hunt. Did it finally arrive today? What was in it? Anything of value?"

"I don't know. There's been a slight delay, and so I—"

Wally's interruption was quick and impatient. "Well, when are you going to get it and find out what all the commotion is about?"

"Soon." She hedged the answer. There was a temptation to confide in Wally, but Rebecca was reluctant to share the unveiling with anyone else. If Wally knew the trunk had already been delivered, she'd be over before Rebecca had time to drink the rest of her juice. "Very soon."

Wally sighed, obviously disgusted with the delay. "Did you say four-thirty?" she asked.

Rebecca confirmed the time and waited for her friend to respond one way or the other.

"I'll juggle my schedule and meet you there at four-fifteen. How's that?"

"Thank you, Wally. I appreciate it."

"Think nothing of it. You know how I love to give my opinion about anything. Maybe you can repay the favor by helping me with my book over the weekend." A note of pleasure entered her voice. "It's shaping up nicely. I can't wait to get back to it."

"Don't let me keep you, then. I'll see you tomorrow."

"Yes. Four-fifteen. Bridgette's."

"Right," Rebecca said. "Good night and thanks." She replaced the receiver and pressed her lips together. Taking the clips from her hair, she tossed her head to free the auburn waves. She rose, took a sip of juice and moved to kneel beside the trunk.

As she inserted the key and turned, she thought of Quinn and wished she could have invited him to stay. The moment was made for sharing, like the television commercials for coffee where a man and a woman took a moment to enjoy the sunrise or to relax after a party over a cup of specially prepared coffee. Rebecca smiled at the image in her mind's eye of herself sitting in Quinn's big chair, sipping hot chocolate. A nice, nice memory, she decided. Even if she wasn't particularly objective.

The key turned protestingly, squeaked, and then the lock clicked open. She heard it echo with the rusty sound of disuse. It was unlocked now. All she had to do was open the lid. But for several minutes she waited, running her hand over the rough, dusty surface and wondering when the trunk had last been opened. And who had last touched it. Rebecca felt a curious affection for the trunk and its past owner or owners.

She pushed the latch and then, with great care, pushed back the lid on its hinges. The smell that filled her nostrils was old but not unpleasant. It was musty, but still held the faint scent of lilac and honeysuckle, flowers pressed by time and tradition into a familiar, ageless fragrance. There were memories in the trunk—Rebecca could feel them—but not much else. She smiled when she saw the fabric covering the inside of the trunk. Tiny purple flowers on a white background, faded, of course, but very similar to the curtains that Rebecca remembered had hung in her grandmother's back bedroom.

She ran her hand along the side and felt the crisp texture that came with age. She touched the rounded tarnished studs that might have been brass and then lifted a hat from its place on top of a button-front beige sweater. The hat was black straw with a lavender cabbage rose on the band. Rebecca suspected it had been in and out of fashion at least twice since its creation, but she rather liked the whimsical tilt of the brim. A pearl-tipped hatpin was stuck through the crown, waiting and ready for use. Rebecca touched it, her smile deepening, and then carefully she placed the hat on the bed behind her.

There was another hat, a cream-colored pillbox with a net veil, and a dark blue beret. She placed the pillbox hat on the bed, too, then examined the beret. It looked like the type of hat worn by members of the air force. There was even a darker spot on the front, as if it might once have sported the silver wings emblem. No way to tell now, though, Rebecca thought and laid the beret aside.

Next she took out the sweater and on impulse lifted it to her nose. Again she was reminded of her grandmother, and she thought, although she wasn't positive, that it had a lingering fragrance of tea roses, a sweet scent she associated with so many childhood memories. There was another sweater in the trunk, same style, different color, and there was a pair of pointed-toe shoes with a squatty heel.

What kind of person had worn these clothes? Rebecca tried to visualize a woman wearing the hat with the cabbage rose trim, tried to imagine the sweater and the shoes as fashionable and new, purchased to complement a dress or the color of the woman's hair. Rebecca liked the idea. She liked the picture she'd created in her mind's eye. Her grandmother would have worn the hat, she thought, and have been proud of it, too. With a reminiscent smile, Rebecca gently placed the shoes on the floor and placed the clothes on top.

At the bottom of the trunk, beneath where the clothes had lain, Rebecca found a yellowed book of poetry, a dozen or more letters tied with a faded pink ribbon, and two notebooks of similar size and appearance, both black with gold etching and both with worn bindings. After glancing at the poetry book and the packet of letters, she laid them aside. She leaned into the trunk and lifted out one of the notebooks, then sinking back on her heels, she placed it in her lap and opened the cover. It was a photograph album, the kind with black construction paper pages and black lick-and-stick corners that fit around the photograph to hold it on the page. Her parents had one like it, filled with black-and-white photos of their honeymoon vacation at Niagara Falls. The few pictures in this album were not familiar, but Rebecca felt as if she'd just run into an old and dear friend.

Here was the woman she'd imagined only moments before. Only she wasn't exactly as Rebecca had pictured her. She was a girl, really. Certainly younger than the style of the sweaters and the pointed-toe shoes would indicate. But the hat could have been in any one of the photographs and not looked out of place. Leaning over the pages, Rebecca tried to determine facial features and the color of the young woman's hair.

Black-and-white photos, however, held their secrets well, and, although Rebecca spent several minutes looking at the album, she could only ascertain that the young woman had a wide, appealing smile and a perpetual expression of mischief. In almost every shot, there was an attractive older man who seemed to have eyes only for the woman beside him.

Lovers. Rebecca didn't know how she could tell that from a couple of dozen faded prints, but she had no doubts about the intensity of these two strangers' feelings for each other. It made her feel like an intruder just looking through the album.

But she kept turning pages, being careful not to tear the fragile sheets, poring over the pictures, trying to see glimpses of the life these two people had shared. As often as not, the background of the photos was the ocean. No. Rebecca took a closer look. There were no whitecaps, no waves, so the water must be a lake. Somewhere. No way of guessing where the lake might be. It could have been anywhere in the world. Not that it mattered. She was sure it hadn't mattered much to these lovers, either.

"Together" could have been engraved in gold on the album's cover, because it was obvious to Rebecca that the couple in the photographs knew how to enjoy each other's company. Had their lives been happy? she wondered. Were they still lovers all these years later?

Rebecca, for the second time, felt as if she were intruding on a private and intimate moment. This album held pictures that had meaning to someone. Probably the woman, because in the few notations written below certain photographs the handwriting was flowery and feminine. The kind of handwriting that a woman who would wear a black straw hat with a purple flower ought to have. Rebecca smiled at the thought and turned the last pages of the album more quickly than she really wanted. The time was slipping away, and she couldn't stay awake all night imagining the background and life-styles of the trunk's previous owners.

At the back of the album she found some folded papers...documents, maybe. She laid them in her lap for later perusal, put the album on the floor beside her and returned to the trunk. As she picked up the other notebook, she heard something fall and leaned over for a second look. Something shiny caught her eye, and there, in the far corner, she spied a ring, spinning in the shadows before coming to rest in its own forged circle.

She retrieved it and held it in her palm, turning it to the light, captivated by the unmistakable, rich gleam of gold. It was worn smooth in places, but the design of twining roses could still be easily discerned as could the inscription on the inside of the band. "Cripple Creek 1899," it read, followed by faint initials that looked like "THH" or maybe it was "TWH." Rebecca couldn't be sure. There was a second set of initials, "MMS," which were smaller than the first but bolder, as if the inscription had been made at a later date.

Rebecca turned the ring again before she slipped it onto her finger and examined it from that angle. It was pretty, she thought and then immediately discarded the description as frivolous. The ring was more than pretty. It had character, a story of its own etched into the design. Rebecca could almost believe she felt the bond this ring represented to someone. Maybe the couple in the photographs.

Impulsively she reached for the album and again leafed through the pages. Nothing, she decided a little later, although what she'd expected to see she couldn't imagine. Few pictures were clear enough to see details like a ring on a finger. With a sigh that turned into a yawn, she placed the album back into the trunk and stretched the stiff muscles in her back, which was beginning to ache.

It was late, and she decided to go to bed. After all, it was fairly apparent to her now that the trunk wasn't going to yield any dark, mysterious secrets. Not unless there was a hidden compartment containing diamonds or emeralds or a deed to the U.S. Mint. Rebecca yawned a second time, and, with a glance around, she began putting everything back into the trunk. It would all be here tomorrow, she thought, and maybe by then she would be able to connect the pieces of this puzzle.

She picked up the second notebook, absently tucking the documents inside the back cover as she opened it to the front, expecting to see more photographs. There was only one. On the inside cover, the picture portrait of the young woman from the photo album looked back at her. There was no smile now, just the innocent, eager expression of someone who loved and had been caught in a moment of revealing the emotion. Beneath the photo was a caption, written in precise, bold letters. "Molly Margaret Summer," it read. "May you always be near to the sunshine."

Intrigued, Rebecca turned a page and realized the notebook was a diary. There wasn't anything so obvious as a "Dear Diary," of course, but the date—June 14, Sunday—written in the top right corner and the entry below were evidence enough.

It is very blue tonight. Even the nightingale sounds lonely. How Thede would tease if he could hear me. He would put his arms around me, and we would laugh and laugh... That's the trouble with the lake house. We have been here too many times together. So when he has to be with them and cannot be with me, I am doubly alone. And I hear noises that I never hear when he is with me. Like the nightingale.

With a thoughtful frown, Rebecca turned a few more pages before closing the book and getting to her feet. The evening's discoveries tumbled through her mind and formed a line of possibilities. *Aunt Molly. Molly Margaret Summer. Thede.* Two sets of initials inscribed in a gold ring. The connecting threads of two lives. Memories placed lovingly inside an old trunk. Memories that Rebecca could only guess about now. Memories that she couldn't imagine would generate a burglary of her apartment.

The possibilities made her feel restless, but Rebecca didn't know why. She had never met Molly Margaret Summer; they were never likely to meet. So why did she feel like an uninvited guest at a lovers' tryst? If this Molly was the

"Aunt Molly" of Quinn and Scott Forsythe's imagination, then didn't she, Rebecca, have a right to read the journal and discover, if she could, what connection these people had to each other? Like it or not, she was involved, and there didn't seem any point in being timid about reading a diary. No matter how personal it might seem.

With that in mind, she placed the journal on the bedside table, put everything else back in the trunk, closed it and then got ready for bed. As she brushed her teeth, she felt the weight of the ring and considered taking it off, but she didn't. So far it was the only thing she'd found that might have any real value, and she decided to take it to a nearby jeweler the next day for appraisal. Not that she expected it to be worth much monetarily, but at least she'd feel like she was doing something. Besides eavesdropping on the written love affair of two people who had in all probability lived years before she was born.

For a moment, Rebecca stared at her mirrored reflection; then she returned to the bedroom and the journal. Before she opened it, though, she reached for the telephone and, without giving herself too much time to think, she dialed.

"Hello?" Quinn's voice was deep and even, husky, but not with sleep.

"Hello, Quinn. This is Rebecca." She wanted to say more, she wanted to say something that would explain, in a word, why she'd called. But she didn't know what that word might be. "I . . . hope I didn't awaken you."

"No. I often work late at night."

"Oh."

The quiet slipped into a few seconds' pause. "Is anything wrong?" he asked. "Are you all right?"

Suddenly she was. "Yes. I just wanted to say good-night and . . . thank-you."

"For?"

"Today. For understanding about . . . things."

"I'm a very understanding guy. Wait, you'll see."

A ripple of pleasurable anticipation flowed through her. "I'm beginning to."

There was a hesitation, a long, considering moment. "I enjoyed being with you today," he said finally. "So did Emily. She's been spelling your name all evening."

"Has she really? How sweet." It was, Rebecca realized. She had little hands-on experience with children, but maybe they weren't as difficult as she'd always supposed. "I guess Emily's asleep now."

"She'd better be. I tucked her in hours ago."

Rebecca wished he were there to tuck *her* into bed and then immediately backed away from the thought. Time to gather her common sense and say goodbye. But she couldn't quite get the words together.

"Why weren't you in bed?" She caught her mistake. "Oh, you told me you were working, didn't you?"

"I wasn't working. I've been sitting here thinking of you."

Her heart stopped, then raced like a hummingbird's wings. "Why?"

"That's a tricky question," he said, and she could feel the smile in his voice. "I'm not sure I should answer."

But he had. She knew it and so did he. "No," she said. "Probably not."

"I'm glad you phoned, Rebecca. Are you sure you're all right? You're not scared staying in the apartment?"

"I'm not scared. I called because I thought I heard something, but it was nothing."

"What did it sound like?" he asked, his tone alert and cautious.

A wistful bit of melancholy tugged at her heart. "A nightingale."

"A nightingale? In town? You must have imagined it."

Her lips curved softly. So softly. "Maybe I did."

"Good night," he said. "Call me if you need anything."

"Yes, Quinn, good night."

She replaced the receiver, wondering where her impulse was leading her. Or if it was impulse at all. Maybe it was a matter of heart over head, something with which she had little experience. She was practical by nature. She had plans for her life. And she had just placed an impractical, un-planned phone call to a man for no better reason than that she wanted to hear his voice.

Nightingale, indeed. He must think she was crazy. She was beginning to wonder about that, too. Whatever the ex-planation, though, her earlier restlessness was gone, and she opened the journal and began to read, no longer feeling like a third party, but a part of the overall flow of life. And lov-ing.

Chapter Nine

Of all the days to be called into the boss's office, Rebecca thought as she nervously smoothed any possibility of wrinkles from her linen skirt. She wasn't her usual career-oriented self today. She knew that. And she was painfully aware of the amount of company time she'd daydreamed away in the five hours since she'd come to work.

"Good luck." Nancy, secretary for all the sales representatives in the office, offered a smile and the thumbs-up sign as Rebecca walked through the reception area toward the elevator and her upstairs meeting.

Rebecca wished she could be as positive, although she really had no qualms about facing the president of the company. In fact, on any other day she would have welcomed the opportunity. But her mind was not on Lady Laura Lingerie today. Her thoughts centered more on the words she'd read in Molly's diary the night before. Words that lingered like a winsome melody and that would not leave her alone. Words of love and longing and surrender and sacrifice. Words about a love affair that was both forbidden and unforgettable.

The elevator doors opened onto the executive offices, and Rebecca tried to kick her concentration into high gear. It would never do to let the company president know that she wasn't interested in what he had to say. Well, actually she *was* interested. She just couldn't keep her attention on business at the moment. But she would, she promised herself as she stepped into the inner sanctum.

Five minutes later, she stepped out again, smiling softly at the commendation she'd just received. It felt good to know that her hard work for the company had been noticed and appreciated. It also reaffirmed her career goals and the idea that she was making progress up the corporate ladder. So why, instead of wanting to rush back to her desk and work even harder, did she wish she could slip out of the office and go home?

This sudden attack of restlessness didn't make sense. The way her thoughts kept returning to Quinn didn't make sense, either. It seemed that no matter which way she turned she was reminded of something he had said or the way he'd looked or the feelings he evoked in her. Feelings that were certainly not as intense as those described in Molly's journal, but feelings that Rebecca realized were just as real and just as special.

But Lady Laura Lingerie and Quinn Kinser had nothing in common, and she, Rebecca reminded herself firmly, needed to keep that in perspective. There were all kinds of sales calls she could make this afternoon in order to keep her attention on her career. And that was exactly what she would do. Right up until four o'clock, when she would leave the office to meet Wally and Scott Forsythe. Then, perhaps, later she would be able to see Quinn. Talk with him. Watch the crooked smile that slashed the solemnity of his dark beard and made her heart beat a little faster.

With a disgusted sigh, Rebecca jabbed the elevator button. Down, she thought. She was going down to her own floor where her own office was located and where she would call Jimi Lee Denarro, the buyer for Edward's Clothing stores in Jefferson City. If anyone could get her mind back on business, Jimi Lee would be the one to do it. Yes, Rebecca thought, she would phone Jimi Lee and confirm their appointment for the next day.

"Business as usual," Rebecca whispered to herself in the solitude of the elevator enclosure. "Do you hear that, Quinn Kinser? It's business as usual. And you can tell your Aunt Molly, too."

"I DON'T KNOW WHY you like this place, Rebecca," Wally said. "There are at least half a dozen restaurants nearby that offer more atmosphere."

"Atmosphere, maybe." Rebecca moved over a step, letting a couple get past her on their way through the café's lobby to the front door. "But square foot per square foot, Bridgette's has more charm."

"At the moment, I'd settle for a cup of coffee and a sandwich. I'm starved. You wouldn't believe how relieved I was to get away from the office this afternoon. It's been a madhouse all day." Wally glanced impatiently past the Please Wait To Be Seated sign. "How long do we have to wait?"

"Oh, probably not long." Rebecca touched the chignon at the back of her neck and hoped the wayward curls would stay in place a little longer. She almost never wore her hair in such a stiff, unyielding style, but for some reason she'd done so today. Considering her command visit to the executive office, it was a good thing she had, Rebecca thought. And she had been glad that she'd had the foresight that morning to choose the crisp buttercup-colored linen suit, which made her feel that she looked more professional than practically anything else in her closet.

Had it really been foresight, she wondered, that had made her want to project her best professional appearance on this day? Or did it have more to do with the unsettled feeling she'd had since finding Molly's journal the night before? Did her choice of sophisticated clothing and hairstyle reflect a wish to offset the unsophisticated yearning for the kind of love that Molly had known? It wasn't a question that Rebecca wanted to explore. Not yet, anyway.

"Is he here yet?" Wally tipped her chin, giving an edge of superiority to her already prepossessing demeanor. In a mint-green tank dress and bright flowered jacket, Wally looked as if she'd stepped off the front page of a magazine rather than coming from her suburban office building. Rebecca admired Wally for a number of reasons, not the least of which was her ability to separate beauty from intellect and still maintain the advantages of both. If only she were a little less rigid about women's place in society....

"Do you even know what he looks like?" Wally continued her visual search of the room, at least the portion which could be seen from where they stood. "Is he going to wear a red carnation or something patently identifiable?"

"I don't think so." Rebecca smiled as the hostess walked toward them. "I told him to sit in the second booth from the window. If he's not already there, that's where we'll wait for him."

"Oh, I see. And what if that particular booth is occupied by someone else? You should have—"

"Hello, Ms. Whitaker," the hostess greeted Rebecca with a welcome familiarity. Then she turned to briefly greet Wally and led the way to the second booth from the window. "I hope your meeting goes well," the hostess said. "Your waitress will be here with coffee in a few minutes."

Rebecca slid onto the bench seat and waited while Wally sat opposite. "I phoned ahead," she explained with a wry lift of her brows. "I often meet prospective accounts here. Once it's down to contract terms, I like to negotiate in my own territory. It isn't always possible, but I've gotten some high-dollar sales contracts while sitting in this particularly charming place."

"Well, tell me what kind of contract you expect to land today with this mystery man." Wally fixed her attention on Rebecca but didn't allow her time to reply. "Do you realize," she said in a tone that seemed suddenly astonished, "that since you bought that albatross of a trunk, men have been coming out of the woodwork? You've opened Pandora's box, Rebecca."

"Kind of exciting, isn't it?"

"Scary, I'd say. I wouldn't trade places with you for a whole month of Tuesday nights off."

"I thought you were on the lookout for a man."

"Only in the name of scientific research."

Rebecca smiled and nodded a thank-you as the waitress set saucers and coffee cups on the table. "I'll bet every woman in this room has a better excuse than that."

Wally sipped her coffee and eyed Rebecca thoughtfully. "All right, what's yours?"

"My what?"

"Don't be difficult. What's your excuse for wanting a man?"

Rebecca shrugged as she lifted her coffee cup to her lips. "If you'd asked me that two weeks ago, I'd have said there was no excuse for wanting a man, but lately... well, I think I might have been missing something."

Wally rolled her eyes and then clasped her hands on the table, leaning forward in a counseling pose. "You're absolutely right, Rebecca. You've been missing the wonderful sense of accomplishment that comes with washing a grown man's underwear. And just think of all the times you've slept straight through the night without hearing a baby cry or the days you've worked without giving a thought to baby-sitters or sick children."

"I didn't say anything about children."

"You didn't have to. I hear this kind of talk from women all the time. 'My biological clock is becoming a time bomb,' they say. 'If I don't find a man soon, I'll never know true fulfillment,' they say. 'I need someone to share my life,' they say." Wally leaned closer, her expression intense. "Do you know what I say? I say—"

"Excuse me, but I think this is my table." The voice was distinctly male. As was the rest of him, Rebecca decided as she diverted her gaze, in unison with Wally, to the man standing beside their table.

He was tall, blond, and handsome. Very. His clothes were eye-catching, casual and trendy. Expensively so. His smile disclosed a boyish appeal similar to that of the current crop of heroes seen weekly on network television. "I'm Scott Forsythe," he said, obviously pleased by the wide-eyed stares he was receiving from both women. "And I certainly hope one of you will tell me the password so I can join you."

"Password?" Wally murmured.

"There isn't one," Rebecca explained, before greeting the stranger with a smile and extending her hand for his handshake. "Hello, Scott. I'm Rebecca Whitaker. This is Wally Sherrow." As he acknowledged the introduction, Rebecca wondered if she should scoot over on the seat and invite him to sit, but before she had a chance to do so, he drew up a chair from a nearby table and sat at the end of the booth.

He looked from Wally to Rebecca and back again. "For a day that got off to a rotten start, things are definitely on the upswing. May I buy you two lovely ladies a drink?"

"This is Dutch treat," Wally stated firmly, settling back against the cushioned bench to widen her field of observation. "Rebecca and I like to pay our own way."

Rebecca saw nothing wrong in letting Scott buy her a cup of coffee. After all, *he* had initiated this meeting, not her. There didn't seem much point in mentioning her opinion, though. Especially since no one gave her the opportunity.

"How refreshing," Scott said, "to find two women who are both as independent as they are beautiful. Will you marry me?"

"Thanks, but bigamy isn't our style." Rebecca was a little put off by his flirty charm. Scott Forsythe was a bit exaggerated for her taste.

That was an opinion Wally didn't seem to share. "Marriage isn't our style, either," she added.

"What a relief. I hate painting picket fences. It just isn't *my* style."

Wally laughed politely. "In that case, Mr. Forsythe, you are in good company."

He paused, drawing his brows into a considering line. "Scott," he corrected. "I don't like formality among friends."

Wally smiled. Rebecca sighed and wished she'd invited Quinn instead of Wally. He would have been more entertaining than this trivial pursuit of a conversation. He was also better looking. Scott might have an edge in a screen test, but for sheer masculine charisma, Quinn won hands down. "Now, Scott," Rebecca said, emphasizing his name, thereby establishing her disregard for formality in this circumstance. "Do you think we can—"

The waitress appeared, ready to take their orders, and Wally asked her to return after they'd had a chance to peruse the menu. Rebecca accepted the delay reluctantly. She wasn't hungry. It was already four-thirty, and she wanted to stop by the jeweler's shop before it closed.

Molly's ring was wrapped in tissue and zippered into the inside pocket of her purse. It was the only tangible object she'd found in the trunk that would have any value, and Rebecca had decided to get the appraisal done as soon as possible. Everything else she had left undisturbed in the trunk. Except for the journal. For some reason that she hadn't been able to analyze, Rebecca had hidden the journal in her bedroom. Placed it out of sight at the bottom of a stack of books in the top of the closet. Which was a silly thing to have done, she thought as she watched Scott flirt with Wally. The journal was Molly's very personal account of her ill-fated love affair. It belonged with the photographs and the other items in the trunk. Rebecca decided she would return it there as soon as she got home.

There really was no reason to keep the trunk at all, she supposed. Except that Scott wanted it and Quinn wanted it, and she didn't know if either of them actually had any right to claim it. There was, or had been at one time, a Molly, but Rebecca had no clue whether she was the Aunt Molly in question. Was she Scott's aunt? Or Quinn's aunt? It was possible she was no relation to either one.

What could they want from the trunk? Rebecca wondered. The question was becoming a perpetual merry-go-round in her head. She must have missed something. And until she found it, maybe it was best to keep everyone guessing. No one except Quinn knew she had the trunk. Not even Wally, who at the moment seemed far more interested in Scott Forsythe's smile than in any body language he was communicating. It would have been better to leave Wally out of this, Rebecca realized belatedly. She should have trusted her instinct and followed proven sales technique. Oh, well, she thought, she would just have to take charge of the conversation.

She didn't get a chance. After ordering a substantial afternoon snack, Wally and Scott—Rebecca wasn't sure which one initiated the topic—began a friendly discussion of politics, which led to a slightly less friendly discussion of why the Equal Rights Amendment had failed, which led, as Rebecca had known it would, to a symposium of Wally Sherrow's carefully sculpted views on men and their role in the defeat of legislation that was near and dear to her heart.

"And the most frustrating thing is to know we're in the right. Men have a lot to gain, but they're too damned scared about losing any of that macho edge to realize the positive effects it will have for them." Wally tapped her fingernail on the tabletop to emphasize her point. "The whole thing just infuriates me."

Scott regarded the tapping fingernail with a frown before lifting a rueful smile to meet Wally's opinionated expression. "You're overly sensitive."

The look of astonishment that settled on Wally's classic features caught at Rebecca's funny bone, but she kept her laughter for herself and merely took a drink of her coffee.

"Well," Wally said a long minute later, "if I could find just one man who had the sensitivity to understand this issue, women's rights would be a moot question."

Scott lifted his hand, palm up. "All right, you've found me. Now what?"

"You think *you*—" Wally almost stuttered, trying to find the words to argue.

"Yes," Scott said with a polite and forceful look. "I think I do. And what's more, I'm very sympathetic to your cause. But *your* problem, Wally, is in blaming all men for the bias of a few."

"A *few*?"

Scott's lips curved in slight concession. "Maybe a few more than that, but—" he held up a finger "—women are gaining a lot of crossover support."

At that point, Wally launched into her second diatribe on the double standards of male rhetoric. Scott took it all in with a vaguely bemused expression, but at an ominous pause in the conversation, he took a stand. "I think, Wally, that you may have some valid points hidden in there somewhere, but for the life of me, I can't see them. In fact, as far as I can tell, your *assumptions* about men are in need of some very basic updating. Where did you get the idea that a man of the eighties—myself, for example—would be threatened by your ambitions?''

Wally looked stunned, and as she struggled for words, Rebecca pressed her lips tightly together to keep from laughing. She had to hand it to Scott. Anyone who could reduce Wally to silence, no matter how briefly, deserved a grudging respect.

"How do you feel about it, Rebecca?" He turned his attention fully to her for the first time, and Rebecca found herself responding with a smile. "Has Wally convinced you that men are responsible for the suppression of your gender, despite the well-established but overlooked idea that women have a mind of their own?"

"That is *not* what I said." Wally, oddly enough, sounded less angry than intrigued.

To Rebecca's surprise, Scott ignored Wally, and that was something that seldom happened. "I think women as well as men are responsible for their own actions and for their own happiness," Rebecca answered, trying not to let her smile curve too wide.

"Ah," Scott raised his brows and nodded solemnly. "My Aunt Molly would like you. You're two of a kind."

Aunt Molly. Rebecca's brows lifted. He had spoken in the present tense. How interesting. "Where does your Aunt Molly live, Scott? Maybe I'll meet her someday."

"That isn't likely. She's a strange old bird. The last time I saw her, she was going to Mexico City to see the ruins." The curve of his mouth matched the wry shrug of his shoulders. "She's the black sheep of the family."

"Really?" Rebecca took a sudden and inexplicable dislike to his tone of voice. She didn't much care for his choice of words, either. "And you think that she and I are two of a kind?"

He had the grace to look embarrassed. "I'm sorry, that was a tactless thing to say, wasn't it? I only meant that Aunt

Molly shares your views on responsibility. She's always saying that people make their own happiness and their own unhappiness.''

''She's right,'' Wally said with just a hint of defensiveness in her voice. ''I tell my patients that all the time. The problem is they don't ever seem to *hear* me.''

''Patients?'' Scott turned a quizzical gaze to Wally. ''Are you a doctor?''

''I'm a psychologist.''

''She earned her doctorate last year.'' Rebecca had felt obligated to add the information, although Scott didn't appear to be listening.

''I'm impressed. Where did you attend graduate school?''

In a matter of minutes, they had uncovered a mutual acquaintance, and Rebecca had lost control of the conversation. She glanced at her watch and reasoned that she'd given Scott enough time to present his case. It wasn't her fault that he was easily distracted. As the waitress arrived at the table, Rebecca seized the opportunity to excuse herself.

''I'm sorry to rush off,'' she said, ''but I have an errand to run before five o'clock. You understand, I'm sure.''

Scott half rose from his seat when she stood. ''But we didn't discuss the trunk. I'd like to buy it if you—''

''It hasn't been delivered yet, has it, Rebecca?'' Wally opened the top half of her chicken sandwich, removed a slice of onion, and reached for the salt. ''She has had the most incredible experience, though. It seems that you are not the only relation of this eccentric Aunt Molly who is interested in recovering the trunk. Why, just the other day—''

''Wally.'' Rebecca warned her friend with a cautioning look and a bit of very expressive body language. ''I'm sure Scott doesn't want to hear about *my* experiences. Why don't you tell him about the book you're writing instead?''

Wally pursed her lips consideringly. "You're absolutely right, kiddo. I don't know why I didn't think of that myself." She turned a pensive regard to Scott, then smiled. "How do you feel about relationships?"

"Yours or mine?"

Wally put her sandwich back together as her lips tilted upward in anticipation. "Can we talk?" she asked.

Rebecca wanted to roll her eyes. Or laugh. Or something. Leaving Wally to her own devices seemed the only solution, though. She had only wanted to let Wally know that the trunk and the mystery surrounding it was not something she wanted discussed with Scott. She'd certainly never meant to place him in the precarious position of lab rat, which apparently was the idea Wally now had.

"It was nice to meet you, Scott," Rebecca said. "Call me in a few days, and we'll discuss the trunk, all right?"

"Yes, of course. I'm only sorry we didn't—" He started to get to his feet again, but Rebecca motioned him back to his seat.

"Don't give it a thought. Enjoy your—snack." She started to walk away, then paused. "Oh, uh, Scott? The password is scientific experiment. Watch out for it."

He looked puzzled, Wally looked unperturbed, and with a wave of her hand, Rebecca walked to the front register and paid the tab.

"You must have gotten the contract," the hostess said with a smile.

Rebecca glanced back at the second table from the window. "Love is just a set of circumstances. Did you know that?" At the woman's blank look, Rebecca smiled. "Never mind. Just keep the coffee hot for Barbie and Ken, would you?"

THE JEWELRY STORE was crowded for a weekday afternoon, and Rebecca wandered around, looking in the display cases as she waited to see Mr. Antonelli. There was a tray of antique rings, but none of them were as interesting as the one she had in her purse. In fact, nothing in the shop really captured her attention, with the possible exception of a man's plain gold watch that for some reason reminded her of Quinn. Did he have one like it?

Rebecca shook her head. She didn't know, and it didn't matter. She was thinking about him too much, anyway. If the sight of a watch brought him to mind, then it was time to—

"Crowded in here, isn't it?"

Rebecca turned to see a small, fragile-looking woman standing beside her. She smiled politely in response. "Yes, it is," she said, returning her attention to the display case.

"I'm looking for a gift," the woman said, placing a hand on the glass counter. "A special gift."

Rebecca nodded absently and then gradually became aware that the woman was wearing gloves. Not finger-warming cold-weather gloves, but fine white summer gloves, the kind she vaguely remembered her mother wearing years and years ago. Rebecca took a second look at the woman, noticing the frail bone structure, the wrinkled skin, the outdated style of the purple dress and the gaudy turban hat atop a head of red, wispy hair. The hat was red, too, but it didn't match, and the woman seemed blithely unconcerned by her garish fashion statement.

"Could you help me choose, dear?" The woman's voice was low, well-modulated and rich with character. When she smiled, Rebecca forgot about first impressions and the impulse to tell this stranger that she didn't work in the jewelry store and couldn't help in any way.

"What did you have in mind?" Rebecca asked instead.

"A ring, I think." The red hat and head bobbed. "Do you like rings?"

"Yes. In fact, that's why I'm here now."

"Are you buying a ring?"

"No. I brought a ring in for appraisal."

Thin lips pulled into a wrinkled approval. "What a good idea. No one knows the value of things these days. I've seen grown men act like children because they didn't know the value of what they were fighting over. It's refreshing to meet someone who has the good sense to ask for a second opinion when it's needed."

In or out of context, Rebecca couldn't see the point, but she realized this woman expected her to agree. She sidestepped a direct response and said, "Let's look at the tray of rings over there. Maybe something will strike your fancy."

"What a quaint expression," the old lady said as she walked to the display case Rebecca had indicated. Her glance at the rings was cursory. "Do you like that purple one? It's an amethyst. I used to have one bigger than that. I don't remember where it is, though. Do you like—"

She was interrupted by a man's voice. "Miss Whitaker? I am Antonelli. Where is the ring?"

All business. That's one of the reasons Rebecca liked this shop. Everything was treated as a business transaction should be treated. If only the little woman with the hat and gloves would move on, Rebecca thought as she opened her purse and produced the ring for the jeweler's inspection.

He took it, held it in his palm, then held it up to the light. "Nice," he said. "May I have a couple of days to examine it? We are very busy today, and I would like to have more time. Is this agreeable to you, Miss Whitaker?"

"Of course." Rebecca tried to ignore the concurring nod of the woman in purple who stood companionably beside her. "May I have a receipt?"

Mr. Antonelli took a pen from his pocket, a claim check from the cash register, and after making a note, he handed the slip of paper to Rebecca. "Thank you," she said, sliding the receipt inside her purse at the same time she turned to leave. Unfortunately, she didn't allow enough space, and she bumped into the elderly lady. Rebecca dropped her purse in an effort to keep the woman from falling.

"I'm so sorry." Rebecca looked for any sign of injury and resolutely kept silent about the woman's failure to stand back in the first place. "Are you all right?"

"Fine." The lady bent and began picking up the items that had fallen out of Rebecca's purse. "Here you are, dear. Take care of yourself, now." She handed over the purse. "You've been a great help. Don't worry. I'll find my amethyst somewhere. Rings always turn up in the right place." And with that, she walked away.

Nonplussed, Rebecca watched and hoped the woman knew where she was going. She certainly didn't seem aware of where she had been. With a regretful sigh for the vagaries of old age, Rebecca left the jewelry store and headed for home.

QUINN TAPPED HIS FOOT. He braced himself against the wall, rubbed the back of his neck and tapped his foot again. He crossed his arms at his chest, drew a deep breath and stared hard at the tinted glass doors of the apartment complex lobby.

She should have been here by now. He'd called her office and been told she had already left. That had been forty-five minutes ago. Now where in the hell was she? And why in the hell was he upset?

He uncrossed his arms, then impatiently crossed them back. What exactly was it about Rebecca that had him tied in knots? The question had been bothering him all day. Maybe longer. Maybe since she'd phone him—quite unexpectedly—the night before. Her voice had been so soft, so quietly sensuous, coming through the wires into his bedroom. He wondered if she would be so soft, so sensuous *in* his bed. The image had lingered like a fragrance ever since. There was more to it than that, though. Quinn had known too many women to be taken in by a simple physical attraction. Rebecca was . . .

He paused, considering, letting all the seemingly small but important discoveries he had made about her come freely to mind. Even Emily, who was notoriously picky in her opinions, thought Rebecca was special. Well, he reminded himself, Emily hadn't *said* special. The word she'd actually used was "ex," an abbreviated version of "excellent," which meant fantastic or wonderful or special or something like that. He couldn't keep his vocabulary current with preadolescent trends.

He couldn't seem to keep his mind on working, either. It wasn't as if he didn't have stories to write, deadlines to meet. It was just that he found himself thinking about Rebecca instead. How she looked. What she said. The way her brown eyes sparkled when she laughed. The concentration she'd displayed in trying to learn the rules of a child's soccer game.

Shifting his position, Quinn tried to find a more comfortable spot upon which to lean. He was past the age for standing in lobbies and daydreaming about a woman he barely knew. Except that wasn't entirely true, he reasoned. He had learned more about Rebecca in the short span of their acquaintance than he'd learned about Diane during the nine years of their marriage. It was amazing, really, that just when he'd thought his life was settled, smooth, and on an even keel, he should meet someone who changed his way of thinking. That kind of thing didn't happen, he knew. It took time to fall in love, to develop a solid foundation for a relationship.

The doors to the building opened, and Rebecca entered. His heart jumped, and he decided that perhaps it didn't take as much time to fall in love as he'd always assumed it did.

She smiled when she saw him, and he slowly straightened away from the wall. Hell, he didn't care if he missed a hundred deadlines.

"Hi," she said. "What are you doing here?"

"Waiting for you."

"Any special reason?"

Approximately a couple of thousand, but he wasn't going to say that. "I wondered if you'd like to have dinner?"

"Now?" Rebecca was suddenly conscious of her appearance. The suit still held its crisp, cool lines, and her hair still bore a reasonable resemblance to the smooth chignon of the morning, but she knew the hectic pace of her day showed.

"Unless that's a problem."

He moved closer, and Rebecca caught her breath at the warm rush of awareness she felt. Quinn was such a welcome sight at that moment. She was not so much tired as mind-weary. Question after question had been tumbling through her thoughts all day. Questions about Molly and the trunk. Questions about Scott Forsythe and the trunk. Questions about Quinn, period. None of that seemed to matter now, though. "I'm glad to see you," she said, putting the thoughts into words. "And I'd love to go to dinner. Just let me go upstairs and change into something else."

Quinn swept a cursory glance over her attire. "You look 'excellent' just as you are. That's Emily's term, in case you wondered. If it wasn't for a small technicality, I'd be happy to wait all evening for you, if necessary. But you see, I have to squire my daughter and four of her friends to another friend's house where six loud, giggly little girls are going to spend the night. A slumber party, I think they call it. And as the only parent who has a van equipped with extra seat belts, I'm responsible for pickup and delivery. Emily volunteered my services. At any rate, if I'd left five minutes ago, I'd only be running ten minutes behind schedule, but as it stands—"

"I understand." Rebecca felt an inexplicable bubble of laughter in her throat. "You want me to ride shotgun on this expedition. After which, you will take me to dinner."

He lifted his eyebrows and his shoulders in a rueful shrug. "If we're more than twenty minutes late, neither one of us will get any dinner. The little darlings will burn us at the stake."

"Then let's go." Rebecca decided her suit was suitable for the occasion, after all. It didn't make any difference what she was wearing, only that Quinn had wanted her company enough to come to her residence and wait for her, making himself late in the process. "Where is Emily now?" she asked as they walked outside together.

"Probably halfway up the living room wall by now." He moved briskly, setting a pace that Rebecca thought she could match as long as he wasn't parked too far away. "But she'll be so glad to see you that she'll forgive my tardiness."

"Are you sure about that?"

"Absolutely." He moved ahead to unlock the door of the van. "Emily is 'a piece of cake.'"

Rebecca tilted her head. "Is that another of Emily's special terms?"

"No," he said with a grin as he held the door open for Rebecca. "That happens to be one of mine."

Chapter Ten

Emily's behavior, by anyone's terms, was *not* a "piece of cake." Instead of being glad to see Rebecca, Emily made a point of ignoring her. Instead of readily introducing her friends, Bethany, Kristen, Kim, and Amy, Emily waited until the delay was obvious and embarrassing. Instead of being the polite, rather shy child Rebecca had known up to this point, Emily produced an entirely new side of her personality. She was pouty, rambunctious and unruly. She seemed unimpressed with her father's stern looks and was equally determined to pay as little attention to Rebecca as she thought she could get by with.

She got by with quite a bit, but when the van stopped at the house where the party was to be held, Quinn made a point of keeping Emily after the other girls had gone inside. Rebecca couldn't hear what he said, as she stayed in the van and Quinn and Emily stood outside, but it was apparent by Emily's chastened expression that she regretted her rudeness. Or at least for being scolded for it.

Rebecca felt a certain sympathy for the child. It couldn't be easy being an only child with only one full-time parent. And if the truth were known, Rebecca thought, Emily was probably very sensitive about any woman in whom Quinn showed an interest. It would be only natural for a child of her age to be fearful, even resentful, when a serious relationship entered the picture.

Was it a serious relationship? Rebecca wondered. It could become so, she supposed, but at this stage it was a little early for the word "relationship" to be tossed around. If it wasn't serious, though, why was Emily showing signs of being a threatened baby bird? Had she picked up on the feelings that Rebecca and Quinn had not as yet acknowledged?

It was the second time she'd asked herself that question, and Rebecca realized that every moment she spent with Quinn deepened her involvement with Emily, as well as with him. The attraction she felt for him had a double edge. Emily was as much at risk as either of them, and Rebecca felt overwhelmed by the responsibility. Did Quinn feel like that? she wondered. Torn by wanting someone with whom to share his life and yet afraid of introducing someone into Emily's life who might not always be there?

Complications. Rebecca sighed with the thought. If she had any sense, she'd jump out of the van and run away, screaming hysterically, as fast as she could.

"I should have made her skip the party," Quinn said as he got into the van again.

Rebecca lifted her eyebrows. "What would that have accomplished, besides making everyone miserable?"

He turned to her with a frown that slowly disappeared behind a frustrated sigh. "It might have persuaded her to apologize to you for being so rude."

"I doubt it. Besides, as far as I'm concerned, she doesn't need to apologize. I can remember being eight, and it wasn't the easiest time of my life. Emily has a lot to cope with as it is. Don't pressure her about me."

Quinn placed a hand on the steering wheel and stared thoughtfully out the window for a minute. "Do you know what she said? Why she didn't *feel* like being nice to you today? She said you had on ugly clothes. Now does that make sense? Sometimes I think raising a child is nothing more than an endurance test.''

Rebecca offered consolation with a slight smile. ''And at the moment, you think you're flunking, right?'' She reached over and placed her hand on top of his. It felt warm and large beneath her touch, and a shiver of response wound its way up her arm. ''I wouldn't worry too much about Emily, Quinn. She's just feeling a bit vulnerable. I'm only guessing, but maybe my clothes bother her on a level she can't quite comprehend. If her mother wore suits similar to the one I'm wearing, then maybe Emily is afraid that if she lets herself like me at all, I'll go away...just like her mother did.''

Quinn's hand flexed into a tight fist of tension before relaxing and turning to cup her fingers in his palm. ''That's a heavy-duty assumption, Rebecca.''

''That's what comes of having a psychologist living across the hall. The idea is probably just presumptuous. I don't have children, so I'm only guessing.''

''Believe me, *having* children doesn't make anyone an expert. It's all a guessing game. The more I think about it, though, the more I think you could be on the right track. Diane put her career ahead of everything else, me and Emily included, and she took great pains to look and dress professionally at all costs.''

He said it matter-of-factly, as if the anger and bitterness he must have experienced had long since dissipated. Still Rebecca felt it was only fair to state her opinion. ''Having a career doesn't necessarily make anyone a 'professional.' What a woman wears has less effect on the image she projects than the attitude she has about herself and her job. And that goes for men, too.''

''Somehow I knew it would.'' His smile curved tenderly, just as his fingers curved over hers. ''For the record, I don't care what you wear...a suit or one of those dainty frills you keep on the sofa, but I—'' He paused and a trace of blue mischief sparked deep in his eyes. "That's a lie. I'd rather you wore the underwear."

Rebecca met his teasing look squarely. "It's lingerie, Mr. Kinser. Get your terms right. That can make all the difference between a sale and a shutout."

He squeezed her hand so gently that she wondered if she had imagined the pressure. "I will definitely keep that in mind. I would hate for you to shut me out."

His voice didn't change, neither did the tilt of his smile, but an intangible whisper of seduction wove its way into the air. Rebecca felt it, recognized it and responded to it within the space of a heartbeat. "I don't think I could. Not now."

He held her gaze, his eyes midnight-blue in the stillness, and her eyes were a warm cinnamon brown, looking for a reflection of feelings too new and tender for words. The moment slipped into another as winter slips into spring. Almost unnoticed, but welcome. So very welcome.

"Do you have any suggestions for dinner?" he asked in a husky whisper.

Rebecca pressed her lips together and shook her head.

"How about somewhere we can talk?"

This time she nodded, and then, determined to stop behaving like a love-shy adolescent, she cleared her throat. "I'd like that."

He released her hand and turned the key in the ignition. "Then I know just the place."

Rebecca half expected him to take her to his home, but instead he chose to drive to Laclede's Landing and have dinner on the steamboat that had been permanently moored along the redeveloped riverfront area. The music was jazz, the specialty seafood, and Rebecca discovered a sentimental, romantic streak in her erstwhile practical nature. Over the candle-glow of a brass lamp, she found herself staring into his eyes as if she had found an oasis after too many days in the desert. She kept losing track of the conversation, what there was of it, anyway. Quinn seemed as reluctant to break the mood as she.

They ordered a dinner neither of them really wanted, and when it came, Rebecca wondered why they were skirting around the game of seduction. Especially since she knew as well as he did that the conclusion was not in question. She didn't know quite when the decision had been made, maybe during that moment of silent sharing in the van after Emily had gone inside. Maybe it had been made earlier, when she'd seen him standing, waiting for her, in the lobby of her apartment building. Maybe it had been inevitable since the first time they'd kissed. Not that the time mattered. She wanted to make love with Quinn, and she knew that tonight presented the opportunity and the mood.

The candlelight, the intimacy of the surroundings, the rhythm of the music, and the way Quinn looked at her, made the world a narrow, self-contained, very private place. Add to that the powerful chemistry of physical attraction plus the sometimes soothing, sometimes restless pace of their friendship, and Rebecca thought she'd probably never had much choice. She didn't believe he had set out with the predetermined intention of taking her to his bed, but she had no hesitation about finding her own way there. Quinn was unlike any man she'd ever met before. He had character and strength, direction and self-confidence, deep thoughts and a sense of humor. So many qualities she respected and admired, yet she was fully aware of the romantic fantasies she had built around him.

It was odd, really, that she, who prided herself on being practical, should create such delicious little fancies. But she had, and she knew that making love with him would either accelerate or satisfy the desire. And she was ready to find out just how much of her heart she was risking.

"Is your food all right?" Quinn leaned slightly forward, his expression one of concern. "You've hardly touched it."

Rebecca, caught in the midst of her own provocative thoughts, glanced at her plate and the fork that rested lazily in her right hand. "Oh, it's fine," she said. "Really." She felt suddenly shy, as if he could read her mind. "I...guess I'm not very hungry."

Quinn could identify with her on that, although he'd managed to eat a moderate bit of the lobster he'd ordered. Rebecca couldn't have done much more than taste hers. It was the tension, he knew. That quiet, exciting, scary anticipation. It had started so softly that he'd been only vaguely aware of the mood change before they reached the restaurant. But when she'd smiled at him, her face bathed in the subdued light, her hair a captive to the flickering glow of the lamp, he'd felt the stirring passion begin.

"You're not worried about Emily's behavior, are you?" he asked. "I can assure you that she—"

"No. No, I wasn't thinking about Emily. I was—" She paused to toy with her food and to smile her appreciation when the waiter refilled her glass. The waiter moved to another table, another intimate dinner for two, and Rebecca let her gaze drift back to her companion. "I was thinking that this would be a romantic setting for a proposal."

A proposal? That wasn't what he'd expected to hear. What could she be thinking about? A blush stole into her cheeks, and he ceased to care *what* she was thinking and wished only that she might be thinking of him. He wanted to touch her...tease her...love her. He made a show of looking around the room, assessing the possibilities for a proposal. "Yes, I guess it would be."

Pressing her lips together, Rebecca speared a bit of food and lifted it to her mouth. "Where did you propose to your—" The word stuck in her throat, and she gave up trying.

"It's all right. You can say it. Ex-wife, Diane. Either term will do. Personally, I try to avoid calling her anything. Except, of course, around Emily, in which case I refer to her as 'your mother.'" He stroked his dark beard as his mouth tipped with amusement. "You know, I'm not sure I did propose to her. That's been so long ago. I think she wanted to get married, and so I married her." He shrugged wryly. "Great reason, huh? I should have known it couldn't last."

"How could you know that?"

"I couldn't, but hindsight is twenty-twenty, and I've always thought I should have seen it coming."

"Her leaving, you mean?"

His expression sobered, he knew, but he couldn't seem to prevent it. "I'd much rather talk about you. Has any man ever proposed to you in a romantic place like this?"

"The most romantic moment in my life was when the boy down the street gave me a bouquet of daisies, told me he loved me and that I could pull off all the petals to prove it."

"And did you?"

Her smile curved. "Of course. What woman could resist such a test? As it turned out, he did love me. Daisies would never lie."

"You probably cheated."

"I probably did."

He sipped his drink and regarded her pensively. "Come on, Rebecca, I can't believe there haven't been other romantic moments."

"Offhand, nothing else comes to mind."

"Not even *this* moment?"

She lifted her eyes to his, caught again in that sudden swirl of desire. "You know how special this moment is, Quinn."

His breath hung in his throat, and his heart pulsed a strong, responsive chord. "Yes, I guess I do."

There didn't seem to be much he could say after that and, although he turned his attention to the lobster, his appetite was nonexistent, that is, his appetite for food. "Would you mind if we left?" he asked. "I can ask the waiter to package your dinner and—"

"No." Rebecca dropped her hands to her lap. "I mean there's no need to take it with us. I'm not hungry."

"Then you're ready to go?"

"Yes."

The word held far more meaning than its simplicity could signify. Quinn motioned to the waiter and paid the check. He slipped his arm around Rebecca's waist as they left the steamboat restaurant and made their way to the car. She said nothing, and he welcomed the silence. He wanted her to think, wanted her to be sure. For all the nervousness coursing through his body, he felt confident about his own reason for wanting her.

He was falling in love with her. He thought it had begun the first moment she'd peeped through the slit in the door and told him he wouldn't have any luck selling encyclopedias. He had known he was in trouble when she laughed and when she had turned to him for comfort after her apartment had been broken into.

"Wally is writing a book," Rebecca said once they were in the car and were driving away. "On the theory that love doesn't really exist except in imagination."

"Sounds like a bubble gum theory to me. Put enough air into it, and the bubble bursts." He glanced at her. "You don't believe that nonsense, do you?"

"No, not really. There's a little corner of my heart that wants to believe in romance and happily ever-afters."

"Good." His hand left the steering wheel to capture hers. "There is romance in the world, Rebecca. Trust me. We may have to make our own 'happily ever after,' but the romance is a lagniappe, a little something extra."

She liked that, liked the way he held her hand, liked the way his voice caressed her. Wally could have her theories and her experiments. Rebecca would take the "little something extra."

WITHOUT ASKING her preference, Quinn drove to his house and parked the van in the garage. He turned to her in the darkness and brushed his fingers along the nape of her neck, pulling free a few rebellious strands of hair in the process. Beneath the slow circling of his touch, more strands escaped, and he wound them around his finger. "Alone, at last." His tone was teasing, but his touch was not. "Colleen is taking advantage of Emily's absence to spend the night with friends. So it's just you and me."

"You sound as if being alone is a rare occurrence for you." Rebecca tried to ignore the scintillating shivers working their way down her spine. "Doesn't Emily spend any time with her mother?"

"Two weeks in the summer and alternate Christmas vacations. Diane moved to Minneapolis, so she's not a constant figure in Emily's life."

"Oh." Rebecca didn't know what comment to make, but she felt a twinge of resentment toward Diane Kinser. "Has she remarried?"

"She's one-hundred-percent committed to her career. That doesn't leave room for anything else." His thumb skimmed a path along the base of her neck around to the sensitive hollow of her shoulder. The collar of her blouse offered no resistance as he moved it aside, and the silky fabric intensified the sensation of his touch.

Rebecca swallowed, feeling warm and cherished, but trying to maintain control of her rapidly beating heart. "I disagree, Quinn. Aren't you one-hundred-percent committed to your career? And yet you still have room for Emily."

"No, Rebecca. I'm totally committed to my daughter. Don't get me wrong. My career is important to me, too, but I believe in balancing my commitments and my responsibilities. There's room in my life for much more than it already holds.''

A meditative quiet settled between them, a silence filled with unspoken needs and the steady building of desire. She wanted to ask if there was room in his life for her, but she couldn't, not without asking herself if there was room in *her* life for him. And for Emily.

A soft breath eased past her lips, and the stroking movements of his thumb stopped. He leaned across, cupping the back of her neck and pulling her gently toward him. Her heart raced like a wild animal's at the moment of capture, and then his mouth gentled her resistance, banished her apprehension.

His beard rubbed against her chin, tickling, stimulating, but the pressure of his kiss made the tactile sensations recede beneath a rush of melting warmth. She lifted her hand to cradle the curve of his jaw and again experienced the wiry-soft, seductive feel of his beard. Every sense was heightened, her pulse was a rhythmic resonance to desire, and the only thing that mattered was the taste and the scent and the feel of Quinn's lips against hers. She opened herself to the exploring thrust of his tongue, and arched her body against the restraining seat belt, seeking to be closer to him, to the source of such intense pleasure.

He began a slow massage of her neck and gradually eased the kiss to a tender parting. For a long minute she stayed where she was, eyes closed, still savoring his touch, then she opened her eyes. Quinn watched her with an expression of cautious wonder, and Rebecca couldn't restrain a quietly appreciative smile. ''That was nice,'' she whispered. ''Very nice.''

''Yes, it was.'' He ran his hand across her cheek and traced the outline of her mouth with a fingertip. ''I didn't intend to let things get out of hand like that, though.''

She coyly arched an eyebrow. ''You didn't?''

"No, I didn't." He matched the teasing in her voice. "I intended to wait until we were inside the house."

"Oh."

"Does it bother you—" he asked as his fingertip retraced the path from one corner of her mouth to the other "—that I want to make love with you, Rebecca?"

Her stomach dropped with the declaration, and an odd pulsing ache filled the space. "No." Her voice trembled, and she repeated the denial. "No. I think I'd like to go inside now."

He drew a long, ragged breath before pressing the promise of a kiss against her lips. Unbuckling his seat belt, he took the keys from the ignition and opened the door. As he got out of the van, Rebecca copied his actions and was stepping to the ground when he reached her. He put his hands on her waist, and she turned into his arms.

Shyness coupled with desire as she slipped her arms around him and laid her head against his chest. It felt good to be held, to be so close to him, to hear the pounding of his heart. An inexplicable push of tears welled up behind her eyes and then retreated to form a lump in her throat. What was it about Quinn, she wondered, that made her feel so cared for? She was independent and had her own inner sources of strength. She didn't need anyone to take care of her. So why was she blissfully content in the protective custody of his embrace? Was it possible that Quinn derived the same pleasure and sense of security from her?

Quinn tightened his hold, then released her, only to capture her hand in his. Together, silently, they walked from the garage into the house. There was no hesitation, no awkwardness, as he led the way to the bedroom door where he stepped back to let her enter first. The room was dark, but with a touch of his hand, Quinn turned on and dimmed the light to a soft, golden illumination.

Rebecca could barely make out the color of the curtains and the carpet. Bathed in a glow as pale as a moonbeam, everything took on a shadow of anonymity, casting a mood of intimate mystery into the air. Quinn placed his hands on her shoulders and kissed the top of her head. She leaned back against him with a sigh, letting the emotions inside her flow with carefree abandonment. When she felt his fingers working at the pins in her hair, she raised her hands to help. In a minute the russet waves spilled through his fingers and settled about her shoulders.

Quinn stroked her and then bent his head to kiss the back of her neck. Not content there, he transferred the exquisite sensation to the indentation just behind her earlobe. The pleasure streaked downward, igniting a thousand nerve endings on its way.

The weight of her clothes was obtrusive and heavy, and she began to work her jacket off without disturbing the seeking movements of his lips and tongue. When he sensed her intent, he helped ease the coat from her shoulders, down her arms and to the floor. Then, carefully, as if he didn't want to startle her, he turned her and began the slow, steady unbuttoning of her blouse.

Rebecca watched his face as his knuckles brushed against her breasts. He glanced up, met her eyes, and a spiral of hot, sweet longing coursed through her veins. She didn't look away, but held him hostage with her steady gaze as his hands worked on the buttons with unfaltering insistence. When the material parted to reveal a strip of honey-light skin broken only by a sheer lacy bandeau, Quinn released a shaky sigh and dropped his eyes to the swell of her breasts.

His hands slid inside the opening he'd made, pushing aside the blouse as he went, touching first the smooth, satiny flesh at her waist, then expanding to grasp her rib cage, and then moving unhurriedly upward. His palms cupped her

breasts, lingered for a heartbeat, before completing the re-
moval of the blouse.

Standing before his appreciative regard, Rebecca reached
behind her to unfasten the zipper of her skirt and let it slide
soundlessly to the floor. In half-slip, bra and panty hose, she
anticipated his next wish and placed her hands at his waist.
She lifted her chin and awaited the reassurance of his kiss.

When it came, she positioned her fingers at his waist and
pulled his shirt free of his slacks. She encountered a cotton
T-shirt beneath the crisp fabric and pulled it free, as well.
Then she explored and caressed the smooth texture of his
skin, following the same path as his hands had traced on her
body. Upward her fingers moved, exulting in the wiry texture of the hair on his chest, noting that it was as soft and
stimulating as his beard.

His breath stirred a new sensation against her forehead,
and when she looked up, he smiled and quite expertly un-
hooked her bra. The straps slipped down her arms without
assistance, and she released her hold on Quinn just long
enough to let it fall from her wrists to the floor. As her
hands returned to his waist and the buckle of his belt, he
maneuvered her to the edge of the bed, and ever so gently,
pressed her down onto the mattress.

Reluctantly she relinquished the progress she'd made with
his belt and allowed him to make short work of his clothes.
He tossed his shirt, T-shirt, slacks, socks and underwear on
top of her discarded clothes, and Rebecca wondered when
he'd taken off his shoes. She was still wearing hers, but with
a quick flip of each foot, her pumps dropped to the floor.

"You're so brown," she murmured, absently mentioning the tan that covered his muscular body everywhere except between the waist and upper thighs. Her hand lifted of
its own accord to investigate that inviting area of skin that
the sun had not kissed. But just as her fingertips grazed his
stomach, he stepped out of reach, intent on removing the

rest of her clothes. She arched her hips to assist his efforts, and soon every barrier was gone, every part of her bared to his caressing gaze.

Rebecca had thought the seduction began long before they'd reached the bedroom, but as his hand trailed upward from her ankle along her slender calf, behind her knee and along the inner curve of her thigh, she realized her mistake. *This* was seduction, this drowning in the sensuous massage of his touch, this whirling, frantic racing of her pulse, this deafening beat of her heart.

She couldn't breath and didn't care. With every movement he heightened her awareness and stripped away her doubts. He touched her, drew back, kissed her, slowly retreated, then returned to the irresistible torture. His tongue created tiny wet circles on her skin as he discovered every shy, sensitive spot on her body. Her hands would not be still, but found little contentment in the touches he allowed her to give. He was too intent on exploring her, too determined to taste every inch of her.

Finally when the ache inside her had reached a melting heat, Rebecca pushed against his chest, catching him off guard and rolling him onto his side. Then it was her turn to explore, to discover his pleasure points, and to bring him to the edge of reason. Stroking hands, legs, tangling over and around each other, lips and tongues melding together in a kiss born of passion and deep longing, all combined in a furious hunger for knowledge and intimate satisfaction.

His eyes met hers as their bodies joined, and Rebecca experienced the sweet, welcome warmth of his possession . . . body and soul. The caress of his gaze was as much a part of her pleasure as the rhythmic stroking of his body inside her. She felt loved. Completely, tenderly, passionately loved. When the fiery heat of desire had burgeoned into a blaze of intense and uncontrollable flames, she held him close and let the fire consume her in the same instant it seared through him.

With all the beauty of a summer sunset, the heat ebbed one slow degree at a time until they lay content and momentarily satiated in each other's embrace. Rebecca listened to his irregular heartbeat and wondered if this was how it felt to fall in love.

After several hushed minutes, Quinn raised himself on his elbow and smiled into her eyes. "You, Rebecca Whitaker, are the most beautiful person who has ever come into my life."

The well of tears returned and Rebecca blinked them away. "What a lovely thing to say, Quinn. Thank you."

"It came from the heart." He bent his head to kiss her lightly on the lips. His hand strayed to cup her breast and to trace a circular pattern around the tip. "Will you stay with me tonight?"

She put her hand at his chest and duplicated the motions of his fingers. "Of course. You didn't really expect me to leave now, did you?"

He groaned softly as his nipple hardened at her touch. "No," he said with some effort. "I do have the keys to the van."

"Keep them." She pressed him onto his back again and positioned herself above him. "Before the night is over, you'll be glad to take me home." With a challenging lift of her brow, her hand moved lower to tease and rekindle his desire.

This time his moan was in earnest. "Look, Rebecca, you may be a heck of a salesperson, but your timing is off."

"Really?"

A minute slipped past before he sighed. "All right, so you're one hell of a salesperson, but this doesn't mean—"

She laughed and withdrew her hand. "I only wanted to prove my point and clarify all that misinformation you had about traveling salesladies."

His smile curved with devilish intent. "Misinformation?" He pulled her down until her lips were only a breath away. "I never even imagined anything half this good."

The kiss that followed proved his point.

Chapter Eleven

"What a *beautiful* morning." Quinn drew back the drapes with a flourish, and Rebecca opened one eye in a cautious squint. It probably would be a beautiful morning, she thought as she drew the covers over her head. But from her vantage point, it was still too early to tell. "Come on, Rebecca." Quinn came to the end of the bed and gently jiggled her foot. "Don't tell me you're not an early riser. I thought all you salespeople were up and on the road before the sun rose."

"Today the sun wins."

"You're mumbling." He tugged at the sheet above her head. "What did you say?"

She lowered the sheet but kept her eyes shut. "Go away. It's too early to be talking."

"It is?" He chuckled and pressed a warm morning kiss to her temple. "Then what do you suggest we do?"

"Go back to sleep." She turned over, drawing the covers with her.

"Nope. I'm going to take a shower. Care to join me?"

It was almost tempting, but Rebecca couldn't force her protesting body into movement. "No." She knew she was still mumbling and that, by and large, she sounded exactly like the grumpy person she was at this time of day. It was simply unfortunate that Quinn greeted the dawn with such enthusiasm and energy. When she heard the sound of the shower spray in the adjoining bath and then the unmistakable notes of his husky baritone singing "God Bless America," she sighed and forced her droopy eyelids up.

Sunlight was barely visible on the other side of the window, and a glance at the bedside clock radio revealed the reason. It was a good forty-five minutes before the morning should have started. Rebecca yawned and stared at the ceiling. She was a sleepyhead, and she knew it, but this was the first time she'd actually wished she weren't. It would have been nice to awaken—slowly—in Quinn's arms, to have snuggled against his warm body, and to have his touch be the first sensation of the day.

Rebecca's lips curved with pleasure at the thought, and a world of sweet memories flooded her mind. Last night with Quinn had been so very special. A flush of pleasure tingled through her body as she remembered, and after a minute she pushed back the covers and, on an impulse, went to join Quinn.

As she opened the shower enclosure door, the patriotic chorus came to an abrupt finale. "I thought you needed some harmony," she said with a shy smile. "I do my best singing in the shower."

"Then, please," he said, gently pulling her inside with him, enclosing her in his arms and the steamy spray of water. "I was just about to start the second verse."

Rebecca lifted her lips to meet his. "I know a better place to start."

"Hmm." He accepted the kiss and then drew her closer for a more thorough demonstration. "Let's go back to bed," he suggested a moment later.

"Too late." She reached behind him for the washcloth. "I'm awake now."

He frowned playfully and then sighed aloud as she began a slow massage of his back. "Have I told you this morning that you're wonderful?"

"Not while I could hear you."

"What? It's too noisy in here." He turned off the spray and cupped her shoulders, bending to nuzzle the moisture drops on her skin. "Now what did you say?"

A sensual awakening was rippling through her, and she couldn't remember what she'd said. Or why. She tilted back her head to allow his lips access to the sensitive hollows of her neck. "Mmm," she murmured.

"I certainly agree. It's far too early for this kind of thing."

She opened her eyes wide in protest. "No, it isn't."

He smiled, tenderly teasing. "Don't you have to go to work?"

She shook her head and pressed closer to the slick, wet surface of his body. "I'm going to Jefferson City." Her hand moved, seemingly of its own accord, to brush across his hips. "On business."

"What a coincidence." He caressed her spine with a zephyr-soft touch of his fingers. "I have business there, too. Perhaps we can drive over together."

"Perhaps." It was a mere breath of a word, sliding past her lips on a pleasured sigh. "I'll have to go to my apartment."

"Now?"

"Later." She smiled before cupping a hand at the back of his head and encouraging him to lower his mouth to hers. "Much later."

"Mmm," he agreed. "Definitely later."

LATER CAME ALL too soon, as far as Rebecca was concerned, but after breakfast, which Quinn insisted on cook-

ing, they drove to her apartment so she could change clothes
and pick up her sales case for the trip to Jefferson City.

The hallway was quiet as they stepped from the elevator.
Even Mrs. Albridge's door was firmly closed, and there was
no familiar squeak as Rebecca fished in the bottom of her
purse for the door key.

"It makes me nervous not to have her eavesdropping on
us," Quinn said with a grin. "You don't suppose Nathaniel
Duncan, the force behind Pete's Pizzeria, slipped up here in
the middle of the night and oiled her hinges, do you?"

Laughing at his nonsense, Rebecca found the key. But as
she started to insert it into the lock, the door of her apartment swung open. Silence wafted from inside, and her heart
quickened with a host of all-too-familiar feelings. In slow
motion, she turned to Quinn.

He met her look, sharing a wordless conversation before
shifting his attention to the door facing and broken lock.
"I'll be damned." He moved past her into the apartment,
twisting the doorknob as he passed, his anger evident in the
set of his jaw and the stiff, unyielding set of his shoulders.
"Who in the hell . . . ?"

The muttering faded as he walked through the living room
and out of Rebecca's vision. She followed with reluctant
footsteps and the beginning fragments of a hundred questions. She saw nothing amiss in the living room—just like
before—and she sank onto the sofa to ponder this new de-
velopment.

Up until now she'd basked in an obviously false security.
With Quinn, at his house, it had been so easy to forget the
mystery surrounding the trunk, to pretend that no one had
intruded into her safe and ordered life. But now . . .

Rebecca surveyed the room around her, and the only
thing she could think of was that she wouldn't be able to
keep her appointment with Jimi Lee Denarro. And what
would the president of Lady Laura Lingerie say then? Re-

becca told herself not to be silly. Even if she couldn't meet Jimi Lee for lunch, she had a perfectly legitimate reason. Surely the company president wouldn't hold her responsible for this. Burglaries and break-ins were an everyday occurrence, weren't they? It wasn't her fault that she'd been chosen twice for . . .

"I think you'd better come in here," Quinn said from the bedroom.

Her imagination went haywire, and she almost ran the few steps to the doorway. Nothing. At least, there was nothing to indicate the type of disaster she'd imagined. Quinn watched her closely as she surveyed the room, looking for whatever had caused his concern. It was the trunk, she realized. The lid was open, and it looked as if everything had been taken out and then haphazardly tossed back in. As she moved toward it, she noticed that the top drawer of her dresser was ajar. Not more than half an inch, but she knew she hadn't left it that way.

A quick inspection of all the drawers revealed a methodical and oddly neat disturbance. Her clothes were still folded and stacked as she'd left them, but everything had been moved around. Not a lot, but enough that she could tell someone had searched her room. The puzzling part was that she could find nothing missing. Even when she knelt in front of the trunk, she knew she would find everything there.

"What was he looking for?" Quinn mused as he peered over her shoulder into the trunk. "What was in there in the first place?"

"Not much." Rebecca sifted through the clothing items, touched the photograph album and remembered the journal. But why would anyone want that? She rose immediately, almost hitting Quinn's chin with the top of her head. Going to the closet, she opened the door and took a deep breath. It had not been disturbed. She caught sight of the notebook's distinctive binding almost hidden beneath the linens on the closet shelf and, without a word, she stepped back and closed the door. "Nothing there," she said to Quinn's puzzled look. "In fact, nothing seems to be gone."

"I don't understand this." He shook his head and looked—wistfully, she thought—at the trunk. "Would it be all right if I..."

"Go ahead." She nodded toward the trunk, giving her permission for him to investigate the contents. At this point, she didn't think it mattered. Whatever had been the object of interest, the intruder had either found it, or it had never been there to find in the first place. Rebecca simply was out of ideas. The journal, at least what she'd already read, couldn't be of any monetary value. The ring was at the jeweler's, but she knew it couldn't be worth a tremendous amount of money. Certainly not enough to make breaking and entering worthwhile. That left...what? A couple of hats, a couple of sweaters, and an old photograph album. "I just don't know," she said aloud, although she was talking to herself. "I just don't understand any of this."

Quinn rocked back on his heels, giving up the fruitless search through the trunk. "Are you sure there's nothing missing?"

"No, I'm not sure." She sat on the edge of the bed and clasped her hands. "But I can't tell. Everything seems to be where I left it."

"Well, then, does anything about this strike you as odd?"

"As a matter of fact," she replied tersely, "everything about this strikes me as odd. Even the fact that I was with you both times someone broke into my apartment." The thought hadn't crossed her mind until the words left her mouth, but she realized it had been nagging at her all along, and she was glad she'd brought up the question.

"What is that supposed to mean?" He, on the other hand, didn't sound glad. He sounded somewhat angry with her.

"Why don't you tell me?"

"I can't, damn it!" He rubbed his beard with agitated strokes and made a visible effort to maintain control. "You can't believe I had anything to do with this. The whole idea is—well, it's ridiculous. In fact it's downright insulting."

The anger of insult was winning in his battle for control, but Rebecca didn't really care. She wanted some answers. "You're the one who lied about why you wanted to buy the trunk. You're the one who invented Aunt Molly. You're the one who—"

"Now, wait just a damn minute. I've already apologized for that. And I did *not* invent Molly."

"All right, then. Scott did. The two of you are in this together, and I—"

"Scott who?"

"Don't give me that. You know very well who he is. For Pete's sake, you both told almost identical stories about your sweet old Aunt Molly. There's no use pretending—"

"I do *not* know anyone by the name of Scott. If I was going to pretend, I'd have made up a better name for a cohort than Scott!"

"Right," she agreed, "you made up Molly instead."

He stood up slowly, taking his time, his expression one of fast-disappearing patience. "Rebecca, for the last time, Molly is a real person."

"Then take me to her."

"I can't. I don't know where she is."

Rebecca arched her brow. "Checkmate."

He thrust his hands into his pockets and took a step toward her. "No, only check. Just because I don't know where she is that doesn't mean she isn't very much alive and well. The last time I saw her she was at the airport. As far as I know, she lives there, and when she isn't there, I don't know where to begin looking for her. She'll show up again. It's only a matter of waiting for her."

"And I suppose in the meantime I can feel safe and secure here in my apartment? No, thanks, Quinn. I want some answers from you, and I want them now."

His lips tightened with irritation. "What do you want to know?"

"Who is Scott Forsythe?"

"I don't know."

She turned, frustrated and angry with his evasion. "I don't believe you."

"I can't help that. I do not know anyone by that name, and I do not know how he came to tell you the same story I did. Unless..." His voice trailed off into a thoughtful silence, and then, amazingly, he began to laugh. It wasn't the laugh she had learned to look forward to hearing—the deep, throaty rumble of amusement—but it wasn't devoid of humor, either.

"Molly Summer is one hell of a lady," he said finally. "I think she's pulled off quite a charade."

Rebecca sighed loudly. "Would you *please* tell me what is going on?"

With another chuckle, Quinn shook his head and then glanced at his watch. "We can still make it to Jeff City before twelve, if we leave now. I'll tell you everything I know on the way. Then I don't have to worry about you getting mad and not listening to the whole story. You'll be a captive audience."

"I think I am, anyway." She ran indecisive fingers through her hair as she considered her options. "I would like to make that appointment."

"Let me call Colleen and tell her I'm not sure when I'll be home. That way I won't have to worry about Emily." He went to the telephone, dialed, and in a matter of minutes, had his obligations fulfilled. "Now, what do you need?"

What she needed at that precise moment was not something she was going to mention. She was upset with him.

Why did she long to be back in his arms? "I want to change clothes, freshen up, and—" she glanced around the room "—get as far away from this place as I can."

His lips curved with understanding. "I'll go downstairs and talk to the building manager and the security guard, if I can find him. I may even phone our friend at the local police station. I'll do everything I can to make sure this doesn't happen again. Twice is more than enough." He started for the door, then glanced back. "Now, don't worry."

Easy for him to say, she thought. Easy for him to take charge, too. In all fairness, though, she hadn't done anything to discourage his protective instincts. On the other hand, he hadn't given her any answers, either. She couldn't think of one convincing reason to believe he was as much in the dark about the two break-ins as she was. Considering all the evidence, he could be guilty of getting her out of the way so someone else could get in her apartment.

Her knuckles tightened. If she followed that line of thinking, then she had to wonder why he'd made love to her. Obligation? Sort of a "beyond the call of duty" type of reasoning? No. She didn't believe that. Wasn't Wally always telling her she was a good judge of character? That she should rely on her instincts? Rebecca stood and began taking off her clothes. She would have some answers soon, one way or another.

Thirty minutes later, when she walked into the living room, Quinn was nowhere to be seen. She heard incriminating noises in the kitchen and followed the sound of an irritatingly cheerful whistle. He had made coffee and was pouring it into a thermos. He smiled when he saw her. "For the road," he said, indicating the coffee.

She nodded and returned to the living room, trying to work up a good head-clearing anger. When the effort proved too difficult, she settled for a cool nonchalance. If Quinn could treat the whole thing casually, then so could she. The memory of his touch, his kisses, whispered through her senses, and she resolutely put such thoughts on hold. This was not the time to be swayed by emotion, she told herself. And it was not the time to let him know he had any such power over her ability to reason.

"I'm all yours." He stood in the entryway, waiting for her.

She walked to his side, picked up her sales case and preceded him through the doorway. "Mine?" she asked sweetly. "To do with as I like?"

"Absolutely." He closed the door. "What would you like to do with me?"

"Right now is not a good time to ask that. I don't think you'd like the answer."

"Live dangerously. Give it a try."

Rebecca shot him a haughty look. "That is wishful thinking, Mr. Kinser. Trust me, you wouldn't like it"

"I *would* like for you to trust me, Rebecca. And you'd like it, too. I'm really a very trustworthy guy."

"Save it for the road," she said, which would have been a terrific exit line if only the elevator hadn't opened just then to reveal a smiling, eager-to-please superintendent.

"Perfect timing," the superintendent said. "I'll get that lock fixed pronto, Miss Whitaker. Don't you worry about a thing. Got a dead bolt right here in my bag. They're gonna have to bust your door down to break in next time."

"How reassuring." Rebecca walked into the elevator and turned just in time to see the man wink at Quinn in a typically male communication. She would die, she decided, before she would utter one word of appreciation to either one of them.

No one seemed to expect her thanks, however. The building superintendent exchanged a few incomprehensible words with Quinn, handed him a key and waddled on down the hallway to her apartment. Quinn took his hand off the elevator door and stepped inside, jabbing the button for the first floor as he smiled at her. "Here's the key to the dead bolt," he said. "It will be installed and working by the time we get back. The janitor said you could pick up the extra key later."

Rebecca bit back her thank-you, tucked the key in her purse and finished the ride in silence. Quinn seemed to understand that this was not the time for trivial conversation, and he apparently didn't mind waiting until she was ready to talk.

"I'll drive," she announced once they were outside. "You can leave your van parked here, and we'll take my car." Her pause was only long enough for him to blink in surprise. "It's an allowable business expense."

"Oh, of course." Quinn decided not to mention that he could count the trip as an expense, also. If she wanted to take charge and sit in the driver's seat, he wasn't going to raise a fuss. "Where is your car?"

She led the way to the apartment building's covered parking area and unlocked her economical but sporty Honda. Without a word, Quinn got in on the passenger side, buckled his safety belt, and prepared himself for the silent treatment. He wasn't sure of her reasons, but he knew she was angry with him. Being married to Diane had taught him the subtleties between a woman's view of an argument and his own more forthright approach. He didn't particularly like the game, but he did know the rules.

When Rebecca glanced his way before they'd even left the city limits, he straightened in the seat, ready for the opening attack. "I'm sorry," she began, and he was on instant alert. This was not the way an argument was supposed to begin. Diane had certainly never opened with an apology.

But Rebecca apparently didn't know that she was going at this backward. "It was inconsiderate of me to accuse you of—" Rebecca gave him another hesitant glance "—well, I don't believe you had anything to do with the break-ins at my apartment. I hope you will understand that I was upset and you were the only one close enough to lash out at. But it wasn't fair.'' She paused again, pressing her lips into a line that made him want to kiss her until the tension was gone. "I do know you better than that, Quinn, and I apologize not only for saying it but for thinking it.''

He didn't know how to answer. He'd expected another round of accusations, and he'd been prepared to defend himself, to reassure her that she could trust him. Now that it wasn't necessary, he felt like laughing. He didn't, but he couldn't resist mentally thumbing his nose at his ex-wife. "Thank you, Rebecca. I'm glad you feel that way. I would never do anything to hurt you.''

She said nothing for several minutes. "Now will you tell me what you know about Molly Summer?''

"Molly Summer is not my aunt," he began, settling back against the seat and casting back through his memory for details. "I only said she was because I thought it made a more believable story." He glanced at Rebecca and knew there was still a small, but definite credibility gap between them. Oh, well, he thought, here we go. "She does live at the airport. At least for all practical purposes. The first time I saw her, I thought she was waiting for someone to come for her. But after seeing her on several consecutive trips, I began to wonder if she had anywhere else to go.''

"Do you travel so much that you know who's supposed to be at the airport and who isn't?''

"I'm an investigative journalist, Rebecca. I have to do some traveling. But besides that, the airport is a great place to make contacts, and I do quite a bit of interviewing there. You'd be surprised at the information I've been able to gather because I was in the right place at the right time. Flight delays and layovers have made many a story work for me.''

He would have liked to talk more about his work, but told himself there would be time for that later. A lot of time, he hoped. "So, back to Molly. I felt sorry for her at first, but she didn't waste any time in curing me of that. I bought her dinner one night, and she told me she had more money than she could ever spend. I didn't believe her. I mean, she spent her days—possibly her nights, too—in an uncomfortable chair at the airport. She wore clothes that might have been expensive at one time, but . . ."

He grinned and shook his head at the remembrance. "Well, everything about her had obviously seen better days. When I offered to take her home, she refused, and when I tried to slip some money into her bag, she told me in no uncertain terms just where I could put it. Finally I stopped trying to help and started enjoying what she had to say. That's when she told me about the trunk."

"My trunk?" Rebecca asked. "The one I bought at the auction?"

"Yes. The one that contains nothing except an old woman's sentiment."

"What did you think would be in it?"

Quinn tapped his fingers against his thigh and released a soft sigh. "A story." He started to say more, to tell Rebecca about Molly's claim of a diary that outlined the inside scoop on a decades-old political scandal. But he'd built his career on a rule of thumb—never discuss the details of a story until the proof was in his hands. He kept his own counsel at all times, and he wasn't going to bend the rule now. Especially since Rebecca had already told him nothing was missing from the trunk.

"Molly Summer has led a very interesting life," he said. "I hoped to be able to write about her, but now I don't know if I will. I'd like to look at the photographs. If you don't mind."

"Of course." Rebecca wondered if he knew about the journal. Had Molly told him? Should she?

"You might want to slow down a bit." Quinn interrupted her thoughts, calling her attention to the rapidly accelerating speedometer gauge. "This stretch of road makes a great speed trap."

"Right." She took her foot from the pedal and concentrated on setting the cruise control. "I'd hate to get a ticket."

"They're not a tax-deductible business expense, are they?"

She smiled and impulsively reached for his hand. It was the first time she'd made the gesture, although it wasn't the first time she'd wanted to do so. Having him close gave her a good, warm feeling. If it hadn't been for the recent disturbing memory of a second broken lock on her apartment door, Rebecca thought she would have forgotten about the trunk, Molly, and the rest of the world.

Except for Quinn, of course.

And maybe Jimi Lee Denarro.

It would have been nice, she decided, if this trip was strictly for pleasure, if she could just enjoy Quinn's company. But someone had to tell her what was going on, and although she didn't have much insight yet, she felt sure that eventually the pieces of the puzzle would come together.

"I still don't understand why you went to so much trouble trying to get the trunk, Quinn. If Molly told you about it, why weren't you at the auction?"

"I wasn't sure she hadn't made up the whole thing—trunk and all. So when she told me where the trunk was stored, I didn't rush right out to find it." He shrugged a wry concession. "Not the sign of a hotshot reporter, huh?"

"Everyone's entitled to one mistake."

"Only one?"

She answered with a tilt of her lips. "So when you discovered the trunk *had* been in storage but had been sold at auction, you tracked it to me."

"Yes. Once I knew that Molly had been telling the truth about at least one thing, I had to find out if there was anything really worthwhile inside the trunk. I'll admit I'm disappointed that there isn't."

"I'm not sure of that, Quinn. Someone has broken into my apartment twice. There has to be a reason."

"The only thing I can figure is that Molly told someone other than me about the trunk. I wouldn't put anything past her. She enjoys the comedy in human nature more than anyone else I know." He traced the outline of Rebecca's hand with a gentle finger. "Now it's your turn. Tell me about this Scott and how you came to hear his Aunt Molly story."

Rebecca had to fight the sweet tingles filtering up her arm in order to gather her thoughts and present a coherent account. "Scott Forsythe called the other day and asked if I had purchased an old trunk at an auction. He said it belonged to his aunt and that he'd like to get it back for her. I arranged to meet him at Bridgette's yesterday afternoon after work."

"That's where you were."

Aware of the edge in his tone, Rebecca glanced at him before continuing. "Yes. He met me and—"

"He called while I was in the apartment with you, didn't he? You made the arrangements over the phone." The pause was heartbeat brief, but significant just the same. "Why didn't you tell me?"

"I didn't think it concerned you."

His eyes turned coolly, critically blue. "Thanks a lot, Rebecca."

"Look, Quinn, some strange things have been happening to me lately. Old trunks and nephews who aren't really nephews at all, phone calls and broken locks. How was I supposed to know you weren't involved in Scott's attempt to get the trunk?''

"You said you knew me better than that."

"Now. A lot has happened since then."

It was the closest she'd come to mentioning the new aspect of their relationship, and he wanted to know more about how she was feeling. "Does that mean you're beginning to trust me?"

She glanced at him and moved her hand in his grasp. "I guess it does."

"You won't be sorry, Rebecca."

Her pulse began to race through her veins. They weren't talking about the trunk anymore. She recognized that. She just didn't know if this was the time to admit the emotion that was fast taking control of her heart. "We have to give it time," she said and hoped he would understand.

His silence gave her no clue to his thoughts, but when he kept hold of her hand, she thought perhaps he did understand her conflict. After a couple of quiet minutes had ticked past, Rebecca decided to return to the safer topic of buried treasure and broken locks. "We still don't know why Scott Forsythe wants the trunk."

Quinn followed her change of subject without protest. "And we still don't know who broke into your apartment or why."

"Do you think—"

"I could have—"

They spoke at the same time and stopped, each giving the other first turn. Rebecca laughed a little, easing her recent tension. "I don't think Scott had anything to do with the break-in. He doesn't look the type."

"Oh, not the dark Arabic type, huh?"

Rebecca frowned at him. "He's too fastidious, too...oh, I don't know. Wally liked him and—"

"Wally was with you when you met him?"

"Yes. I asked her to lend me some support and the benefit of her experience." Rebecca shook her head and moved the hand Quinn had been holding to the steering wheel. "She wasn't much help, though. If I didn't know her better, I'd say she fell head over heels for the man."

"That makes me feel better."

"What? That she fell for him?"

Quinn leaned his head against the headrest and crossed his arms at his chest. "No. That you didn't."

Rebecca sighed and flipped the air conditioner to high. "But we still have no idea what's going on. With the trunk," she clarified quickly. "We don't have any answers."

Quinn liked the sound of that "we." He liked it very much. "I know where to get answers, though. Molly can tell us. All we have to do is find her."

Chapter Twelve

Jimi Lee Denarro did not look like a woman who would wear sheer lace and ribbons. In fact, Quinn thought halfway through lunch, she looked like a woman who would sleep the same way she showered...nude...simply because it made sense. She was a beautiful woman, tall, buxom, and proud of it. Her clothes were tailored, tasteful, and professionally feminine. He suspected that she harbored a secret disdain for those women who purchased the frilly bits of lingerie that Rebecca sold to her. He recognized, though, that Ms. Denarro was one savvy businesswoman and she would never underestimate the public's taste.

It was apparent to Quinn long before the polite conversation turned to real business that Rebecca didn't underestimate her opponent, either. She seemed to know exactly when to ask Jimi Lee's opinion of the clothing industry as a whole and the lingerie market in particular. She seemed to sense when the moment was precisely right to mention Jimi Lee's intractible, hard-to-get-along-with boss, and she gave just the proper mixture of sympathy and understanding in her response.

Quinn watched Rebecca and knew he was down for the count. It was amazing, really, considering the short time he'd known her, but he was sure, nonetheless, that she was going to be a part of his life for a long time to come. At least if he could persuade her to be a part. He thought back to Emily's show of temper and wondered if Rebecca would even want to take on the package deal he and his daughter represented. But then, there were certain benefits to the situation, too, he told himself. Emily was a wonderful person, just a little immature yet. Why wouldn't Rebecca love her?

Good question, he thought as he asked a passing waiter for more coffee. Almost as good as asking Diane why she *didn't* love Emily. The thought angered him, as it always did, and stirred up the residual resentment he felt toward his ex-wife and her obsession with her career. By rights, he shouldn't have fallen so hard for Rebecca, who was obviously and openly involved in her work. But it was different somehow. He wasn't sure why, but it was not the same with Rebecca.

Give it time, she had said earlier, and he hoped that time would prove him right, would set their relationship into a give and take sharing of every area in their lives. He wanted that. For himself. For her. For Emily. He didn't believe he was asking for too much. *Give it time.* The words repeated softly in his head. *Give it time.*

As the waiter returned to the table and refilled the coffee cups, Rebecca slanted an appreciative glance at Quinn, and he decided that he could afford to give her all the time she wanted, as long as she didn't take too long.

"Would you bring me the check, please?" Rebecca asked the waiter and hoped that Quinn wouldn't make any objection. She'd kick him in the shin, she decided, if he made a move toward the check. "You don't mind if we go back to your office now, do you, Jimi Lee?" Rebecca turned her attention again to her customer, although it had never fully strayed in the first place. "I want to show you the new Star Shine bikini briefs and matching bras." She smiled intentionally. "You know I can talk for hours about Lady Laura Lingerie and still not be able to do justice to our product."

"I know you're going to sell me a half-dozen items I never intended to buy, and I'll have to spend hours convincing my boss, *dear* Mr. Pryor, that the lingerie will sell at the exorbitant prices we have to charge for it." Jimi Lee patted the corner of her mouth with her napkin. "I wouldn't even carry Lady Laura if it wasn't for you, Rebecca. I can get the Ophelia brand for a lot less, you know."

Rebecca calmly took one last sip of her coffee and set the cup on the saucer. "But then you'd be stuck with an inventory of inferior products, and your customers would have to look elsewhere for quality lingerie. You and I both know that Mr. Pryor wouldn't like that."

Quinn made an odd noise—something like a muffled laugh—and Rebecca nudged his foot under the table. Jimi Lee raised her carefully shaped eyebrows in Quinn's direction, and then an equally careful smile shaped her lips. "She's really very good at this," Jimi Lee said. "Sometimes I wonder why I don't just sign a blank order and let her fill it in any way she wants."

"That sounds dangerous to me." Quinn leaned back, coffee cup in hand, his eyes darkening to an amused blue. "You could end up with a lifetime's supply of underwear and disastrous storage problems."

"At the very least," Jimi Lee agreed.

Rebecca shook her head and watched the waiter approach the table with the check. "Give me credit for having more integrity than that. I'd make sure the lingerie was shipped at regular monthly intervals, which would allow more than enough time for the inventory to be depleted." She smiled at Quinn and at Jimi Lee. "Lady Laura Lingerie doesn't have a long shelf life. The sales figures clearly show how popular our lines are and how well they move...no pun intended."

Quinn did laugh then and made no effort to hide it. A quiet delight swept through Rebecca at the sound, and she realized how very much she appreciated his supportive presence at this meeting. For some reason, Jimi Lee Denarro made Rebecca nervous, and she seldom felt that she'd given her best pitch to the woman. But this time had been different. She'd felt more in control of the situation from the beginning, and she was confident of getting an excellent order. Had Quinn given her that edge of self-assurance? Or had his incredibly blue eyes simply provided a distraction that Jimi Lee couldn't ignore?

It didn't matter, Rebecca thought as she paid the bill and made the first move toward ending the luncheon. Now the bartering began. She only hoped she could maintain the advantage.

"I THOUGHT IT WAS all over but for the shouting when we left the restaurant," Quinn said later as they drove toward St. Louis and home. "When we went back to her office and you started pulling out all those samples, it certainly surprised me."

Rebecca smiled in contentment, with the stress and uncertainty of the sales trip now behind her. Keeping one hand on the steering wheel, she adjusted the radio to a softer background, easy listening station. "Lunch is just the preliminary round. The main event is what happens afterward."

"I saw that for myself." His appreciative glance stirred her own feeling of pride in the sales order she'd received. "Your presentation was so good that *I* wanted to order a little bit of everything. And heaven knows what I'd do with ladies' lingerie."

Rebecca laughed, just because it felt good. "Thank you, sir. That's the kind of compliment we traveling saleswomen love to hear."

"I shouldn't have been surprised. Jimi Lee did say you were very good at your job."

"She did, didn't she?" Rebecca's lips tipped up ever so slightly at the corners. "Well, no matter what her faults, Jimi Lee Denarro would never lie about a business associate."

"Right. She'll just complain about her own lack of resistance when you start pitching sales."

A pleasantly relaxed silence settled into the small interior of her car, and Rebecca tried to remember the last time she'd felt so inexplicably wonderful. After a thoughtful moment, she decided the last time had been mere hours before when she'd awakened in Quinn's arms. Which brought up an interesting point: would he stay with her tonight? Was that what she wanted?

An unqualified *yes* echoed through her mind, and her smile tucked deeper into the line of her mouth. It was strictly for herself, of course. She wasn't going to tell him the direction of her thoughts, at least not now. The savoring of emotions, the anticipation of his touch, were feelings she wanted to hold on to for a while.

"You know, Rebecca, it's funny," Quinn's voice interrupted her private interlude. "I was so proud of you this afternoon, so thrilled to be with you that I could hardly sit still." He paused. "I don't remember ever feeling like that before."

"Not even with your first wife?" Rebecca wished she hadn't phrased it like that. "First" implied that there was or would be a second, and she didn't want to see that possibility. She didn't want to be a second wife. Or a second anything, did she? "I meant your ex-wife," she corrected. "Didn't you ever accompany her on business trips?"

His grimace pulled his beard and moustache into lopsided contact at one side of his mouth and conveyed a wry skepticism. "I wasn't invited. She said I would only be bored and that she wouldn't have time to entertain me. Corporate accountants have to keep their minds free of clutter." His gaze swung to the side window and beyond. "It took several years before I finally realized that Emily and I were the clutter she referred to."

"Is that when you divorced?"

"No. That's when I started looking for a solution...marriage counseling, compromises, anything that would keep the family together. It was the wrong approach, but I was idealistic then and thought that she would come around to my way of thinking. By the time I stopped caring, she'd received the job offer in Minneapolis, and the divorce was anticlimactic."

Rebecca looked at him for a long moment, before returning her attention to her driving. "It must have been a terrible time for you. How old was Emily?"

"Five."

"I don't understand it." Rebecca shook her head, wondering how Diane Kinser had been able to separate her life from her child's—no matter what her reasons. And why had she felt she had to choose? "I'm sorry for her. She had it all: you, Emily, a home and a career."

"She thought there was more." Quinn lifted his brows and shrugged. "And I hope she finds it. I sincerely hope she finds it."

"No regrets?"

"Dozens. I'd be lying if I said otherwise, but none of them have anything to do with wanting her back. Our relationship was over long before the divorce." He placed his arm along the back of Rebecca's seat. He didn't touch her, but she was aware—shyly, deliciously aware—of his nearness. "It's just that sometimes," he continued, "I wish Diane would be more considerate of Emily's feelings. There are times—"

He didn't finish the sentence. Just broke off the words in midthought, and Rebecca didn't have to look at him to see the rigid set of his jaw, the latent anger in his eyes. She felt it, knew his frustration, recognized his sense of helplessness and, despite her wish not to, shared his concern for Emily. "It must be hard for you, Quinn. Our society isn't very sympathetic toward single fathers, is it?"

He smiled slightly. "Oh, we're making progress, I think. Being a single parent isn't easy, but it isn't the worst situation I can imagine, either."

"So you're not thinking about marriage?" It was out before Rebecca had time to stop it, and she would have done almost anything to recall the question.

"I didn't say that." He regarded her with a probing blue stare that melted her already soft resistance. "I do think about getting married again. Lately, I've thought about it quite a bit. But under no circumstances would I get married in order to provide Emily with a mother figure. Or even to provide someone who could share my responsibilities."

What could she say? Rebecca decided there wasn't any casual response, so she maintained her listening silence.

"Don't get me wrong. There are bound to be some crossover desires, a certain amount of expectations, that will play a part in any decision I make. I like the idea of marriage—one man, one woman, a future to plan, a home to build. But I realize that any good relationship constitutes hard work and commitment. I'm not scared of that, but I'm cautious about Emily's ability to accept another person into our family."

Rebecca found a smile, somewhere, to ease her tension. "I think you're underestimating the adaptibility of females, regardless of age. Emily may not like sharing your attention at first, but I can't think she'll be a tremendous problem."

"You can say that after her performance in the van?" He chuckled. "She can be a problem, all right. It all depends on the way the situation is presented to her."

"Then perhaps you should stay single."

The pause that followed was thoughtfully long. Far too long.

"Something to consider, isn't it?" Quinn settled back against the seat, crossing his arms at his chest and closing his eyes as if he were tired or had lost interest in the subject. Rebecca wanted to argue. She didn't know why and flatly refused to analyze her impulse to challenge his ready acceptance. After all, she'd been the one who introduced the topic of marriage, and she'd been the one who remained noncommittal about her own views.

The problem was that she was no longer sure what her views were. She didn't know how she felt about marriage or children or her career. All the edges that had been clearly defined once, had blurred, becoming a vague promise of a whole. But did she have to choose among them, or could she check a combined choice of "all of the above"?

Diane Kinser had had it all, Rebecca thought. And it hadn't been enough. "My career is very important to me," she said, knowing that he knew, but wanting to reinforce the goals that had kept her going for a long time. "I can't imagine that my feelings about it will ever significantly change."

Only the upward pull at one corner of his mouth revealed that he was listening and not asleep. "I wouldn't worry about it."

"It could be a problem."

"For who?" He yawned and ran his hand over his beard.

Rebecca wanted to stop the car and let him walk the rest of the way to St. Louis, but she could hardly tell him she didn't like his attitude. She didn't know what his attitude was. She didn't even know what she wanted him to say.

Marriage was the farthest thing from her thoughts…except that she and Quinn had just been discussing it. In a round-about way. The realization scared her a little, but intrigued her a little more. Was it too late to enroll in Wally's Tuesday night therapy group?

"Do you want me to drive?" Quinn asked, his voice a husky blend of relaxed masculinity and easy control.

"I can manage, thank you. Go ahead and take a nap if you want."

"I'd love to, believe me." He kept his eyes closed. "But I'm tracking down Molly Summer in my head and trying to decide where to look for her."

"Try the airport." Rebecca couldn't resist adding a touch of skeptical sarcasm to the words. An old woman living at an airport was just a bit much, even when she gave Quinn the benefit of the doubt. Molly Summer was either very clever or Quinn was very gullible. "She can't live there, you know."

Quinn opened his eyes and turned his head to frown at Rebecca. "I think Molly can do anything she damn well pleases. Once you meet her, you'll think so, too."

"Then let's go looking for her."

"Now?"

"Is there a better time?"

He shook his head and resumed his former position. "If you're game, then so am I. There's nothing I like better than roaming the concourse with a beautiful woman who wants to hold my hand."

"Quinn," Rebecca said with a sigh. "I wish you'd take this seriously."

"I thought I was. You do want to hold my hand, don't you?"

"I've been waiting all day for the opportunity."

"Then you're in luck. I might even let you take me to the concession area for dinner."

She cast him a frown that he couldn't see with his eyes closed. "I took you to lunch."

"That was business. This is for fun."

Of course, she thought. This *was* for fun. Life had thrown an adventure right into her arms, and all she could do was ask serious questions. Perspective, Rebecca told herself. Keep perspective. "All right, Mr. Kinser, we'll test out the concessions, but remember, the main event comes after you've been wined and dined."

His lips curved fully at that. "That, Ms. Whitaker, is one hell of a sales pitch."

THE AIRPORT WAS CROWDED, even for a Friday evening. Rebecca didn't really think there was much chance of finding one small elderly lady, no matter how eccentric, in the jam of busy people. Quinn, on the other hand, was undaunted. He seemed to know exactly where to look and for whom. And he did it with such an air of expectation that Rebecca found it hard to maintain even a tiny doubt about his sincerity. Which was one more clue, Rebecca reasoned, to add to the mounting evidence in favor of Molly Summer's incredible story. Either that, or Quinn was in a hurry to bypass the search and find food.

When they had walked for what must have been fifty miles, from one end of the airport to somewhere near the other end, Rebecca gave Quinn full marks for diligence and asked him to please let her sit down. With a grin, he suggested they forget about the fifty-cent concessions and opt for one of the restaurants.

It was the best idea of the day. The restaurant Quinn chose was almost as noisy as the airport corridors outside, but Rebecca found it a delightful respite. They talked for a while about places they'd been, of other places they would like to see, and the conversation drifted gradually through a sharing of philosophies and goals for the future into the everyday happenings of life.

Emily's name flowed freely in and out of the discussion, but it wasn't intrusive. In fact, it dawned on Rebecca halfway through dinner that she mentioned Quinn's daughter almost as often as he did, and she wondered if he had noticed. Like a far-off echo, she could hear herself discussing with Wally and other friends the issues of children versus career, motherhood versus a vice-presidency. How had she progressed from addressing the pros and cons of such choices to this casual but oh-so-crucial discussion of second-grade arithmetic and a little girl's dream of dancing in the Nutcracker Suite?

The realization that she genuinely cared settled around Rebecca like a cloak, a little heavy on the shoulders, but wonderfully warm just the same. She was involved, deeply involved, with the Kinsers, father and daughter. It didn't matter that she was still unsure about the issues, and it didn't matter that she hadn't as yet analyzed her feelings. Quinn mattered. Emily mattered. Time would take care of the rest.

As they left the airport, Rebecca handed Quinn the car keys. He took them without comment and drove to her apartment. When he spoke, it was of trivialities, as if he were aware that Rebecca's thoughts were private and not ready for sharing. At the apartment, he collected the extra key to the dead bolt and escorted her to her door.

There was a moment of absolute quiet when he touched the doorknob and a soundless, mutual sigh of relief when it was clear the lock had not been disturbed. A door down the hall made an eavesdropping squeak, and suddenly Rebecca felt comfortably secure. "Mrs. Albridge," she whispered against Quinn's ear as he bent to unlock the door. "Quick. Act like you're delivering pizza."

He straightened slowly, eyeing her with a mischievous challenge. "I have a better idea." He drew her into his arms and pressed the challenge to her lips. One hand slipped around her waist, the other slid beneath the thick weight of auburn hair at her neck. In a heartbeat, Rebecca forgot about her curious neighbor. She forgot about the break-ins. She forgot about breathing. Nothing intruded into the magic of the moment, of Quinn, of belonging exactly where she was.

He tasted of wine, and the lingering scent of airport smoke and flavors wafted elusively past her nose. She relaxed as she had been unable to do all day. The tensions, the uncertainties, even the pleasures of the past several hours blurred with the demanding delight of his kiss. As her arms moved to encircle his shoulders, she wondered how she had lived all her life without ever once knowing this feeling existed, this special emotion that Quinn had brought to her heart. This, she thought, was what Molly had meant when she wrote in her journal, *"Loving Thede is the best thing I will ever do... and I will do many things. But nothing else will be so sweet."*

Rebecca drew back. *Loving? Was this loving?*

Quinn's eyes met hers in the still, quiet hallway. "I've been wanting to do that all day."

"You have?" Her voice was a murmur, hardly worth the breath it required. Thoughts whirled through her head, feelings vied like multicolored ribbons for her attention. "Was it worth the wait?"

He caressed her cheek with a gentle fingertip. "Yes," he said simply and then again, "Yes."

"Do you think it's safe to go inside?"

"That depends." He smiled, holding her with the tenderness in his eyes. "Safe is a relative term, you know."

The door down the hall squeaked again. Mrs. Albridge was having trouble hearing, Rebecca thought. She could tell by Quinn's expression that he was thinking the same thing, and she took a step forward, taking him with her into the apartment. Inside, she reached for the light and tried to close the door with her foot. Quinn assisted by giving the door a firm push with his hand and capturing her fingers just as she found the switch. "Would you like for me to search the apartment?" he asked. "Make sure it's safe?"

She nudged her way back into his arms. "If I say yes, will you stay?"

"Forever. Or until morning. Whichever comes first."

Nestling closer, her cheek against his chest, Rebecca simply enjoyed the contentment that washed over her. "That sounds fair enough. Any other qualifications?"

"I think you have them all."

"There's just one thing..."

"Don't worry, I'll respect you tomorrow morning."

She stepped on his toe. "I'd rather you brought in my sample case. We left it in the hall."

"We did? How impractical. What were we thinking about?"

"I don't know about you, but I was preoccupied."

"Funny. So was I." He cupped her shoulders and eased her away from him so that he could see her face. "You're the best thing that's happened in my life for a long time, Rebecca. When I find Molly, I'm going to kiss her."

"Wouldn't it be better to kiss me?" Rebecca tipped her chin, offering her lips to him.

He touched them, barely brushing her mouth, his beard tickling across her chin. "Good point, but first things first." He opened the door, reached down for her sales case and lifted it inside. When the door was closed and safely locked again, he turned back to her. "Now, what were you saying about kissing?"

She began unbuttoning her blouse. "I think we should go into my office."

"Ah, the main event. I remember now." A pulsebeat of excitement throbbed at the base of his neck, and the sight of it sent an eager thrill fluttering in her stomach. "Are you going to show me the new Star Shine lingerie?"

She reached for his hand. "Not exactly."

"Something irresistibly seductive, then?" He followed her across the living room. Her blouse drifted to the floor just outside the bedroom doorway, and Quinn watched it fold into a pool of silk.

"I don't think you'll be able to resist." Rebecca turned around, walking backward and still tugging on his hand, pulling him with her toward the bed. "You saw me in action today. You know what a sales pitch I have."

His throat felt suddenly dry. "I saw," he said. "I know."

Her skirt slid past her hips and thighs and calves to droop around her ankles. She stepped free of the material and tugged the half-slip she wore down and off. Her hose were thigh-high, elasticized at the top, and so sensuously seductive he couldn't have looked away if he'd tried.

He didn't. He simply watched, not breathing, his heart pounding with a primitive drumbeat as she slowly removed first one and then the other. She straightened, and with a smile that he only glimpsed, she pirouetted before him. "This, sir, is Lady Laura's latest line of bra and brief."

Quinn decided it was time to stop standing on the sidelines and get into the act. He moved forward, and Rebecca came into his arms, her lips curved with laughter, her eyes alight with humor. She laid her cheek against his chest and hugged him. "Did I scare you?"

"You bet. I was afraid you were going to ask me to order a dozen of each. And as beautiful as you look in Lady Laura's finest, I think it's a little early in our relationship for me to buy you . . . that kind of thing."

Rebecca thumped his arms with her fingers. "How traditional, Quinn. I'll bet your mother taught you that it would be terribly improper to purchase lingerie for a woman who wasn't your wife." When he didn't answer immediately, Rebecca laughed again. "She did, didn't she? Well, don't worry about it because I can buy my own underwear."

"That's because you get a discount."

She looked up at that. But when she saw the teasing expression on his face, the grin tugging at his mouth, she smiled. "And a few free samples, besides."

He reached behind her and unfastened the bra. As it fell away from her skin, he bent to her breast and warmed it with his tongue. He moved to the other breast, wetting it, puckering the nipple to a rosy willingness. He trailed moist kisses upward to the base of her neck and across the hollows of her shoulders.

Sighing, Rebecca sank onto the bed, her body pulsing with the need he had created, and which only he could assuage. He pulled back then, removed his clothes quickly and lay down beside her on the bed. Her briefs were gone, shed in the eagerness of seduction, and now there was only skin against skin, warmth against warmth. She gave herself to him and accepted his tenderness in return. He offered a slow, gentle possession that she shared with whispered words and pleasured sighs.

And when the loving ebbed to a soft afterglow of fulfillment, Rebecca wondered if she would ever know another moment as sweet.

Chapter Thirteen

Quinn left early with a muffled explanation about Emily and Molly, one or the other. Maybe both. Rebecca floated to the edge of a pleasant sleep to nod her understanding, feel the touch of his lips at her temple, and then she was asleep again. When she awakened later, her memory coyly refused to tell her the predawn events, so she contented herself with remembering the midnight caresses, the passion that had burned like a hot summer sun, the sweet warmth of an afterglow that had enveloped them.

Stretching her legs straight beneath the sheet, Rebecca wondered if Quinn was remembering, too. Was he home? she wondered. Or on his way? A glance at the clock revealed a fast-disappearing morning. No time to miss him now, she thought, and resolved to shower, dress and catch up with the housework.

She'd managed to finish everything except the kitchen, when Wally rang the doorbell. "You're not going to believe this, Rebecca," Wally said even before she was inside the apartment. "But our conspicuously absent building supervisor was just outside in this hallway. He spoke to me, no less. Can you imagine?" She followed Rebecca to the kitchen, pulled out a chair and sat at the table. "Well, you know me. I could never live with myself if I passed up an opportunity like that. I told him every single problem I've had with the dishwasher, and then I suggested that while he was in the neighborhood he ought to take a look at it. And what do you think?''

Rebecca smiled over her shoulder as she prepared the coffee she knew Wally was going to ask for the minute she caught her breath. "I can't imagine."

"Well, he looked, he apologized, and he fixed it! Just like that." Wally propped her feet on an adjoining chair. "After months of leaving messages and of hearing rumors that there really was a janitor in the building, one day he appears in the hallway, and voilà, a miracle of modern plumbing simply happens."

"An amazing story," Rebecca said with a laugh. "Are you sure you didn't dream the whole thing?"

"I don't think my subconscious is that original. No, he definitely was in my apartment—round little body, jangling keys, toolbox and all."

"What was he doing in the hallway?"

"Checking locks, he said, which sounded like as good a reason as any I could think of."

Rebecca leaned her back against the countertop and let her lips curve with a soft smile. "Quinn probably asked him to check."

"Quinn? Of the incredibly blue eyes? The man who is only interested in that piece of junk you refer to as an antique trunk?"

The smile grew wider, and Rebecca was in no hurry to answer. The coffee smelled good, so very good. "The same Quinn," she said. "But he isn't *only* interested in the trunk. He thinks I'm a wonderful saleswoman."

"Good heavens, Rebecca! You've fallen for him, haven't you? Did I tell you this would happen? Didn't I say 'Come to the Tuesday therapy group'?" Wally waved her hands in abject dismissal. "You should have listened to me. The scientific method is much safer."

"Than what?" Wally was so determinedly, wonderfully wrong, and Rebecca felt like giggling because she knew it, and Wally didn't. "You shouldn't underestimate tried and true emotions, Wally. After all, I'm the one who has a new dead bolt lock on my door, not to mention janitorial protection."

Wally's brows drew into a sobering frown. "Dead bolt? I didn't notice. When did you do that?"

"After the second time someone broke into my apartment."

"You're kidding." The frown changed to amazement on Wally's model-perfect features. "What happened this time?"

Rebecca moved to the cabinet, took out two mugs and filled them with the freshly brewed coffee. "It's so strange. I came home yesterday morning, and when I—"

"You *came* home? Now that is strange."

Pursing her lips, Rebecca turned and placed the coffee cups on the table before seating herself across from Wally. "Not so strange, considering that I am a fully liberated single woman, over the age of twenty-one, who accepts complete responsibility for her actions."

Wally's smile began slowly. "Absolutely correct, except for the *fully* liberated part. I haven't given up hope, though." She took a sip of coffee. "All right, so you came home yesterday *morning*...early or late? Alone or was someone with you?"

"What difference does it make?" Rebecca didn't try to hide her impatience. "*You* weren't home."

"I have to work for a living."

With a sigh, Rebecca fixed Wally with a pointed stare. "Do you want to hear this story or not?"

"Yes, of course. I just can't resist ribbing you a little. Ever since you met this man, you've been so touchy about things."

Had she? Rebecca wondered and then dismissed the possibility. What did Wally know about anything, anyway? Especially men? "As I started to say, I came home yesterday morning—and yes, Quinn was with me—to find my apartment door open and the lock broken. Whoever broke in this time didn't tear up the doorframe like before, but that hasn't been much comfort."

"I'll bet. Do you think it's the same person? Was anything taken?"

Rebecca ran her finger around the rim of her coffee mug. "It could be the same person. I feel like it must be. I just don't have any idea who or why. Nothing was taken, but everything was moved around this time. As if whoever it was had been looking for something specific. I'm at a loss, though, as to what it could be."

"What was in the trunk?"

Pursing her lips, Rebecca considered the question. "Some hats, a couple of sweaters, a photograph album, some letters, a journal, a ring...stuff like that. But nothing so valuable that it could be worth the trouble of breaking into my apartment twice."

"Value is in the eye of the beholder, Rebecca. Just because you can't see it doesn't mean it isn't there." Wally took another drink, then stared pensively at the steam curling above the rim of her cup. "You're sure it has to be the trunk? There's nothing else different, nothing missing now that was here before you bought the trunk?"

"No. The trunk has to be the object. Or rather, something that was in the trunk when it arrived."

"And the trunk was locked then, right?"

Rebecca went completely still with the thought. "It was locked when I bought it. I distinctly remember the notation on the receipt. But, Wally—" she leaned across the table as if she'd discovered a secret "—there was a key. One of the deliverymen gave me the key. He said—" she struggled to remember "—he said it had fallen on the ground when they took the trunk off the moving van and some lady picked it . . ." *Some lady? Molly?* No, the idea was crazy. Rebecca knew it was too ridiculous to consider. But it wouldn't go away without a hearing. "You don't think it could have been— No." She shook her head at Wally's mystified expression. "No, forget it. It couldn't have been her."

"Who? Come on, Rebecca, I'm about to fall off this chair trying to follow your line of reasoning. *Who* couldn't it have been?"

"Molly." Rebecca stood to refill her coffee cup, although she'd hardly taken more than two swallows. "Molly Summer."

"Scott's aunt?"

"I suppose there's always that possibility of kinship, but at this point, I'm not interested in family ties. I just want to know what is so important in that trunk."

Wally crossed one ankle over the other and settled comfortably into the chair. "Well, what did Quinn tell you?"

Rebecca resumed her seat. "About what?"

"The trunk," Wally said with a sigh. "Why did he want to buy the trunk?"

Oddly enough, Rebecca couldn't remember. Not for a full minute. "He said he thought there was a story. He's a writer, and when Molly told him about the trunk, he thought it might be worth looking into. Except that he waited too long, and then I had gone to the auction and—"

"This guy has you buffaloed, doesn't he? Get to basics, Rebecca. It isn't like you to ramble. What did he expect to find? Specifically?"

"I'm not sure." With a start, she realized it was true. Quinn hadn't been specific. He'd said he had hoped there would be a story, or maybe he'd said he'd hoped to find evidence to support the stories Molly had told him about her interesting life. Had he been looking for the journal? No, she reasoned, that was simply a diary of Molly's love affair with Thede.

"There's the journal," Rebecca said, putting her thoughts into words, although they were more for her own reassurance than for Wally's information. "He doesn't know about that. I took it out to read and never put it back into the trunk. I haven't mentioned it to Quinn, but all I've read so far is personal. Nothing that could provide the kind of material he writes. And the photographs in the album are ordinary. Nothing special there."

"At least, nothing you can see. Don't overlook anything, Rebecca. Something in that trunk is worth a hell of a lot to someone."

Rebecca smiled ruefully as she tapped a fingertip against the tabletop. "Now, if we could just substitute an item for 'something' and a name for 'someone.' A plus B equals solution. I was never that good at algebra."

Wally offered her understanding with a nod before returning to the attack. "Anything else? A journal and a photograph album certainly don't seem like promising clues, but there has to be a link. The clothes—what did you say? Hats? Sweaters? Are there any pockets?"

"No, nothing like that. There was a ring. But I can't believe it's worth—"

"Where is it? Maybe it's solid gold or a priceless gemstone."

"It's at the jeweler's for appraisal, but believe me, Wally, that ring can't be valued at more than a few hundred dollars—and that's probably stretching the amount. Even twenty-four carat gold isn't priceless. There's no gemstone on it. It's rather plain."

"Dead end."

"I'm afraid so."

"Back to the album. Maybe the photographs are being used for blackmail, and—"

"You've been watching Perry Mason reruns again. The album was and is now in the trunk. If that was the object of the search, why wasn't it taken?"

"You're right." Wally stood, frowning at her inability to solve the mystery. "Well, what about the letters? Is there anything in them?" Shaking her head, she answered her own question. "I guess if they're still in the trunk, they're not valuable, either. But wait, I once read this book where a stamp was the motive for murder. Stamps can be worth a lot of money, you know. Do you think that maybe—"

"Wait and I'll go get them." Rebecca stood and started for the bedroom with Wally close behind her. She really had no illusions that a stamp was going to tell her anything, but at this point every possibility had to be considered. It only took a glance at the packet of letters, though, to cancel the whole idea.

"No stamps," she said, holding up the still-tied letters to show Wally. "These are all written on that thin, bordered paper they used during the war. V-mail, I think it was called. So the stamp theory is another dead end." With a sigh, she dropped the letters back into the trunk and closed the lid.

"It's certainly strange." Wally turned and led the way to the kitchen once again. Absently she picked up her coffee mug, took a drink and then placed it in the sink. "I'm all out of ideas, Rebecca. We'll just have to keep thinking about it, I guess." There was a pause that lasted as long as it took for her frown to reverse. "Sorry I can't stay longer and help you puzzle this out, but I have to go. Scott is meeting me at the Arch, and I need to get dressed."

She was dressed, but Rebecca chose not to mention that. "A date? With Scott? At the Arch?" she teased. "Lo, how the mighty have fallen."

"Don't be ridiculous. Scott is perfect for my experiment. I couldn't have asked the gods to send a better subject."

Rebecca smiled with her own opinion. "I take it you're wearing your tweed suit—à la Barbie doll?"

"You're cute, Rebecca. Starry-eyed, but cute." Wally moved to the doorway. "When I'm a famous author, appreciated by thousands of women who have read my book and learned they do not need men, you'll wish you'd listened to me."

"I'm counting the days."

"Good for you, Cinderella. Just try to keep your foot out of that glass slipper in the meantime."

"You worry too much about me, Wally. Especially considering that *you're* the one who's playing with fire. Experiments go haywire sometimes, you know, and the results aren't always what you might expect."

Wally stepped into the kitchen again, shaking her head as if that gesture alone lent credence to her theory. "Not this time," she said firmly. "I have mapped out a plan so simple, so foolproof that there's no room for surprises. Men are easy, Rebecca. You just don't realize... Why, I have Scott Forsythe wrapped around my little finger already."

She held up the digit in question, and Rebecca thought it looked a bit fragile for the task, but then what did she know. Quinn could probably say the same thing about her. Not that she believed for a moment that she'd lost any of her independent philosophy, but he certainly had her contemplating ideas she'd never seriously considered before. She hadn't planned it, hadn't been fully aware it was happening. But here she was, half—maybe more—in love with him. And Wally was on an emotional edge herself. If she only knew it.

"And how do you feel about being able to manipulate Scott so easily?"

"I'm not manipulating him." Wally frowned in her own defense. "I'm only placing the two of us in certain controlled situations and observing the results. It's very interesting."

"I'm sure it is. Just be careful with your variables. Emotions are unpredictable, at best, and I think you're asking for trouble when you underestimate their power."

"Who's the doctor, here? Really, Rebecca, I can't believe you'd worry about me. I have everything under control. When reduced to its simplest form, falling in love is nothing more than being in the right place at the right time. Or the wrong place at the wrong time, whichever way you choose to look at it. I happen to think that when women finally grasp that idea, we'll see some real progress in the equality of male-female relationships."

Rebecca mulled that over as she took a drink of coffee and came to the conclusion that her friend was hell-bent on taking her liberal views to the extreme. And in Rebecca's humble opinion, Wally was asking to be proven wrong. Or maybe, Rebecca thought, that was only her own newfound perspective on romance speaking. *"Lagniappe, a little something extra,"* Quinn had phrased it. What would Wally make of that? She lifted her coffee mug in wry salute. "Then, for women everywhere," Rebecca said, "I wish you luck, and may you never live to meet your waterloo."

"I'm not going to live to complete my experiment if I don't get ready to meet Scott. He's taking me to the brewery this afternoon. To show off his office, you know."

"Brewery?" Rebecca straightened, placing her cup on the table, some niggling suggestion of an idea hovering at the edge of her thoughts. "Does he work there?"

Wally adjusted the hair comb in her blond hair. "He *owns* the Bartlett-Summer Brewery. At least, he owns part of it . . . with his cousin. I'm not sure of the split. We haven't discussed his business all that much. Anyway, he's taking me on a personal tour of the place." She smiled coyly. "Wrapped around my finger, remember?"

Rebecca nodded absently. She was trying to put together the connection. *Scott Forsythe. Molly Summer. Aunt Molly. Bartlett-Summer.* There were references in the journal to the "family" business. Could it be the brewery? How could she find out? Rebecca wondered. Was there more information in the journal? What about the papers that, with only a perfunctory glance, she'd slipped inside the back cover of the notebook? And even if she found a link between Scott and Molly and the brewery, how did that tie in with the trunk?

"Don't look so concerned," Wally said. "After you read my book, you'll be able to do the same thing."

Rebecca lifted a blank look to Wally's grin. "Do what?"

"Wrap that man, Quinn What's-his-name, around your finger."

"Thanks, but I'll pass." Rebecca stood, deciding to escort Wally to the front door. "I prefer to keep my pinkie free and clear of that kind of responsibility."

"I think you missed the point, but we'll argue technicalities later." Wally walked swiftly to the front door, opened it, and as an afterthought, she let her gaze examine the door and frame. "It has been broken, hasn't it?" Her finger traced the faint evidence of damage and the new lock. "Do you think I can get one of these?" Wally shook her head in answer to her own question. "No. The chances of finding that janitor again are about as good as winning the lottery."

"Probably worse." Rebecca hesitated, considering her next move. "Do you have plans for later?" she asked. "Maybe you could bring Scott here this afternoon after you've toured the brewery. I'd like to talk to him about the trunk."

"I'll ask him," Wally said as she walked across the hallway to her own apartment.

Rebecca closed the door and then returned to her bedroom to stand thoughtfully regarding the trunk. What was she missing? There had to be an answer here somewhere. Maybe the documents did hold a clue. And, she thought, the only way to find out was to look through them. Decisively she opened the closet door and reached up to the shelf.

The journal was as she'd left it, hidden high in her closet. Taking it down, she carried it to the bed and began to leaf through the pages. She caught herself pausing to read entry after entry, even though there was no reference to the Bartlett-Summer Brewery or to a nephew named Forsythe. In Molly's life at that time, Rebecca concluded, there hadn't *been* anything except her love affair with the man she called Thede. There were other names scattered throughout the narrative, but they made no more of an impression than a handful of pebbles tossed into the ocean.

Realizing that the day was slipping away, Rebecca backtracked through the journal, trying to find the vague references she'd noticed before. It took time, but eventually she found it. "As far as I'm concerned," Molly had written, "the family business belongs to them. I want no part of it." And on another page . . . "Papa never cared about Dot and me. He only cared about his recipe and the family business. I wonder if he even cared for Momma. How could he have felt about her as I feel about Thede?"

Rebecca looked further, but found no other mention of Molly's family or what their business might be. A recipe could certainly refer to beer, and Summer wasn't an everyday name in the St. Louis area. Rebecca sighed. Only possibilities. Nothing conclusive. But at least it was more than she'd had when the day began.

Looking up from her reading, she stared pensively at the old trunk, wishing it could tell her the answer. That it was within her reach, she didn't doubt. She just couldn't see it. Not yet. But wait . . .

Rebecca moved off the bed and retrieved the photograph album. What else might provide a clue, she asked herself before decisively taking the stack of ribbon-bound letters and the poetry book in hand. Settling back on the bed, she examined each item with careful meticulation. The photograph album yielded a black-and-white picture of Molly and another woman on the beach…somewhere. The woman was younger, but there was a certain resemblance. On the back was scrawled, "Dot and me. Soaking sun on the island."

So, she reasoned, Dot most probably was Molly's sister. Which explained nothing. Frowning, Rebecca put the album aside and examined the slim volume of poetry. There was no inscription, only printed poems, only sentiment. The book went on top of the album, and Rebecca turned her attention to the letters. Just because there wasn't a million-dollar stamp waiting to be discovered, it didn't mean the content of the letters couldn't be enlightening.

She felt a bit like a spy, reading the words Thede had intended just for Molly, but soon she was involved in his descriptions of Europe and what was happening in the war. Nothing really detailed, though. Rebecca knew that mail during wartime was subject to censorship. She glanced at the postmark on the envelopes. Nineteen forty-four. World War II. Almost the end of the war, at that. Had Molly received letters since the beginning and only saved these? Or had there been others that had been lost over the years since? Impossible to know, but somehow romantic.

Funny, how the passage of time added a poignancy to objects that had been ordinary only a few decades earlier. Nothing in the trunk was uncommon, and yet from the letters to the hats, every item had a special touch of romance. Molly Margaret Summer had lived and loved. That was a lot of emotion to be locked inside an old trunk.

Knowing she had to continue her search for…something, Rebecca resisted the impulse to look through the packet of letters again. Instead she tied them with the original ribbon and put them aside. What was left? Pressing her lips in a smooth line, she reached for the journal. The papers. The ones she had stuck in the back of the notebook. Maybe here she'd find what she needed. The papers rustled crisply as she opened the back cover and took them out. Documents, she realized almost immediately. How had she come to overlook them before?

Carefully, gently, she unfolded the sheets. The crease had become permanent, leaving a faded strip across the middle of a marriage certificate. "Dorothy Kathleen Summer" and "Ralph Wade Forsythe." Progress at last, Rebecca thought with a sigh. Scott Forsythe had told the truth: he did have an Aunt Molly.

The next document was a little harder to decipher, but Rebecca decided it was a stock certificate, made out to Molly Margaret Summer. Bartlett-Summer was legible at the top of the paper, but the date and the rest of the record had faded into obscurity. But Rebecca now knew that the family business was the Bartlett-Summer Brewery. And she knew that Molly had a sister and a nephew. Slowly the pieces of the puzzle were beginning to fit.

The last two papers were handwritten and less formal. They contained, in short semilegible passages, the information that Eli Summer had become an American citizen, and that he, together with Joseph Bartlett, had founded the brewery in the year of 1910. The only other pertinent information Rebecca discovered was that Molly also had a brother, John Eli Summer, who had died in the war.

And that, she decided, looking over the things spread across her bed, was that. She still didn't know what, if anything, was missing. She still didn't know who had broken into her apartment. And she still didn't have any idea why.

Lifting the hair at the back of her neck, she pondered the problem and let the cool air caress her skin at the same time.

Quinn. She would simply call him, tell him what she'd found and hope he could make some sense of it. Besides, it had been too long since she'd heard the husky sound of his voice. Too long since she'd drowned in the dusky blue of his eyes.

Without hesitation, Rebecca reached for the telephone.

"Daddy isn't here," Emily said in a voice that communicated both acute boredom and a sad wistfulness. "I don't know when he'll be back."

Rebecca felt a tiny tug at her heart. "So, what are you doing, Emily?"

"Nothing."

"Oh, I see." She smiled to herself. "Well, what have you been doing?"

"Nothing."

Rebecca decided to try a different tack. "What would you *like* to be doing?"

"I don't know."

"Is Colleen there with you?"

"She's cleaning the kitchen cabinets. I broke a dish, so I can't help anymore."

The tug on Rebecca's heart came again, a little stronger this time. "I'm sure Colleen knows you didn't do it on purpose."

"Maybe." Emily's tone grew softer and sadder. "She told me not to come back to the kitchen, and now there's nothing to do."

Rebecca had the distinct feeling that she was being suckered into a little game of childish blackmail, but for the life of her, she didn't know how to avoid it. "What about your friends? Can you call them?"

"They're all gone. Out having fun." There was a forlorn sigh. "No one's home but me."

All right, Rebecca thought. She shouldn't fall for this. She realized that, but—well, she couldn't help it. Besides, if

Quinn wasn't home and apparently wasn't going to be for a while, she might as well spend her afternoon "out having fun." "I'm by myself, too, Emily. Maybe I could come over, and we can keep each other company. Would you like that?"

"I don't know."

So much for enthusiasm. "If you don't want to, that's fine."

"What would we do?"

The emphasis was on "do," Rebecca realized, and she searched her memory for activities she'd enjoyed at Emily's age. But the only thing that came to mind was Wally's remark about the St. Louis Arch. "How about a trip to the Arch?" she asked Emily. "I haven't been there in a long time."

"The Arch?" Emily paused, as if considering the question. "Can I get a soda?"

Rebecca thought that over and decided it was only remotely similar to a bribe. "I think we can manage that."

"Okay, I'll go. What should I wear?"

This could be more complicated than she'd imagined, Rebecca thought, but if it helped establish a budding friendship with Quinn's daughter, well . . . "Wear whatever you like. I'll be at your house in thirty minutes. Will you be ready?"

"Yes." That one syllable sounded more enthusiastic than anything else Emily had said so far. "See you in a few minutes. Bye."

Rebecca replaced the receiver with a thoughtful look. Not at all the conversation she'd planned to have when she'd picked up the phone, but not bad as a substitute. The whole afternoon and a fair portion of the morning still lay ahead. Why not spend some time getting acquainted with Emily? Quinn and the trunk and all the questions could wait. She and Emily were going to the Arch.

IT DIDN'T WORK OUT quite the way Rebecca thought it would. By the time she reached Quinn's house, Emily had changed their plans.

"Amanda called," Emily explained matter-of-factly. "She invited me to go to the movies, and then her mom is going to a party, but her dad will take us to play miniature golf...if Amanda can talk him into it. You didn't really want to go to the Arch, did you, Rebecca?"

Rebecca sensed that this was a pivotal question, but she had no idea which way she was supposed to pivot. She wished she'd read Dr. Spock or whoever was the leading authority on kids these days. Considering that she had no experience to fall back on, Rebecca decided to be honest. "Well, actually, Emily, I was looking forward to it."

"Then can Amanda go with us? And you can drop us at the movies afterward?"

"I can't believe your dad would want me to 'drop' you at the movie theater."

"Amanda's mother will meet us there." Emily's expression conveyed that *anyone* would know that. "Dad has let me do that lots of times."

Rebecca doubted the "lots of times" part of that statement, but she didn't feel it was a point worth pursuing. "What has Colleen said?"

"She said I could go if I wanted, but she didn't have time to take me. And Amanda's mother can't come to get me until just before the movie starts, and that's two hours."

The picture, and Rebecca's place in it, was coming into focus. "Well, what if you and I pick up Amanda, go to the Arch, get a soda, and then we'll meet Amanda's mother at the theater?"

"That's a good idea." Emily's smile curved like a rainbow, and Rebecca decided that being manipulated by an eight-year-old had its silver lining.

"I think so, too. Why don't you phone Amanda and ask? I can talk to her mother, if you want."

Emily started for the telephone but stopped. "Thanks, Rebecca. I know Amanda's mother won't care. I told her you were a friend of Daddy's and that you drove carefully." She picked up the receiver and dialed, speaking in a grown-up manner to someone on the other end about the change in plans.

It was a nice gesture, Rebecca thought, even though she knew the phone call to Amanda was simply to confirm plans already made. After all, she remembered being eight. With a half smile, she sought out Colleen to verify her approval of the afternoon's events. Colleen thought it was a wonderful idea and went on with her cabinet cleaning. Rebecca did ask if Quinn should be called, but Colleen informed her that Mr. Kinser wouldn't be in until three, and he wouldn't care, anyway. Emily often went places with Amanda and her parents.

And that, Rebecca decided, was that. Nothing else to do except to see what else Emily could talk her into doing before the afternoon was over. But Emily seemed happy with her accomplishments, and she, with her friend Amanda, went out of her way to keep Rebecca entertained. By the time they met Amanda's mother, a charming and attractive woman only a little older than Rebecca, the girls had managed to tour the Arch, have a soda, and were ready for popcorn.

After relinquishing her responsibility to Amanda's mother and waving goodbye to Emily, Rebecca went to a nearby public telephone and called Quinn. He was home and was delighted that she'd phoned. After she'd answered his questions about just how she'd come to take Emily and her friend out for the afternoon, she said, surprising even herself somewhat, that she'd enjoyed being with his daughter more than she'd thought she would.

"She's a delightful little person, isn't she?" Quinn asked, although he obviously required no reply. "I've always been partial to her, myself."

Rebecca laughed. "Perfectly understandable. Of course, how could she be anything except delightful? You're her father."

"Ah, flattery. I love it. Whatever you want from me, just ask."

"How about a couple of hours of your time? I have some things to tell you."

"Concerning what?"

"The trunk." A noisy car rattled past, and Rebecca leaned closer to the phone. "Can you meet me at my apartment? I'm not sure if what I've discovered is really important or not, but—" The car stalled, and the engine began to churn, creating more noises than before.

"Never mind. You can tell me all about it when I get there. I'll be at your apartment within the hour."

Chapter Fourteen

"Now," Quinn said when Rebecca opened the apartment door not quite an hour later, "start at the beginning and tell me everything."

Rebecca felt the corners of her mouth going, felt the smile starting deep inside, and yielded to the pleasure. "Hello, stranger. Where have you been all my life?"

"Peddling encyclopedias door to door." His beard parted to reveal a grin that untied a curl of longing inside her. "You could be my first sale."

"What an honor. Won't you come in?" She stepped back, drawing him inside with a coy smile and a most tempting pout on her lips. It would, Quinn decided, be crazy to try and resist such an invitation. He followed her lead, giving the door a push with one hand as he reached for her waist with the other.

The kiss began as a teasing welcome, but quickly fanned the ready embers of a scarcely banked fire. Quinn gathered her close to him, delighting in the soft, delicate feel of her in his arms, sharing in the eagerness of her greeting, responding to the need to touch and be touched, love and be loved. Rebecca was so giving, so willing to meld to his wishes, and yet he never felt as if he were taking anything away from her. How good it was just to be with her. And how much better to know she wanted him to be there.

When he allowed her a moment to catch her breath, she took unfair advantage and tugged at his beard in protest. "I think this is highly unethical behavior for a door-to-door salesman," she said. "You could get in big trouble."

"I'm already in trouble. The question is, should I, or should I not, pursue a career in soliciting?"

"Leave it to the professionals like myself, Kinser. There's no room in this business for amateurs." Rebecca laughed, and taking his hand, led the way into the living room.

He stopped her halfway there to press his lips against her temple and offer another hug. "I've missed you. The airport is no place to go alone."

"The airport? Did you find Molly?"

He shook his head. "No luck. I suppose all we can do is wait for her to show up...somewhere."

"Well, my luck has been a little better than yours. Besides the fact that I was priviledged to escort your daughter through St. Louis's tourist attraction, I had a very interesting conversation with Wally this morning."

"I want to thank you for that," he said.

"Think nothing of it," Rebecca replied airily. "I have conversations with Wally all the time."

"That isn't what I meant. I think it was very nice of you to entertain Emily today, even though you must have figured out what a con artist she is."

"The possibility did occur to me once or twice, but as soon as we got the plans all straightened out, I had a really delightful time. I didn't think eight-year-olds would be that much fun."

"Knowing Emily and Amanda, they were trying to impress you. It's their way of setting you up for the next con."

Rebecca shrugged in guilty admission. "We've already made plans for next weekend. I hope you don't mind."

"I hope you'll include me in your plans."

"Sorry, you'll have to arrange that with Emily. She's in charge."

"I can handle her," he said with confidence as he perched on the edge of the sofa and crossed his arms at his chest. "Now, let's go back to your conversation with Wally."

Rebecca leaned over the back of the sofa, clasping her hands in front of her. "Wally came over this morning for coffee, and we talked about the trunk and the new lock on the door, and the two break-ins, and who and why and that kind of thing. But as she was leaving, Wally mentioned that Scott owns a part of the Bartlett-Summer Brewery. With a bit of investigating, I found out that Scott Forsythe was telling the truth when he claimed Molly Summer as his aunt, because in the trunk there are some documents that substantiate his claim. And Molly, believe it or not, has shares in the brewery, too. Her father founded it."

"*The* Bartlett-Summer Brewery that makes my favorite beer?"

"I don't know of any other by that name." Rebecca tilted her head to the side, teasing him with a lifted eyebrow. "Didn't Molly mention that to you?"

"If she did, I wasn't paying attention. She told me several times that she could buy anything she wanted, but I didn't believe it, of course. I mean, the dresses she wears aren't exactly designer originals." He stroked his beard and wandered toward the sofa. "Do you really think she is the heiress of Bartlett-Summer?"

"All I know is what Wally told me this morning about Scott. The rest I've pieced together from things I found in the trunk."

"What things? A few old love letters and a photograph album?"

Rebecca frowned at the quick suspicion in his voice. "As a matter of fact, yes, I did look through them. I also examined three or four documents that were with the journal."

Quinn turned to face her, his heartbeat quickening with excitement. "There *is* a journal? Molly kept a journal?"

She had never seen him so animated, but before she could reply, there was a knock and then the sound of Wally's voice. "Hey! Anyone home?"

A sigh slipped past Rebecca's lips as she resigned herself to the role of hostess. It wasn't that she minded: after all, she had asked Wally. Timing. It was just bad timing. "Come on in," she called and tried to convey an apology to Quinn.

Wally paused in the doorway like a queen whose tiara would tip off if she nodded her head. "What good is a dead bolt, Rebecca, if you don't close the door?"

"Not much, obviously." She motioned Wally into the room and smiled a greeting at the man who stood behind her. "Hello, Scott. It's nice to see you again. Quinn Kinser, I'd like you to meet Scott Forsythe."

Quinn stepped forward to seal the introduction with a handshake, and Rebecca silently compared the two men. One dark, one blond, both tall and well-built, they looked equally at ease with themselves and the situation. Scott was dressed in the latest style of men's leisure wear, and in Rebecca's opinion, he was just a shave away from being an extremely good-looking man. Quinn, on the other hand, hadn't been blessed with a perfect profile, and his slacks and sport shirt were traditionally casual, but the roguish arch of his dark brows and the devil-may-care slash of a smile against the wiry thickness of his beard put him several points ahead of Scott in sheer seductive masculinity.

Never one to hang back, Wally moved in on the men. She extended her hand to Quinn. "I'm Wally Sherrow, Rebecca's across-the-hall neighbor, and such a dear friend that she forgot I was here."

Quinn accepted the hand and the information without a blink. "I've heard a lot about you," he said.

"Rebecca has mentioned your name to me, too...once or twice."

"Has she?" Quinn met Rebecca's eyes and smiled. "Then we have something in common, don't we?"

Rebecca leaned against the sofa, resting her palms behind her on the cushioned back. "Scott, you and Quinn have something in common, too. He's acquainted with your Aunt Molly."

With a look of surprise, Scott turned to face Quinn. "Is that right? How did you happen to meet her?"

"At the airport."

Scott nodded. "Probably on her way to Madagascar or some other obscure destination. Aunt Molly is a character. She pays no attention to me or my cousin, Robert. Just goes her merry way, doing what she wants, saying anything she pleases, and generally acting like she was forty years younger than she is. Robert wants to clip her wings, but I don't know." He shrugged. "She's not hurting anyone. Why shouldn't she enjoy herself?"

"Why, indeed?" Quinn murmured, and Rebecca realized suddenly how much he cared for the lady under discussion. "When I met her, I thought she lived at the airport. She never seemed to be going anywhere. And she was always alone."

The words had an accusing edge, but Scott didn't seem to notice. "She has a house. She just doesn't stay in it. Says it's ugly and that she doesn't like the color. I offered to get it painted, but she insists on a god-awful color, and frankly, no reputable painter will take the job."

Quinn chuckled. "Purple, right?"

"Ah, you do know Aunt Molly."

''She's a delightful lady. And quite a storyteller besides. No one could listen to her for very long and not be enthralled.''

''Her life has been eventful, that's for sure. Did she tell you she was a courier during the Second World War?'' Scott smiled at Quinn's look of amazement. ''Ask her about it. She'll be happy to enthrall you with that story. Of course, no one in the family has ever known for sure if it's true, but it's a whale of a tale.''

Wally stepped forward and placed her hand on Scott's arm. ''It sounds like your aunt is a liberated woman. I'd like to meet her.''

''So you shall.'' Scott gathered her hand into his. ''I'm not sure you'll be too crazy about her views on men and relationships. I know she's not going to let you get by with the nonsense you like to pass off as liberated thinking. But once the two of you get past that, you'll get along famously.''

''You have a lot of nerve,'' Wally said, but not with any degree of real irritation. In fact, Rebecca thought, her voice sounded rather complacent. Even her expression, as she looked up at Scott, seemed more amiable than argumentative. Rebecca's lips curved. She hoped Wally liked eating crow, because it was becoming obvious that the black feathers were soon going to fly.

''Do you know where your aunt is now, Scott?'' Rebecca asked. ''Have you talked to her recently?''

''I have no idea if she's even in the country. The last time I saw her was three months ago at the board meeting.'' He paused, looking from Wally to Rebecca to Quinn as he explained. ''I operate the brewery with my cousin, Robert Summer. He owns a third of the stock, I own a third, and Aunt Molly has a third. She doesn't want to be involved in the business, but she never misses a board meeting. She likes to listen to Robert and me argue, I guess. Anyway, at the last one she told us she'd lost her favorite ring and that she would sell her shares to whichever one of us found it. You can imagine the furor that created."

Quinn laughed aloud and then looked properly apologetic as he attempted to conceal his amusement behind his hand.

Unperturbed, Scott continued. "Robert and I have a different approach to practically everything, so the chance to have controlling interest in the company was more than just appealing."

"And the search was on." Wally slipped her hand from Scott's grasp and walked to the rocking chair. She sat down and crossed one leg over the other and clasped her hands expectantly. "How did you happen to track the ring to Rebecca?"

Scott shifted his admiring gaze from Wally with just the faintest hint of reluctance. "You *did* find the ring?" he asked Rebecca. "Wally said you'd taken it to a jeweler's for appraisal."

Rebecca didn't want to confirm what he already knew, but she couldn't think of a good reason not to do so. "Yes, I'm supposed to pick it up one day next week." Which was an outright lie. She could pick it up anytime she wanted. She just had an inexplicable aversion to handing over Molly's ring to Scott, no matter what the ethics of the situation. "Obviously," she continued, "the jeweler won't have any idea the ring's value is largely symbolic."

"That's better than sentiment, I suppose." Quinn moved restlessly, stopping a few feet away from the open bedroom door. He was, either by intention or accident, blocking the entrance to that room and the trunk. Rebecca loved him for the protective gesture, and she wished they'd had time to discuss the trunk, the ring and the journal before company had arrived.

Disguising her resigned sigh, she fixed her gaze on Scott. "Why didn't you tell me about the ring in the first place?

Was it necessary to pretend you were recovering the trunk at Molly's request?''

"You don't know my cousin. Robert has been a step ahead of me in this game since day one. I didn't know whether or not he'd contacted you already, and I wanted to test the water, so to speak, before I jumped into an explanation."

"So where is Robert?" Quinn asked. "If he's been in the lead, why hasn't he called Rebecca about the trunk?"

Scott shrugged. "Beats me. I never try to predict his behavior. For all I know, he might have decided to steal the ring from me once I find it."

"Would he do something so...criminal?" Rebecca straightened, pushing herself away from the sofa's support.

"In a second." Scott snapped his fingers, then shoved his hands into his pockets, pushing back the sides of his jacket in a mannerism straight from television. "Aunt Molly didn't specify rules, you see, and Robert has the extraordinary ability to justify anything he wants to do."

"Not extraordinary. We all have that capability," Wally inserted, for the first time sounding like the psychologist Rebecca knew. "Some are simply better at it than others. But I want to know how you traced the ring to the trunk in the first place."

"Process of elimination," Scott explained. "After I'd searched every logical place, I started looking for the illogical, and sure enough, I found a clue...a check made out to A-1 Mini-Storage in Jefferson City, of all places. It didn't occur to me to wonder until much later why she hadn't mailed the check."

"Sounds like Molly was the one who stayed a step ahead," Quinn said, a suspicious glint of humor in his eyes. "It looks like she's led you on a merry chase."

"But now, at last, the game is drawing to an end." Scott pinned Rebecca with a polite but demanding gaze. "If you'll just give me the claim check for the ring, I'll pick it up."

And in the process pick up controlling interest in the family business, Rebecca thought. That was a lot of money and power to be centered on a tiny piece of paper, and she didn't think she wanted to just hand it over. What if he wasn't telling the truth? What if it was all a hoax?

She looked to Quinn for guidance, saw his hesitation and searched her mind for a delay. "The claim check is in my desk at the office," she lied, lifting her hands in a helpless gesture. "Sorry."

"You can get in the office, Rebecca." Wally stopped rocking and leaned forward in the chair. "I know you've worked weekends before. Why don't we all go down there together, get the check and then have dinner? I'm starving. What about you, Quinn?"

"I'm always hungry," he answered, but Rebecca knew it was an absent reply, and that he wasn't endorsing Wally's suggestion. But even knowing that, Rebecca didn't know how to refuse without accusing Scott of prevarication and making Wally very angry. So what choice did she have?

"We can do that," she said. Maybe something would occur to her on the way. "I'll just pick up my purse on the way out."

"Then let's go. If I don't get to a restaurant soon, the consequences could be frightening." Wally stood up and started toward the doorway. "I need to stop off at my apartment for—"

"Don't tell me I've missed the party..."

Rebecca stopped short at the sound of an unfamiliar voice and turned to see a stranger standing in the entrance of her living room. He was tall, dark and attractive, and for a moment all Rebecca could think of was that she had never had so many handsome men in her apartment all at the same time.

The silence passed swiftly through the room, from one person to the other, before Wally drawled, "Did someone order pizza?"

Rebecca looked at Quinn, who took a protective step toward the intruder just as Scott moved forward. "Robert," he said, "I figured you'd show up here sooner or later."

"Hello, cousin." Robert Summer smiled easily, including everyone in his greeting. "Why don't you introduce me?"

"No need for that," Wally said. "We've met before, remember? Outside in the hallway. You smelled like pepperoni."

"Oh, you didn't like the authentic uniform, huh?" Robert made a clicking noise with his tongue. "I thought it was a nice touch, but then I'm new at this, you realize."

"New at breaking and entering?" Quinn's voice bridged no argument regarding the seriousness of such activities. "I don't think Rebecca found it amusing."

Robert's gaze circled the room and came to rest. "So, you're Rebecca? Hey, I'm really sorry about the lock. I could have gotten in without breaking it, but some lady down the hall kept opening her door, and I didn't have enough time to do it right." His mouth slanted in a mischievous and appealing grin. "I'll be happy to pay for the cost of replacing it."

"Fine." Rebecca put her hands on her waist. "How would you feel about three to five years in jail?"

"Suspended sentence?" he asked with a cautious smile. "After all, I didn't disturb anything of yours. I was only looking for the ring."

"Robert, you fool!" Scott covered the distance between them and stared his cousin straight in the eye. "Breaking and entering is no laughing matter. How could you be dumb enough to risk going to prison?''

''Risking it twice,'' Quinn added.

''Twice?'' Scott's voice increased in volume. ''You broke into this apartment *twice*?''

Robert shrugged, letting his glance stray to Wally and linger there. ''The trunk wasn't here the first time. I had to come back.''

''And what if the police had caught you?'' Scott continued to pursue his point. ''What if Rebecca had been home?''

''I made sure she wasn't.'' Robert smiled just for Wally. ''And as to the police, I would have taken the consequences. No guts, no glory.''

''You're not exactly covered in glory at the moment.'' Wally took her place beside Scott, challenging the newcomer with her best professional expression. Hoping no one would notice, Rebecca took a couple of small steps toward the kitchen doorway.

''Neither is my cousin, here.'' Robert nodded in Scott's direction. ''I notice that he isn't in possession of the ring yet, either.''

''He will be!'' Wally defended Scott with more emotion than Rebecca had ever seen her display. ''If you hadn't shown up, he'd have it already.''

''Well, Doctor, that's exactly why I *did* show up. You see, I don't *want* him to have it. Any more than he wants me to have it. The thing is . . . *I* intend to get it.''

Rebecca hoped he would get everything that was coming to him . . . and more. She edged closer to the doorway and realized with some relief that Quinn was following, as inconspicuously as possible.

''Now wait just a minute,'' Wally said. ''Scott is going to get the ring. He was here first.''

Robert laughed, and Rebecca had to admit it was a pleasantly determined sound. "Yes, but Aunt Molly wanted me to find it. She always liked me best."

"This is ridiculous." Scott bent his head, then shook it from side to side as if he were considering what to do next. "Rebecca? Do you think we could—"

"Yes, I do." She stopped cold and tried to look like she wasn't trying to get away. "We all need a drink, so why don't all of you make yourselves comfortable while I fix something. Any requests?"

"I'll just take the ring," Robert said.

"She doesn't have it." Wally seemed to take great pleasure in telling him that.

"You may as well forget it," Scott said.

Rebecca looked at Quinn and then walked purposefully from the room. He followed her into the kitchen and breathed a heavy sigh. "This is the most incredible thing I've ever witnessed."

"Too bad Molly isn't here to see it."

"No kidding. Now that I've met her nephews, I know why she lives at the airport."

The argument grew louder, and Rebecca glanced nervously toward the hallway and the living room beyond. "What should we do? Call the police? Or let the cousins 'duke it out'?"

Quinn frowned as the angry voices got angrier still. "I say we should get the hell out of here."

"And get Molly's ring," she whispered. "It's time this game got a new twist."

"I'M SORRY, Miss Whitaker," the jewelry store clerk apologized. "Without a claim check, there's no way I can give you the ring. Mr. Antonelli would fire me on the spot if I did."

"But I had it...." Rebecca rummaged through her purse for the fourth time. "I put it in this zippered pocket when Mr. Antonelli handed it to me. It has to be here...?"

"Are you sure you got the ticket?" Quinn tried to aid her frantic search. "Maybe you were in a hurry and left before—"

"I was in a hurry that day," Rebecca said. "But I'm sure I had the paper in my hand when I turned from the counter...." She suddenly remembered. "There was a lady standing next to me, and I bumped into her. My purse fell, and before I could move, she bent down to gather the contents for me. Do you suppose...?"

"...that she took the check?" Quinn considered that momentarily. "It seems apparent that she did. Maybe she gets her kicks by taking claim checks from the rich and distributing them to the poor. Or maybe she just wanted to help and took the thing by mistake."

"Do you recall what she looked like?" The sales clerk sounded sincere and looked as if she truly wanted to be of assistance. "Maybe one of the sales staff here will remember her name."

"She was small. And she had on a red hat." Rebecca waved her hand in circles around her head to illustrate. "A turban-style hat. Oh, and she had red hair. I'm sure it was dyed, but it was still red. She was looking for a ring—"

Quinn made a distracting noise, but Rebecca ignored him. "She asked me to help her decide, but she left without buying a thing. She wore white summer gloves. You know, the kind that were popular years and years ago."

Another, louder noise rumbled from Quinn's throat. Rebecca glanced his way, then continued. "I can't believe I remember this much about her," Rebecca explained to the clerk. "If she hadn't been dressed so oddly... A purple dress. Of all things."

She heard the laughter almost before it was born. When the first chuckle escaped Quinn's control, Rebecca turned to him with a question. A question she didn't get a chance to ask.

He was laughing too hard to hear her.

Chapter Fifteen

"You've got to hand it to her," Quinn said when he finally gained control of his amusement. "Molly has thumbed her nose at the lot of us."

"I don't know how she did it." Rebecca looked from Quinn to the jewelry store clerk, not knowing which one offered the best hope of an explanation. "She looked so fragile and . . . and helpless."

"That's Molly." Quinn chuckled again, shaking his head, his spirits high.

Rebecca smiled because it was hard to resist his obvious delight in this newest turn of events. She had to admit that her heart was feeling pretty light, too. All the way to the jewelry store, she had wished there might be some way to keep the ring from those two selfish men back in her apartment. Quinn had expressed much the same desire, although he hadn't been able to offer any concrete suggestions as to how it might be accomplished. And now, to find that Molly had the situation well in hand—

"Ms. Whitaker? Is there a problem?" Mr. Antonelli asked, approaching the counter where they stood.

"She doesn't have a claim ticket," the clerk explained nervously.

Mr. Antonelli frowned at his employee. "But of course not. The other lady—" he looked at Rebecca "—the one who was with you before. She came this morning."

"And took the ring?" Quinn asked, the size of his smile increasing.

"Yes." Mr. Antonelli drew his bushy eyebrows into a single confused line. "I handled the transaction myself. She had the claim check and was quite charming. We talked for some little time about the ring and its origins. Obviously it means a great deal to her, but I thought she seemed pleased with the appraisal."

"I'll just bet she was." Quinn moved his attention to a display case, but he continued to chuckle off and on.

Rebecca felt some explanation was in order, but she didn't know where to begin. "That's fine, Mr. Antonelli, thank you," she told the store owner. "That's all I needed to know."

Mr. Antonelli didn't want to let it go at that. "But Ms. Whitaker, were you not pleased? The ring is a quality piece of jewelry. It isn't, however, as valuable as you perhaps imagined?"

She laughed. She couldn't help it. "Oh, no. That ring is just this side of priceless, Mr. Antonelli. You just have no idea..."

At that point, Quinn took her arm, and with a nod of appreciation to the sales staff he escorted Rebecca to the door. Behind them, Mr. Antonelli warned his employee about customers who can't distinguish between twenty-four carats and a lead nickel. The doors closed, and outside on the sidewalk, Quinn and Rebecca laughed.

"Mr. Antonelli is going to be unhappy when the nephews show up looking for the ring." She slipped her hand into Quinn's larger one and sighed at the protective warmth of his clasp. "And that poor sales clerk..."

"The nephews don't know where to look, do they? Antonelli's wasn't mentioned by name."

"Wally knows, but if they don't get here soon, the store will be closed, anyway." She glanced at her watch and smiled. "Twenty minutes to five and counting."

Quinn tugged on her hand. "Then why are we standing here like sitting ducks? Let's book it!"

"Is that anything like 'hit the road'?"

"Exactly. Only faster."

They made it to the van in a minute flat, and Quinn was pulling away from the curb two minutes later. At the first stoplight he adjusted the mirrors. At the next he turned off on a side street, made a detour through a residential area and made a production of glancing in the mirrors every few minutes. "I think we made a clean getaway," he said after a while. "Do you think it's safe to go back to the hideout?"

"It might be risky." She joined the game and tried to recall the last time she'd had so much fun. "You know the 'cousins' can be bad customers when they're crossed."

"We can always call in Aunt Molly to get them under control."

"Good idea . . . if we just knew where to find her."

"I'd suggest a tour of the airport, but frankly, I'm sick of the place."

"Then let's head for the apartment and wait to see what develops."

Quinn reached for her hand. "This has been one hell of an exciting afternoon. I'm not sure I can handle much more."

"Get that idea out of your head right now," Rebecca said with a playful squeeze of his hand. "The excitement has only just begun."

"Oh?"

"Trust me. There's more to come."

Quinn wasn't sure what she meant, but he could always hope. "Are you positive I should trust you? After all, you didn't tell me about the journal, didn't even mention it until this afternoon."

She shrugged. "You didn't ask. How was I supposed to know that's what you wanted from the trunk?" She hesitated before narrowing her gaze on him. "You weren't interested in the ring, were you? I mean, Molly didn't—"

"No, she never mentioned a ring or her nephews or any number of other pertinent facts. Scott was right when he said she was an incredible storyteller. It just didn't occur to me that she might have other tales to tell. I thought her one claim to fame would be the story she told me. And believe me, she told just enough about Missouri politics to whet my appetite for more. But all my journalism experience made me skeptical. I only hoped the concrete facts would be in the journal she mentioned."

"There isn't anything about politics. At least, I haven't seen any mention of it yet, and I've read quite a bit. The journal is very personal; I feel a little like I'm betraying a trust by even talking about it. It's a beautiful account of Molly's love affair with a man she refers to only as Thede."

"Thede." Quinn's expression grew thoughtful, then gradually brighter. "Thede, of course." He parked the van up the street from her apartment building and turned off the motor. "Ever hear of Theodore Wilkins Hayes?"

Rebecca frowned, trying to recall the reason the name sounded familiar. *Politics. Hayes.* It clicked. "Ted Hayes? Wasn't he one of our state senators during—" She couldn't remember the dates.

"The late thirties, and some of the most scandal-ridden years in Missouri's history."

"Oh, no." Rebecca felt the disappointment as if she were hearing something bad about a close friend. "Molly's Thede wouldn't have been involved in anything...unpleasant. He seems so conscientious...." Rebecca felt her cheeks warm with a blush. "How silly of me. I don't know anything about the man." Except that he loved Molly. And that he wrote beautiful tributes to her. And that he had known happiness.

Quinn smiled softly. "He was married, you know."

"I figured that, but still—" She broke off the protest with a sheepish look. "I guess it's not my place to make excuses for them. I've never even met Molly, much less Senator Hayes."

"He's been dead for a number of years. So has the scandal, for that matter, and knowing Molly, I'm sure she's had the whole thing in perspective for a long time." Quinn reached out to run his fingers through the auburn hair at her temples and brush it back. Carefully. Tenderly. "And I don't think it's silly that you care about Molly's love affair. In fact, I love you for it."

For a moment she was lost, realizing the feeling behind his choice of words, but not fully comprehending that he had said them. She turned to him with a silent question, seeking the answer in his eyes. His lips curved, and his hand slid to cup the back of her head as he leaned toward her. Their lips met tentatively and then lingered to savor the gentle awareness of the moment and its sweet promise.

"Let's go inside," she said when the kiss had drifted to a reluctant separation. "You can read Molly's journal for yourself."

Quinn felt as if he had just been handed a gift. An unexpected and priceless gift. For whatever reason, Rebecca had kept the journal as her secret. She had had opportunity to confide in him, but she hadn't. Until now. And knowing she cared about Molly's privacy, made her offer to share the journal all the more precious to him. Trust, he thought. He had wanted so much to have her trust. And now...

With another caressing stroke of her hair, he turned to open the door and get out of the van. Just as he came around to her side, there was a squeal of tires, and a car raced out of the parking area and down the street. In less than a minute, another car followed, its engine churning with the effort to catch the first car. Rebecca laughed as she stepped down from the van. "That was the cousins and Wally heading for town."

Quinn glanced at his watch. "They won't make it, but at least we'll have the apartment to ourselves."

"And we don't have to answer the door should anyone knock."

"Good thinking."

They walked inside and chose the stairs instead of waiting for the elevator. But as they entered the apartment, it was immediately apparent that they were not alone. The stereo was playing, and a high, reedy voice was singing along with Madonna. Rebecca stood in the doorway of her living room and stared at the tiny little woman who was sitting on the sofa . . . white gloves, red hat and all.

"Hello," Molly said. "I was wondering when you two would come back."

"Molly Summer—" Quinn took a step into the room, then stopped, shaking his head and smiling broadly "—may I introduce Rebecca Whitaker?"

Molly nodded with all the grandeur of a queen. "We're already acquainted, aren't we, dear?" She graced Quinn with her smile. "Rebecca has been a tremendous help to me."

"Molly, you're a fraud. We've just come from the jewelry store. We know just how much help you've needed— none."

"Wasn't it clever of Rebecca to think of getting an appraisal?" Her bright green eyes smiled at Rebecca. "That man, Antonelli, I like him. He's honest. I could tell by the moustache. Anyone who trims his upper lip that close has got to be scrupulously truthful.''

Quinn rubbed his moustache and beard self-consciously, and Rebecca laughed. ''You're right,'' she agreed. ''Mr. Antonelli is very conscientious. That's why I was surprised he gave you the ring. Even with the claim ticket.''

''But I was with you that day. And he remembered.'' She turned her head toward Quinn, then swiveled it back to Rebecca. ''That was rather clever of me, don't you think? To be at the jewelry store when you dropped off the ring? I was at the restaurant when you met Scott, too. Did you see me?''

Rebecca shook her head, and Molly chuckled. ''I didn't think so. But I was there. Scott didn't see me, either.'' She chuckled again, a gleeful, crackly sound of amusement. ''I had a wonderful time. Good coffee, too.'' She held up both gloved hands and then brought them together in a muffled clap. ''I'm not supposed to drink coffee, you know. But what the doctor doesn't know is that I try never to do what I'm *supposed* to. Makes life interesting.'' Molly frowned. ''Would the two of you sit down? You're going to give me a crick in my neck. And turn off that music, Quinn,'' she ordered in the same breath. ''I was just passing time until you returned.''

Rebecca settled on the sofa beside Molly, and Quinn, after obeying her command to end the music, sat in the armchair. ''That brings up an interesting point,'' he said. ''How did you get in the apartment? Not that it's important. Getting in doesn't seem to be a problem for anyone except Rebecca, who has to depend upon a key.''

''I just told the janitor that I was your aunt and that you had evidently forgotten that I was coming to visit. He let me into the apartment . . . no trouble.''

''If you'd arrived a little sooner, you'd have had plenty of trouble,'' Quinn said. ''Your nephews conducted quite an argument here not very many minutes ago.''

Molly nodded. "They conduct arguments wherever they are. I guess I just missed them." Her thin lips curved with pleasure. "I enjoy incredible luck. Always have."

"That isn't what I heard," Rebecca said with a smile. "Your nephew Scott says you believe we make our own happiness. Doesn't that apply to luck, as well?"

Molly frowned as if she'd never before considered that philosophy. "You could be right, Rebecca. Maybe I'm just a better detective than I thought. What were the boys doing in your apartment, anyway? Besides arguing, which goes without saying."

"They'd both tracked the ring to Rebecca, and each thought he should have the claim check." Quinn sat forward in the chair. "Robert broke into Rebecca's apartment twice, looking for the ring."

"Robert did that?"

When Quinn nodded, Molly sighed and shook her head sadly. "Robert has no shame. He's always been terribly reckless... a lot like me, in fact. But I take no pride in his immature behavior." She reached across and patted Rebecca's cheek. "I'm very glad you're a sensible girl and didn't panic. But now everything has worked out beautifully, hasn't it?"

"Hasn't it?" Rebecca found herself concurring with Molly's assessment, although she had no idea that everything *had* worked out. "At least I guess it has. I'm afraid I'm still in the dark about exactly what 'everything' is."

Molly pursed her lips, the wrinkles fanning around the corners of her mouth in neat rows of good humor. "I suppose you deserve to know the details. But I'm going to tell you right now that I couldn't have planned this better if you'd been in on it since the beginning."

Quinn cleared his throat, and Molly crinkled her nose at him. "I'm getting to it," she said. "Hold your horses." Sitting primly, her back straight, she pulled off her gloves—

one finger at a time. Then she slipped the ring from her bony finger and handed it to Rebecca. "I want you to have this. It was given to me by someone I loved very much, and I have always treasured it."

Just as Rebecca started a weak protest, Molly withdrew the ring and put it back on her own finger. "You can't have it now, though. I'll bring it later. Those idiot nephews of mine will be breaking in here again if they know you have it. First, I'll have to show them it's on *my* finger, and that the game is over. I won."

Quinn cleared his throat. "Uh, we were told you'd *lost* the ring and that whichever nephew found it could have your shares of stock in the family business."

"I *never* lose important items." Molly addressed that issue in no uncertain terms and with a stubborn tilt to her chin. She softened her expression as she turned toward Rebecca. "I admit that I misplaced that amethyst, but it's around somewhere. And it'll turn up. But this ring—" she tapped it with a fingertip "—I knew where this ring was all the time. I just *told* the boys I didn't. Certain privileges come with age, you know. Anyway, I never thought my nephews would be able to find it." With a shrug of her shoulders, she held her hand to the light, turned it to admire the gold band, then carefully she put on the gloves again. "I'm eighty-one years old," she said proudly. "I don't have time for quarreling, you understand. I'll never know why the good Lord saw fit to send me two nephews who like nothing better, but those boys have been arguing ever since they learned to talk. 'Course it's hard to blame them when my sister did everything in her power to spoil them both and then up and died, leaving them for me to straighten out." She turned to Rebecca. "It hasn't been easy. Robert's father, my brother, died before Robert was born. And his mother...she's an airhead. Always has been. Always will be. Now Scott has better judgment than Robert, but not much. My sister waited until she was almost fifty years old before she had him. Too late, I think, to be much of a mother. She tired easily, you see. Then she died."

Molly paused, rubbed one gloved fingertip across another, then looked around the room. "You have excellent taste, Rebecca. Do you like living in an apartment?"

"Thank you." Caught a little off guard, Rebecca shifted uneasily on the sofa, feeling a building affection for this frail old woman who vibrated a magnetic energy. "Yes, I guess I like it."

"Hmm. I've thought about getting an apartment. Is it very expensive?"

"Well, no. Not really."

"Now what is it you sell?"

"Sell?" she repeated automatically.

"Weren't you on a sales trip that day you came to the auction? I heard you talking to the other girl . . . the tall one with blond hair. She was with you and Scott at the restaurant the other day."

"Wally." Rebecca nodded and then her mouth formed a soft, round O. "I saw you at the auction. Of course. You were standing by yourself, and the next time I looked, you were gone."

"I was there to rescue my trunk. I'd hoped Quinn here would do it for me. I promised him first rights to my life story, but I guess he didn't believe I knew what I was talking about."

"Now, Molly—" Quinn interrupted.

"It's all right." She waved her hand to shush him. "At your age, I probably wouldn't have believed me, either. It worked out for the best, anyway. Rebecca bought the trunk, and suddenly my little game had a whole new twist."

"How did you know Rebecca wouldn't throw your belongings in the nearest trash container?" Quinn leaned forward in the chair, clasping his hands, pinning Molly with his question. "She might have lost your ring for sure."

"Pshaw! When you've lived as long as I have, Quinn, you'll know that nothing can happen unless something is at stake. You have to take a chance once in a while. And you can't have any fun if you're always thinking about what you stand to lose. Look at those nephews of mine. Always trying to whip the other one out of something or other. Do you think they're enjoying themselves? Hell, no!" Molly straightened the set of her shoulders and looked as if she were savoring the sound of the words. After a pause, she smiled. "I don't know why Scott and Robert are so uptight. They ought to realize I'm not going to give either one of them my stock. After I'm gone, they'll have to split the shares, and they'll *still* be partners." She chortled at the thought. "Maybe then they'll learn to cooperate with each other."

Quinn laughed. "You're really something, Molly."

"You should have known me when I was younger. I was a real corker then." Molly smoothed the bright purple fabric of her outdated dress with the back of her hand. "I'm not doing too badly now, am I? I've had a marvelous time watching everyone scurrying here and there, playing hide-and-seek with my trunk." She patted Rebecca's cheek again. "I hope you didn't mind getting involved in my little game."

"Oh, no." Rebecca took Molly's gloved hand in hers. "This has been a wonderful adventure, and I wouldn't trade it for anything."

"She got to meet me," Quinn said. "And my daughter, Emily. That's an adventure in itself, isn't it, Rebecca?"

She smiled at him, then looked back at Molly's wrinkled face and the red, wispy ringlets of hair visible beneath the turban hat. "I had never seen a soccer game before I met Quinn. Emily is a good player and a beautiful little girl."

"Quinn is a good daddy," Molly said confidentially. "I can tell."

"By the way I wear my moustache?" Quinn asked.

"Don't be silly. I knew that first day at the airport by the way you talked about her. It was obvious that you already missed your daughter, and she had barely gotten on the plane." Molly turned her green eyes to Rebecca. "Quinn is a lonely man," she said. "I guess you know that."

"I was—" Quinn said, reclaiming the attention of both Molly and Rebecca "—until a couple of weeks ago when I knocked on Rebecca's door. For my part, Molly, I want to thank you for plotting out this treasure hunt. I came looking for a story and found Rebecca."

Rebecca met his eyes, and for the space of a heartbeat, she was lost again in the sweet knowledge that the way she felt about Quinn, the way he felt about her, was special. Very special.

Molly clapped her hands, and for a second Rebecca thought she might put her fingers at the sides of her mouth and whistle her delight. "Does this mean I've made a love-match? That's something I always wanted to do. How wonderful. Will you invite me to the wedding?"

"Whoa!" This time Quinn held up a quieting hand. "It's a little early to be talking about a wedding, Molly. I haven't even told her I loved her, yet."

"Well, what are you waiting for? Armistice Day?" Molly shook her finger at him. "You can put these things off too long now, Quinn. And I'm here to tell you that life is too short to fool around and risk missing the boat. Love is precious. Don't you dare take it for granted."

Rebecca sat, listening, but not listening. Her heart was pounding, her breath came in short, expectant sighs. *He loved her. Quinn loved her.* It was too soon, reason objected, but her heart overruled. *He loved her.*

"I'm going to tell you a story," Molly continued, oblivious to the exchange of shy glances between Quinn and Rebecca. "If you'd read my journal, Quinn, you'd already know it, but since you didn't ... I was in love once—terribly, madly in love with Thede. I knew he was special ten minutes after I met him." She narrowed her gaze on Quinn, making sure he was listening. "I met him at the Williamses' house. *Governor* Williams. He wasn't governor, then. Thede was just a fledgling senator. But there we all were, only I can't remember anyone else's face. Just Thede's. He was married. He never pretended otherwise, but...well, that didn't matter. I spent the next thirty years loving him, sharing him with his family, taking whatever he could give."

She stopped talking, and a faraway expression dimmed the vibrancy of her eyes. "That was a long time ago. It's all in the journal. You can read it if you want."

"Do you regret loving him, Molly?" Rebecca almost whispered the words. She *had* read the journal. She knew what the answer would be. Yet she wanted to hear, wanted to believe.

"No regrets," Molly said. "It wasn't the best way to conduct a love affair, but I'd do it all again if I had the chance. So that's why I'm telling you not to take too much time. Believe me, life goes by faster than you can ever imagine."

"I have the journal, Molly, I've read parts of it, and it's a beautiful story. Sad at times, but very beautiful. Would you like to have the journal back?"

"No. That part of my life is over. Even the memory isn't as sweet as it once was. Actually, I would like Quinn to have it. Who knows? He may want to write about me. I've led a most interesting life, even if I do say so myself." She smiled at Quinn, and stretching her gloves tighter across her fingers, she stood. "I have a couple of other journals, too. I'll try to find them for you."

"Thank you. I'm sure I'll find them fascinating. Knowing you, Molly, how could they be anything less?"

"I'd better be going," Molly said. "I have a dinner date tonight."

"How lovely." Rebecca stood, too. "I hope your date has someplace in mind besides the airport concessions. Quinn loves to eat there."

"Ah, a man after my own heart. You'd better grab him quick, Rebecca. Not that I think he'll get away, you understand. Just don't spend all your time analyzing. If too many women did that, marriage could become obsolete."

"You never married," Quinn pointed out.

"Maybe that's the one thing I do regret." She slipped the handles of her purse over her arm. "Naw. I don't regret that, either. But the two of you might. Just remember to invite me to the wedding."

"Where can we find you? At the airport? The brewery?"

Molly smiled. "Oh, I'll be around." She started for the entryway, then stopped. "What was it you said you sold, Rebecca?"

"Lingerie. Lady Laura Lingerie."

"Well . . ." Molly pursed her lips thoughtfully. "I guess if I ever decide to do any modeling, I'll know who to contact, won't I?"

Quinn began to laugh, but Molly stopped him with a sharp look. "I could do it," she said firmly.

"I don't doubt it for a minute, Molly." He tried to appear chastened, but Rebecca saw through his deception. "Not for a minute."

"I'll be waiting to hear from you," Molly said, and without a goodbye of any kind, she walked to the door.

"I'll be right back." Quinn followed her out to the hallway, and in a moment Rebecca heard his muffled voice, then Molly's higher pitch.

"Young man," Molly said, quite audibly. "I haven't needed an escort in twenty years. And if I ever do I'll call the Boy Scouts. Now get back in there before Rebecca locks the door, and *you* have to break in."

He obeyed and locked the door himself. Rebecca stood, watching him, trying not to smile too broadly at his expression of chagrin. "I'm beginning to understand her nephews' frustration," he said finally. "She's an impossible old woman."

"She's wonderful and you know it."

He pretended to consider that as he narrowed the distance that separated him from Rebecca. "She did bring you to me, didn't she?"

"I remember it as being the other way around. *You* came to me." She slipped her arms around his waist.

"Does it matter?" He pressed his lips to hers, and she didn't want to quibble any further. Magic was in the air. A promise of beginnings stirred new emotions inside her, and Rebecca knew it didn't matter. Nothing else mattered... for the moment.

"I love you, Rebecca," he said when the moment was over, when he raised his head and sought the reflection of himself in her eyes. "I know you're going to say it's too soon for me to know, but it's true. I love you."

Her heart plummeted to her toes, bounced back into place and fluttered against her rib cage with the excitement of a dozen butterflies. "I love you, too," she said very, very softly. "I think so, anyway. It is a little early. I mean, we haven't known each other very long. This might be just infatuation."

"It isn't." He'd said it as if there was no doubt in his mind, and she loved him for being so confident. "But I'm willing to give you all the time you want to make sure. I want to marry you and spend the rest of my life watching you smile and hearing you laugh."

"And if I frown?"

"I don't expect perfection." He kissed the tip of her nose. "Just lots and lots of love."

"And a little romance?"

"Oh, yes, we won't forget about life's little extras. I want you to have all the romance your heart can hold."

She smiled up into his blue eyes, knowing she had never before felt such a sweet, warm desire. "How is Emily going to feel about this?"

"Our getting married?"

It sounded strange and wonderful, scary and exciting, and Rebecca tried to imagine it. "*If* we get married."

Quinn's laugh was a soft caress against her forehead. "Right. Keep that illusion as long as you feel it's necessary," he said. "But *when* we get married, Emily will be fine. She likes you already, and she's really not that hard to charm. You can probably do it with your hands behind your back."

"A piece of cake. Is that what you're trying to tell me?" Rebecca didn't believe it would be easy, not for a minute. On the other hand, she'd never shied away from hard work. "And you expect me to fall for that line?"

His lips formed a wry smile, and she reached up to run her palm across his beard. "I didn't say it wouldn't require some effort. I just said she'd be fine. And she will, you know. After all, I'm a wonderful father. Molly said so."

"Oh, yes, I remember. It had something to do with the way you shave, didn't it? Too bad I forgot to ask her what kind of stepmother I'll make. Maybe I should part my hair on the left side."

"Which brings up an interesting point." He let his glance waver from her face, then—almost as if he were nervous—brought it back. "Would you consider—I know you haven't agreed yet to marry me, but I'd really love to have another child. Sometime. It doesn't have to be right away. Your career is important, and I wouldn't want to—''

She pressed her fingers against his mouth. "We can talk about it. Later. Before my fiftieth birthday."

His smile developed slowly and enveloped her in a loving embrace. "I love you, Rebecca. I meant it when I told Molly I went in search of a story and found the treasure of a life-time instead."

She thanked him for his tribute with a lingering and seductive kiss. "Would you like to see Molly's journal now?"

"Now?"

"It's in the bedroom."

"Oh. In that case, I'll just bolt the door, in case the cousins return."

"Good idea. Maybe we should leave them a note, a clue to Molly's whereabouts."

"Let them find their own clues. You and I are busy following Molly's advice and falling in love."

"Falling in love?" Rebecca inched closer, lifting her lips to his, offering him her heart into the bargain. "Was that her advice? Or is that just another of your pet phrases?"

"I made it up just for the occasion," he whispered. "A little something extra . . . just for you."

Epilogue

It was hot. The middle of September, and it was hotter than it had been the year before. Sam Ellis frowned when he heard the sound of a car engine outside his office. Now why, he wondered, would anybody come out to the mini-storage on a day like this? But he supposed he ought to go outside and see what they wanted. Business wasn't bad, but he couldn't afford to turn customers away just because it was hot, either. With a sigh that rumbled all the way up through his barrel chest, he slicked his hand over his balding head and moved slowly to the door.

A man and a woman were standing outside, smiling and talking to each other and to a little girl with short, dark braids. The couple looked familiar, but Sam couldn't place them. He ambled forward. "Hi, I'm Sam Ellis. Can I help you folks?"

"We're just looking around," the child informed him. "I wanted to see the place where Daddy met Rebecca. So that's why we came."

Sam nodded, as if he understood, and stuck his hands into his back pockets. "You don't want to rent a storage unit?" he asked the man.

"No." The man offered a handshake. "You probably don't remember me, Mr. Ellis. I'm Quinn Kinser. I came here last year looking for a trunk, but you'd already sold it at auction.''

''To me.'' The woman moved closer and memory tapped at Sam's attention. ''I bought the trunk, and you shipped it to me. Do you remember?''

He did. Suddenly he remembered very well. ''Yeah, that's right. Hey, if I'd known there'd be so many inquiries about that old trunk, I never would have auctioned if off.'' Sam leveled a finger at Rebecca. ''First you bought it.'' The finger swung to Quinn. ''Then this guy here comes lookin' for it. Then some other fella calls and offers me a hundred bucks if I can get it back.'' He grinned a bit sheepishly. ''Sure wish you'd sold it back to me, Miss—what was your name?''

''Rebecca,'' she answered with a smile. ''Rebecca Whitaker...''

''Kinser.'' The little girl hopped up and down on one foot, then the other. ''Her name is Kinser, too. Like mine. Emily Kinser. I'm nine.''

Rebecca reached for Emily's hand and squeezed it affectionately. It was hard to believe that a year had passed since the first time she'd been to the A-1 Mini-Storage. It was even harder to remember the person she'd been then...before Quinn and Emily had entered her life.

She'd had doubts in the beginning, but since the wedding two months ago, she had been so happy it was difficult to remember why she'd been uncertain about what she wanted. In the year that she'd known him, Quinn had become such a special part of her every day that she couldn't imagine a day without his good humor and gentle, loving support.

Emily hadn't adjusted overnight. In fact, Rebecca thought there would still be some rough times ahead for her. It couldn't be easy to share the father she'd had all to herself for so long. But all in all, Rebecca thought she and Emily were forming a special bond of their own, separate and apart from Quinn and yet connected by their mutual love for him. Even Colleen seemed more relaxed with Rebecca's entrance into the family. Emily had even noticed it, commenting that she'd never heard Colleen do so much singing. The Kinser family was new, but gaining ground every day, and for her part, Rebecca wouldn't have traded a single minute.

In the beginning of the relationship, Wally had predicted dire setbacks in her career. "No woman can have it all, Rebecca," she'd said. "You'll have to choose between a family and a career. Wait, you'll see." But that hadn't happened. If anything, Rebecca had made a great deal of progress in her work. The wedding had been postponed once because she had had an unexpected sales trip come up, but Quinn hadn't complained. He'd only encouraged her to pursue the promotion she wanted. "Support makes all the difference," Rebecca told Wally. "You'll see."

And as winter melted into spring, Wally began to show signs of a thaw. Scott became a resident of apartment 3-K. He even made friends with Mrs. Albridge down the hall. Wally's book on catching a man by the scientific method was shelved in favor of a little romance. The Tuesday night therapy group had graduated and presumably gone on to find the men of their collective dreams. Or to exercise clubs.

By the time Rebecca and Quinn took their places before a flower-bedecked altar, Wally had changed her tune... several times. "Good for you," Wally had said just before she walked down the church aisle ahead of Rebecca. "You can have it all, Rebecca," she'd said. "Career, husband, a family. I know you can do it." It hadn't dawned on Rebecca until some time later that Wally had had an ulterior motive. If Rebecca could have it all, then so could Wally. Quinn and Rebecca had had a good laugh about all the hypotheses and theorems that Wally was going to have to eat, word by presumptuous word.

Wally hadn't been the only one present at the wedding to offer advice. Molly dropped in for the occasion, dressed in a new lavender dress and wearing the black hat with the cabbage-rose trim. Emily and Molly had struck up a quick and permanent friendship, which pleased Quinn and Rebecca immensely. "Never take your love for granted," was the advice Molly offered before she gave them her blessing. "May you always walk near to the sunshine."

Now, standing where she'd stood a year before, facing Sam Ellis's well-meaning but puzzled expression, Rebecca wanted to laugh aloud because the sunshine felt so very good.

"I'm married, now," she told Sam, thinking as she said the words that they sounded far too ordinary to describe the happiness her marriage had brought into her life. "Quinn and I met because of the trunk, and since we were in Jefferson City on business, anyway, we decided to drop by."

"You selling antique trunks?" Sam looked completely mystified.

"Rebecca sells lingerie," Emily said, pronouncing the word carefully. "L-i-n-g-e-r-i-e. I'm studying for the spelling bee."

Sam scratched his head, and, with a laugh, Quinn took pity on his confusion. "Actually, we're in town so Rebecca can make her last sales calls. She's been promoted and won't be doing as much traveling as before."

"Is that a fact?" Sam wished he'd brought a cigar with him. Fool idea to try to quit smoking the stogies when it was so hot. "Congratulations," he said to Rebecca.

"She got a promotion, married Daddy, and got to be my stepmother all in the same week," Emily announced proudly. "And you helped."

"How'd I do that, missy?"

"Emily. My name is Emily. E-m-i-l-y. And you helped because you sold her the trunk in the first place."

"Oh," Sam said, then he looked again to Quinn for clarification. "What was in that trunk, anyway? Buried treasure?"

Everyone laughed, especially Emily. "There was a ring," she said. "See? Rebecca is wearing it."

It looked like an ordinary gold wedding band to him, but Sam didn't say so. He smiled and nodded because these people seemed to expect him to. "That's nice," he said and decided to try again. "Was that all that was in the trunk? Just a ring?"

"Oh, no," Quinn assured him. "There was adventure and intrigue and a whale of a story. You can read it in a few months when the book is published."

It was too hot for this, Sam thought. "I'll do that. I'll sure do that."

Emily tugged at Rebecca's hand. "We better go," she whispered, and Sam wondered why she suddenly had lowered her voice.

"Yes," Rebecca agreed. "Thank you, Mr. Ellis, for letting us stop by and reminisce for a minute. We can't stay any longer because we're all involved in a wedding rehearsal tonight."

"Aunt Wally is getting married." Emily's mouth curved upward, revealing two toothless spaces in her smile. Sam didn't know why, but he forgave her for interrupting his air-conditioned afternoon.

"Well, tell your aunt I said congratulations to her."

"Thank you," Emily said. "I'll tell her. We're giving her Barbie and Ken dolls for her wedding cake."

"Now nice." Sam tried Quinn one more time. "Is that traditional, nowadays? Barbie and Ken?"

Quinn motioned his wife and daughter toward the van. He leaned closer, but not too close, to Sam's sweaty brow. "Don't pay any attention to that. It's one of these newfangled ideas...putting fashion dolls on the cake instead of the old bride and groom decoration. Sort of like a scientific experiment.''

''Oh.'' Sam didn't understand a word of it, but what did he know? People got crazy when the temperature shot to the nineties. As he watched Quinn Kinser get into the van, Sam thought about the crazy things he'd seen people do. Why, just the other day some funny-looking old lady had rented a mini-storage. All that space for a suitcase. Come to think of it, that old woman had looked kind of familiar, too.

Naw, he thought. Heat. It was just the heat.

Rubbing his head, he walked back into his office.

Harlequin American Romance

COMING NEXT MONTH

#201 PROMISES by Judith Arnold

In the old days it would've been a "happening." When six friends reunited to celebrate the fifteenth anniversary of a college newspaper they founded in the seventies, they renewed old friendships and shared nostalgic memories. For two of them, Seth and Laura, the night held more magic, as their long-term friendship turned to love. Experience the first book in the *Keeping the Faith* trilogy.

#202 DREAM CHASERS by Anne McAllister

Owain O'Neill couldn't pinpoint the urge that led him to Belle River, Wisconsin, to see for himself the child he'd created. A quick look and then he'd be gone—that was what he'd promised himself. But Owain hadn't planned on discovering he was the father of twins—or on falling in love with their mother.

#203 THE HEART CLUB by Margaret St. George

Next to broccoli, Molly hated injustices the most. So when she discovered her gran's Heart Club had been victimized by a patent thief, she solicited the help of part-time inventor Mike Randall and took justice into her own hands. The situation looked bad, but it was about to get worse....

#204 TO ASK AGAIN, YES by Carolyn Thornton

Men. Where could women find decent ones? Ivy had looked everywhere—from blind dates to the dreaded personal ads—and then took matters into her own hands. The result: an original Date Mate T-shirt. Now that the task was done, would Ivy find the man of her dreams?

ATTRACTIVE, SPACE SAVING BOOK RACK

Display your most prized novels on this handsome and sturdy book rack. The hand-rubbed walnut finish will blend into your library decor with quiet elegance, providing a practical organizer for your favorite hard-or soft-covered books.

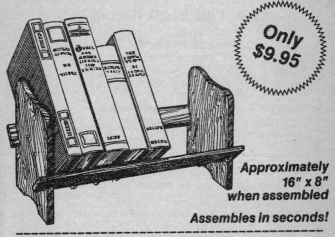

Only $9.95

Approximately 16" x 8" when assembled

Assembles in seconds!

To order, rush your name, address and zip code, along with a check or money order for $10.70* ($9.95 plus 75¢ postage and handling) payable to *Harlequin Reader Service*:

Harlequin Reader Service
Book Rack Offer
901 Fuhrmann Blvd.
P.O. Box 1325
Buffalo, NY 14269-1325

Offer not available in Canada.

BKR-1R

*New York residents add appropriate sales tax.

Can you keep a secret?

You can keep this one plus 4 free novels